OUTFIELD MAGICKED

FARIES AND FASTBALLS
BOOK THREE

BRIGID COLLINS

RON COLLINS

SKYFOX
PUBLISHING
Fantasy

(In Trade Paperback)
ISBN-10: 1-946176-76-1
ISBN-13: 978-1-946176-66-9

(In Hardcover)
ISBN-10: 1-946176-77-X
ISBN-13: 978-1-946176-77-6

CONTENTS

When the Samhain wind blows, the veil between the worlds grows thin.

Throngs of Pattersonville West High School baseball fans filled the stands at Unicorn Field, butting right up against capacity as they shouted and hollered their joy, some leaning out over the rails to high-five their favorite players as the team paraded past them in a happy lap around the infield.

Victory music blared. A crisp fall breeze swirled around the ballpark, tousling hair and tugging at jerseys. A scattering of brittle orange leaves made it over the brightly painted fence to land in the outfield grass, which had been so meticulously mown prior to the final game that even a day later it still sent up fresh scents.

After the parade of an entrance, the entire Unicorns team gathered around the pitcher's mound, grinning and slapping each other on their backs and forming a loose half-moon around the small pedestal that had been set to display the gold cup they'd won yesterday.

Adrien Thorn, who had experienced quite his fair share of fey festivities in his time, found it impossible to stop smiling. The feeling of pure joy that cloaked the place made him want to burst. And not just for what his friends had pulled off on this field. He was also filled with a sense of pride at the ballpark itself. *Unicorn Field,* he thought to himself with a wry sense of satisfaction. As he stood among his teammates, drinking in the cheers, he let himself cast another appraising eye over his handiwork.

It was a truly beautiful place, this park. Perfectly tended and nestled in behind the oak and sycamore trees that made up the small forested area that lined the entire outfield fence. Not a hint of McMasters' presence remained anywhere in the field. The gaudy advertisements for the Ball and Glove store had all been scraped away or painted over, and the tacky, over-detailed archway at the entrance declaring the place "McMasters Field" was torn down and replaced with a beautiful brick archway and a simple banner that gave the field its proper name: *Unicorn Field.* Classic wooden rail fences lined the seating areas and added an old-timey sense of elegance to the place. Fresh coats of white, teal, and blue paint made the concession stands, dugouts, and back fence glow in the sunlight.

Just the way it ought to be.

He was glad he'd managed to get the extra set of bleachers installed as part of his work in improving the field, too.

These changes had made playing the season so much more enjoyable, but today Adrien was especially grateful for the extra time he'd gotten to do all the work, for all the construction businesses that had donated materials, and for all the volunteers who had helped him. Because to him, today felt like a culmination, of sorts. For the first time since 1923, when Adrien himself had led the team to victory, the Pattersonville West High School Unicorns were State Champions.

It felt so right.

If the small, Midwest town of Pattersonville was known for anything, it was baseball. Even their rival towns throughout the tri-state area would admit that no one knew how to root for the home team quite like the fans of Pattersonville West High School's team. Even with the Unicorns' long streak of despair, the city still managed to turn out record attendance of supporters wearing Unicorns jackets, waving Unicorns banners, and singing Unicorns chants at every game.

So, when the Unicorns had a bit of trouble due to the McMasters sponsorship falling through— not to mention strange rumors about disappearances and midnight baseball rituals— everyone agreed when the High School commission said it would be in everyone's best interest to push the start of the season back a few months.

But even with all that, nobody could have predicted the sheer exuberance of Pattersonville's citizenry upon a brisk, sunny day at the beginning of October as their Unicorns, led by star player Emily DeWitt, finally defeated the Marion Bulldogs to become State Champions for the first time in over a century.

Megan Moore, in her article covering the event, described the feeling in the air that day as "magical" and "fey." Those unfamiliar with Pattersonville who read the article as it got passed around the Internet thought that description was sweet, and that it was always nice when the underdogs won for once, then went about their days in mundane ignorance.

Which was fine by Adrien.

The less of that kind of interest, the better.

What Adrien enjoyed most about this day was watching his teammates gather around the trophy, smiling, laughing, and joking. Unlike the rest of his teammates, he'd already known what winning a State Championship felt like. He'd been the one to hit the winning home run on this very field back in 1923.

Then he'd spent the next hundred years trapped in the Fairy Realm.

Though he'd been back here in the mortal world for over a year now thanks to Emily DeWitt, there was something about this newest championship victory that felt like a firm cap on his experience.

He'd finally finished his senior year of High School. Just a month ago, with the help of Mayor Culpepper, he'd even finally turned "officially" eighteen. For the first time, it seemed like his life might go along something like a normal path.

He cast a glance over at Emily, who stood beside him. She grinned back, the not-so-secret-anymore connection they shared passing between them. Ever since the events back in the spring when the Unicorns, joined by a few mysterious fairies, had played a late-night game against the Seelie Court for the powerful artifact known as the Web Gem, everyone knew about the existence of the Fairy Realm and about Emily's and Adrien's experiences there. And even if people outside Pattersonville weren't treating their news as anything more than a silly story from the locals here, people in Pattersonville knew that Adrien really was the hundred-year-old legend they used to tell stories about and that some townsfolk even had a few drops of fairy blood running through their veins.

And they knew about the true power of baseball magic, too.

Well, everyone in Pattersonville did, anyway.

Adrien didn't think the outside world would be able to remain so purposefully ignorant for much longer, especially not if his reporter friend, Megan, had anything to say about it. Sometimes Megan made people uncomfortable, but he liked her a lot. She was nothing if not persistent when she had a story to tell. And, given the way she was flitting around the edges of the field now, snapping pictures for her article about this very event, she was going to have plenty to say about this one.

A swell of cheers rose, drawing Adrien's attention to Mayor Culpepper, who was striding towards the mound with a huge, genuine smile stretched across her face. She was a good fit for the office, Adrien thought. Competent, caring, and capable of making things as serious or casual as the moment called for. For this event, the mayor had dressed in jeans and a windbreaker in Unicorns teal and wore her blonde hair in a ponytail pulled through the back of a Cubs cap.

Arriving at the trophy display, she waved at the crowd, then came to stand beside the team, lifting the microphone she held to her mouth.

"Is there anything better than spending a beautiful day at a beautiful ballpark with a few good friends?" she said.

The crowd whistled and yelled in agreement. Out in the crowd, Adrien caught sight of his family in the front row, Aunt Peg and Uncle Gary jumping up and down just as energetically as his ten-year-old cousin Sydney between them. Seeing them here made his chest swell with happiness. They'd been his strongest supporters from the moment he'd arrived in town claiming to be his own descendant and that support had only grown even more firm as his truth came out. Sydney and Aunt Peg had been the first volunteers to help him bring his vision for the field's renovations to life, too.

Mayor Culpepper let the supporters cheer for a moment longer before continuing her speech. "And speaking of good friends, may I draw your attention to these amazing kids right here? Your Pattersonville West Unicorns, everyone!"

The shouts that invitation elicited would have rivaled the baying of the Wild Hunt.

"I think we can all agree that the baseball these kids played this season was some of the best we've ever seen in Pattersonville," said Mayor Culpepper. "I know I was on the edge of my seat every inning, feeling the magic of baseball flying with every pitch and every hit. And with a group of players like these, that's hardly a surprise. Let's hear it for our seniors, all of whom have spent years playing their best for this team we all love— Emily DeWitt, Benji Amberman, Jamal Douglas, Patsy Pell, Jake Nesbitt, and our very own centurion, Adrien Thorn!"

She turned her bright smile on them as the crowd started up a new set of chants.

"Our boy's back home! Our boy's back home!"

"Strike 'em out, Em!"

"Jake the Rake!"

Adrien let their excitement wash over him. He'd spent much of this past year working as one of the theater kids, and though he'd done some line reads and even taken an understudy role for *Taming of the Shrew*, he'd found he didn't enjoy being on stage quite as much as he did working on the sets. But this moment didn't make him break out in nervous sweat, despite all the attention being thrown his way.

It all just felt like the familiar tingle of baseball magic.

In fact, it felt so much like the baseball magic that he didn't notice the real swell of power happening under the field until tiny lights started twinkling in the air.

Emily noticed it at the same moment he did and cast a startled look his way, eyebrows raised in silent question. Adrien only shook his head, then turned to glare at Benji, their third baseperson and the one most likely to be pulling some fairy shenanigans, given the fact of their fairy heritage and that they were the current caretaker of the fabulous fey artifact, the Web Gem.

But Benji stood still near the middle of the Unicorns' semicircle and gave no more than their usual fairy glow. Their teal-shadowed eyes were staring at the disturbance around home plate, though, narrowed with the same uncertainty Adrien felt.

Adrien looked at the plate, too, fighting a wave of anxious nausea. The feeling of magic was too strong to deny now. People in the stands were starting to notice it, too, their chants fading away in favor of anticipatory shuffling.

Mayor Culpepper kept her voice firm and even. "Let's keep calm, folks. Looks like our neighbors across the way are stepping in to join our celebration."

Adrien admired her calm control. It hadn't been that long since she and the rest of Pattersonville's population had become aware of their fairy connections, after all, and there hadn't been another incident of *co-mingling* since that fateful game in the spring.

A flare of light over home plate made Adrien wince, and when he opened his eyes again, he was completely unsurprised to find that, indeed, a small contingent of fairy folk had joined them on the field.

They were a varied group, with representatives from many of the factions he recognized within the Realm. There was Fennoc, the faun leader of the Small Folk Emily had played with, his shirt and fur as fastidiously clean as always, and his brother, Maddoc, looking rugged and charming with his flat cap perched jauntily over one horn. Beside them stood the sinuous mermaid, Lady Marne of the River Kin, whose scales reflected the autumn sunlight into rainbow sparks. A trio of witches represented the Hag Sisters of the Wood, holding a single crystal between them like a beacon. Behind them, standing tall and proud, was a Centaur Adrien recognized as being a particular friend of Callie McMasters, clearly there to represent the Wild Hunt. There were even a pair of fair-haired, regal-looking elves, their pure white robes and haughty expressions marking them as Seelie Courters.

As Adrien scanned the newcomers, his heart rate rose. Notably, he saw no creatures from the Unseelie Court.

He remained tense and ready for action, though. Even without any of the Unseelie Queen's minions, this lot couldn't be here for anything as pleasant as simply celebrating the Unicorns' championship win. The cost of crossing over, especially now that the Web Gem was on this side of the fairy ring, was too high to do so frivolously.

Something must be wrong.

He heard Emily draw in a fortifying breath, and knew she was on his same wavelength. What trouble had befallen their friends this time? What feats of courage or strength were they about to be called upon to display?

Lady Marne stepped towards the pitcher's mound. Then she met Mayor Culpepper's eye and performed what Adrien recognized as a very correct fairy curtsy from one lady of powerful rank to another.

To her credit, Mayor Culpepper managed a kind of half-bow in return that even the Unseelie Queen would have struggled to find true fault with.

Lady Marne smiled. "To our mortal neighbors, greetings. We beg your forgiveness for the interruption, but Samhain draws near and the festival nature of your gathering was an opportunity for easier travel that we simply could not pass up."

Her voice flowed as smoothly as a river, but with the roar of a waterfall to back it up, ensuring she was heard by every person present within Unicorn Field. A murmur set up through the stands, but it remained soft, as though no one wanted to miss what Lady Marne had to say. Adrien couldn't blame them. Even after a hundred years among them, he still found fairy folk hard to ignore when they were trying to hold attention.

Only Emily was able to break that spell. "Is something wrong?" she said, her tone somewhere between breathless and determined. "Is there trouble in the Realm?"

Lady Marne's smile turned softer. "Not at all. Not of the sort you mean, anyway. Nothing that requires heroism and sacrifice to resolve." She gave a trill of laughter.

Now Maddoc stepped up. "'Tis nigh time for the Fall Season to begin in the Fairy Realm, and we find ourselves short a team."

One of the Seelie elves gave a sniff of disdain. "The Unseelie Court refuses to field a team this year, claiming 'interest in other pursuits' instead."

"Sore losers, more like," said the other Seelie elf in a lower voice.

Adrien stifled a snort. As if the Seelies hadn't behaved as the sorest of losers last season.

Now the Centaur— Trace, Adrien remembered his name was— spoke. His deep voice sounded like stones rolling down a hunting trail. "We of the Realm recognize the Unicorns' recent win in their own championship, and it has been decided amongst all our houses that such prowess, along with our previous interactions, allows us to extend an invitation."

"Double, single, bunt and fumble," the three witches intoned together in an eerie sort of harmony. "Runner score and pitcher grumble. Join our league of fairies humble. To the winner may the Web Gem tumble!"

The murmurs in the stands grew louder, and on the field, the gathered Unicorns shifted as they looked at one another.

An unsettled feeling lodged in Adrien's chest. He hardly knew where he ought to look. The Unicorns, a team of mortals, were being invited to participate in the Fairy League's Fall Season? How would that even work? *Could* it work?

Should it?

Finally, he met Emily's gaze again. She was shaking her head, a frown pulling her face into sharp angles. But to her side, Benji held their head tilted to the sky, looking pensive.

They'd worn that look often since coming into the stewardship of the Web Gem, but now that expression came with a sense of intrigue and something that might even have been hope rather than the uncertain edge of fear that it usually contained.

Mayor Culpepper held up one hand. "Settle down, folks," she said into the microphone. Though she didn't exude the same fairy aura as Lady Marne, she still managed to gather the audience's attention. The stands quieted once again.

"To be perfectly clear," the mayor said, "you are inviting the Unicorns to play in your league for a season? You do understand that, ah, the exact team you interacted with last spring has mostly graduated, yes?"

Lady Marne smiled and waved one hand in casual dismissal. "That hardly matters to us. The love of baseball is all that is required, and we know these players have that in spades. And the fact that the Web Gem itself resides in the Realm of Mortals is enough to say the games can be played legitimately across the portal. So, yes. We do so invite the Unicorns to join us for one season. No tricks, no soul-binding contracts."

"Just a lot of baseball and pure fun," said Maddoc.

Behind him, the pair of Seelies sniffed and folded their arms over their chests.

Emily hadn't stopped shaking her head. "I don't think this is a good idea."

"Aw, come on, Em," said Jake. "Who gets this kind of opportunity?"

The other Unicorns chimed in, too, and Adrien's heart sank to see them so swept up in the enthrall. "No, Em's right. This is courting danger. Don't you all remember what almost happened in the spring?"

Patsy grinned. "Hell yeah, we do. We remember the best baseball game of our lives. This season has been great and all, but that game? That was pure magic."

"And this fairy ring here is totally something the Unicorns should have a say in using, right?" said Jake, pointing at the chalky baseline under his feet. "Maybe if we win this Web Gem, we can pass it down to the next set of Unicorns for, like, protection and stuff. That way, nobody else can get snatched away like you and Em did."

Adrien coughed against the lump Jake's words put in his throat. "I... guys..."

Mayor Culpepper switched her microphone off and stepped closer to the Unicorns. On reflex, the Unicorns closed in, becoming a loose huddle.

"Kids," she said with an almost conspiratorial seriousness. "I know this is asking a lot of you, but I think we should accept this offer. Not only is it good to build relations with our fairy neighbors now that the general population knows about them, but, well, I won't lie to you. Fred McMasters didn't just do a number on your field with his shenanigans in the preseason. He also wrecked a lot of business deals around town. I've been able to keep it out of the news for now, but I'm not sure how much longer that can last. All that money he so generously poured into our coffers turned out to be nothing more than fairy gold, and when we tried to take it to the bank, it turned into leaves and sticks and other stuff I'd rather not mention. It left Pattersonville's economy in shambles. The city is literally broke. We need something to draw in more big-spending tourists, and what could be more enticing than the promise of great baseball games against teams the likes of which nobody outside of Pattersonville has ever seen?"

Emily chewed on her lip. "That's... I don't know, Mayor Culpepper. There's got to be a better way. It seems way too dangerous to expose so many people to the Fairy Realm."

"Oh, no," said Mayor Culpepper. "I don't want that. But if we can arrange to have the Unicorns play their home games here, on Unicorn Field, couldn't anyone come to see those games without even dipping a toe into the Fairy Realm? Besides," she laughed. "What use do fairies have for mortal money, right?"

"We could try to ward the field, too," Adrien said, the words escaping his mouth before he realized they were even there.

"Ward the field?" Emily said.

Adrien felt sheepish. Using just his gaze he tried to tell Emily he was sorry, but her expression said she wasn't having anything to do with it. "Well. We could try. You and me, anyway. My glove. Your ball. Callie's not here with her bat, but maybe Benji can help?"

Exasperation dripped from Emily's posture. "How would we even work this? Going across the ring has a cost, guys. And not the monetary kind."

Benji shrugged. "I don't think it should be too hard. I've got the Web Gem, after all. And as Lady Marne said, it's nearly Samhain. Y'know, Halloween. I've been jumping back and forth between the realms by myself since the spring, and it's been way easier the past week or so. I think I could manage it."

"The barriers between the worlds are thinner around the festivals," Lady Marne said from nearby.

Emily threw her hands into the air but didn't say anything more.

"I'm for it," said Jake.

"Me, too," said Patsy.

One by one, the other Unicorns threw in their hats, until only Adrien remained to comment. Emily stared at him as if trying to beam a message directly into his brain.

Adrien sighed and dug his toe into the dirt. What was he

supposed to do? It was clear he and Emily were outnumbered. This thing was going to happen, regardless of the danger.

The Unseelie Queen isn't playing this time, whispered through his mind. *Maybe it really won't be so dangerous.*

He didn't believe that for an instant. There were many kinds of peril in the Fairy Realm.

But he had the baseball magic on his side. Even now, he could feel the connection he had with his magical glove, even as he'd tucked that glove safely away in his gear bag back home. He wasn't powerless.

And after working on Unicorn Field all summer, he felt so close to this park. He knew its every intricacy like his own backyard. He hated the idea of separating from it now. And the best way to tap into it was to be part of a team playing on it. Besides. He couldn't deny the thrill running up and down his spine at the thought of playing baseball with the fairies again, especially now that he was free of the Unseelie Queen's hold.

His muscles itched to test his true mettle against the teams he'd only half-faced for a hundred years, this time as a Unicorn.

Once a Unicorn, always a Unicorn.

I'm sorry, Em, he thought.

"I'm in."

Emily glowered at him, but everyone else set up a whoop of joy. Mayor Culpepper smiled and tugged at the brim of her Cubs cap, then turned away from the huddle and switched her microphone back on.

"Pattersonville, get ready for the greatest season of baseball you've ever seen. Your Unicorns are playing in the Fairy League this Fall Season!"

TWO

Sitting against the thickest oak tree behind the outfield fence at Unicorn Field, Megan Moore pressed the icon for her bank app on her phone. Her heart pounded with an ice-cold thrill that meshed with the feeling of sharp bark pressing against her back through her denim jacket. On the screen, the numbers seemed to pulse.

There it was. The check from New York had officially cashed. Which meant she was officially a professional journalist.

Some people would say it was just a puff piece. A few inches buried deep in the life section, probably something the editor thought of as quaint silliness rather than hard-hitting news. Fairies in Pattersonville. Right.

But the money was there.

Heat rose to her cheeks. She could barely stifle a giddy yelp.

Keep your composure, Moore, her mother's voice came from inside her head. *Act like you've been there before.*

But she couldn't help herself. After all the work. All the controversy. All the ridicule. After sticking to her position despite everyone treating her like a pariah just for showing up, she was a published journalist.

Screw the *Pattersonville Times*. Megan Moore was going national.

She breathed deeply, savoring the sharp autumn air and the earthy smell of red and orange leaves. Tilting her head back, she looked toward the blue sky and giggled as her Red Sox cap slid over her forehead and as the bark pressed now against the back of her head.

Even better than the money was the note that accompanied it. *Please send more!*

She was glad she was alone. She had, in fact, come out here before even looking at the notification because she hadn't trusted herself to maintain a proper professional demeanor when she read it. To be honest with herself, she hadn't felt this happy since she was twelve, dancing to pop music and crushing on Davy Munroe in the privacy of her bedroom.

Being at Unicorn Field, the place where everything had started for her, was soothing, though. And, in truth, she knew she wasn't really alone here.

Glancing through the outfield slats, she could see Adrien where he was knelt over to maintain a patch of grass along the foul territory of left field. He looked so natural, running fingertips along the grass, then scanning the flat green plane of the field. His dark hair fell over his forehead almost exactly like Davy's blond hair did in the video of "She Looks Like You," which had been Megan's favorite song. Adrien was prettier than Davy Munroe, though. If that was possible.

Maybe it was his genetics. Or maybe it was a century living in the Fairy Realm.

Whatever.

Adrien Thorn was sky-high on the scale of Attractive.

It felt strange to have a— a someone. She wasn't sure what she and Adrien were, really, other than something more than friends. It seemed like he was always showing up around her, and sometimes, when they accidentally touched hands, she saw him jump in interesting ways. But he never asked her out. She was no better, though. The otherwise dogged persistence she felt while she was chasing a lead seemed to fade away every time she envisioned just biting the bullet and asking him out. What would a guy who'd lived a hundred years in the Fairy Realm want with a kid like her?

So, there they were.

Regardless, though, Adrien Thorn made her feel comfortable. He was the only person she'd want to let see the goofy smile she could feel plastered on her face now. Anyone else would be embarrassing. But Adrien had believed in her first. Probably more than her mom, really. Mom was one of those "you can do anything you set your mind to" kinds of people, which was great. But she didn't understand her passion like Adrien did.

On the field, Adrien stood to his full height and ran his hand over his hair. His chest gave a heavy heave, and Megan saw a darkness come over him.

Worried, she stood up, pushed her phone into her back pocket, and brushed off the prickly bits of grass and leaves that had stuck to her pants.

"Hey!" she called out.

She took two steps and leaned with both elbows over the edge of the outfield fence that ran between them.

Adrien smiled at the sight of her, but even as he put his hands in his pockets and strolled towards her, the smile faded.

"Are you okay?" she said as he drew closer.

"I'm fine."

"You don't look fine. I'm a reporter. I can see fine, and that's not it."

"Well," Adrien said, hesitating. "You look like you're doing pretty good, though."

"You could say that." The goofy grin was back, but there was nothing to do for it. "I got paid for my article."

Adrien's expression lit up. "Wow. Congratulations! Next step is the Pulitzer!"

"I accept."

"Ha."

Megan reached up and reseated her Red Sox cap. "It's a good dream, anyway."

"You'll make it happen."

Adrien's voice was tired. Megan looked at him more closely but wasn't sure what to say. She decided to stick with her own news for now and wait for a better opening.

She gave an exaggerated sigh. "I don't know. With stuff coming out about the Fairy Realm every day now, all these other reporters are getting into the mix. I'm going to need another angle."

"Well, at least the mayor's happy."

"No doubt." Megan couldn't really complain. Mayor Culpepper had thrown the gauntlet at her to write as many stories about the Fairy Realm as she could, and she had responded. If things went well, she'd have another couple stories printed in the next few days. But if there was one truism she'd heard about being a real journalist, it was that you're only as good as your last scoop. Now, with the flood of reporters coming into town, the basic story was getting played out and Megan was learning just how real that was. The mayor herself had to put off another interview with Megan because the KTV-10 people had scheduled over her.

"Easy come, easy go, I guess," Adrien said with a sense of fatalism that seemed out of place. He gripped the top rail of the fence, chewed the inside of his cheek, and let his gaze flow around the fence.

Megan instinctively reached across to put her hand on his shoulder.

The pressure brought his gaze to hers, and she saw something like despair writhe in his eyes.

"Seriously, Adrien. What's wrong?"

He pursed his lips.

"You can tell me, right?"

"Can I?"

She removed her hand from his shoulder. "You mean can you tell me without me printing it?" The slight widening of his eyes told her she was right. For the first time, an expression of possible mistrust made her feel bad. "Okay. That's fair. I know I've run with things in the past. But I give you my promise, Adrien Thorn, that I'll do my best to protect you. And, even if you don't trust me fully, you should know that as a professional journalist, all you have to do is tell me it's off the record and I can't use what you say."

"*As a professional journalist...* I like the sound of that."

She drew her phone from her pocket. "I've got the cash to prove it."

Adrien laughed then. "You're quite cute when you're passionate."

Megan glared at him.

He held his smile for a heartbeat longer, but then the corners of his mouth tightened, and his eyes drifted back towards the field he stood on. Megan watched as the muscles in his neck grew rigid with tension.

"Adrien," she said.

"I'm worried about Unicorn Field," Adrien said with a gusty breath. "It's just... with the fairies coming and being open about it to the whole town..."

He shook his head and shoved his hands deeper into his pockets.

Megan leaned further over the fence. "They said they just want to play baseball."

"Right. And Fred McMasters just wants to sell sports equipment."

Megan gave a knowing nod. Fred McMasters, Callie's dad, still owned the biggest sporting goods shop in the city. He'd gotten himself tangled up with denizens of the Fairy Realm in the past and had even tried to use the Web Gem to twist fate to his favor, but after the debacle that delayed the high school season, he'd laid low through the summer and early fall. Nobody had seen him for a couple of months now.

"I wonder where ol' Ball and Glove is?" Megan said.

"Who knows?" Adrien said with a shrug that told Megan he wasn't nearly as curious about it as she was.

"Maybe the Seelies threw him into servitude for screwing up their play for the Web Gem?"

"Could be. Or maybe the Unseelie Queen has her fingers into him. I've seen them all work. I don't trust any of them."

"Even the Small Folk?"

He shuddered. "Power corrupts."

"I understand that."

"I don't want any of them running free in the city."

Megan looked past Adrien to see a glove and ball lying on the ground where he'd been kneeling before. "Is that Emily's baseball?"

"Yeah."

She nodded, feeling the first wispy lines of a fresh story unfurl in her head but knowing for the first time that she wouldn't write it without Adrien's permission. Instead, she let the half-formed sentences dissipate.

The baseball and glove were talismans of a sort. Emily DeWitt and Adrien Thorn's personal *tchotchkes,* for the lack of a better word. They were tied to the Fairy Realm and made some kind of magic that Megan didn't understand yet. If she ever got the chance to bend her mind to unraveling their secrets, they would make for an amazing story in and of themselves. Despite her promise, she fought the urge to let her brain work on that angle. What did it say about her that she was willing to consider killing a story even if it was the truth? She wasn't sure. Dealing with the idea of privacy from the other side of the fence felt uneasy.

Adrien pulled his gaze from the baseball and glove. "I've been trying to figure out how to use them to build a barrier strong enough to keep the fey from crossing the boundaries of the field and coming into the city. I thought it would be simple enough when I agreed to play this season, but no matter what I try, I don't feel anything working." Arms spread and head hanging, Adrien sighed with despondency. "Emily was right. No matter how excited everyone is to play, it's just too dangerous. You would think I'd have learned my lesson by now, but I'm still overestimating my ability to reckon with fairies."

Megan matched his sigh. "I hate seeing you so upset."

"Thanks, I guess." He smiled at her. For a moment he seemed happier. "You know," he said. "You've got a story in you that no one else even knows about."

She glanced at DeWitt's ball and Adrien's glove. "I promised you I wouldn't use it."

"I mean the missing kids."

"Oh." A sudden wave of familiar, terrierlike determination ran through her spine.

The kids. At least seven of them. Each with at least a loose tie to Unicorn Field and possibly its then-undetected fairy ring. Lost over ages spaced far enough between to have blurred the field's impact. Assuming the field had an impact, that is. She'd done that research a few years back when she wrote her initial story about Adrien Thorn — nothing more than a legend to her at the time— but had lost track of it while covering the events of the Unicorns championship season and then the whole thing with the Fairy Realm's invitation. Leave it to Adrien, a boy who'd been kidnapped by the fey, to bring it all back with a single line.

Chasing the leads down would be hard work, which was one reason Megan had focused on the lower-hanging fruit of the championship run, but it would be worth it.

"You're right," Megan said, already feeling the structure of the article fill her mind. "That would be a big story. Maybe even an exposé." Headlines formed in her thoughts. The essence of the chase filled her so fully that she recalled the musky scent of the Wild Hunt as the Huntsman played baseball that fateful night, racing into the darkness to chase down fly balls hit to centerfield. The memory brought another image, too. Callie McMasters, bound up in spiderkin silk and tossed from the game, her magical bat lying abandoned on the ground beside her.

Megan's heart pounded hard again. That sense of focus she got when she was on the right trail of a hunt of her own settled over her. "Maybe you need Callie's bat to complete your ward," she said.

"Callie's bat?"

"You made better magic with the three together in the past, right?"

Adrien hesitated, but the idea seemed to flow through him. "Yeah. You're right. But she's in the Fairy Realm, finishing her contract with the Hunt. It's not like she's just down the road for us to visit." He kicked one foot at the outfield grass as if annoyed at it.

"Right," Megan said. "But I seem to recall certain sources saying something about Samhain making things easier."

"Benji," Adrien said with a wry smile.

Megan gave a grin that was only slightly goofy this time. "Benji says they've been moving back and forth, right? Do you think they can open the gate for us, too?"

"For *us?*"

"I need to do some investigative reporting there," Megan replied. "For the story?"

Adrien laughed again. "I guess I can't really argue if you're following a lead I gave you, can I?"

"No. I don't think you can."

Adrien stood up straight and took on a fresh confidence. "I've got to clean up here. Why don't you text Benji and ask if we can meet at their place at five o'clock? Maybe when we're done, we can go grab a burger and make some plans for tomorrow?"

Megan adjusted her ball cap and squinted up at Adrien—who was now backlit with the setting sun. She smiled.

"It's a date," she said.

CHAPTER

THREE

A crow perched in the big oak tree in the Amberman backyard let out a grating croak.

Benji, who had been making yet another circle around it, gave a startled jump.

The dry grass and fallen leaves crunched satisfyingly under the soles of the amazing new brown faux-leather boots Benji had grabbed on clearance, and earlier they had pushed their fists into the pockets of the silk-lined leather jacket they'd gotten during a bit of retail celebration of the State Championship game. You only live once. It was great to win, but even better to have done it with the same teammates who had started together as first-year losers. The jacket, with its smooth pockets and perfect sheen, felt good in indescribable ways. The wind was making a mess of their carefully styled curls, but that annoyance barely registered now.

Instead, Benji drew in a long breath of crisp autumn air and held it, letting the earthy scent fill up their lungs.

With the exception of Opening Day, the season of Samhain had always been their favorite. It was a blast to spend hours dreaming of costumes and greasepaint, then going out for Halloween.

They were all too old for that now.

Benji let the breath go, feeling good as the air left their lungs.

They shooed the bird. "Go away, little crow. I've got friends coming."

The crow remained, though, peering at Benji with a defiant gaze.

Benji huffed. "Well. Not a lot I can do about it, is there?"

The bird shifted on the branch but still didn't leave.

Benji laughed and shoved their fists back into their pockets. "How about you just not startle me again, all right?"

Megan Moore and Adrien Thorn were due any moment now.

Megan's text, *Adrien and I wanna talk about if maybe you can do us a favor*, had been classic Megan. Intriguing, but low on details. Her way was more than a little annoying, but now that Benji had gotten to know the reporter the secretiveness of her approach didn't bother them so much. As a journalist, Megan would always wait for the right moment to reveal a scoop.

Benji was finding they didn't mind much of anything at all, these days. Having sole care and keeping of a powerful fairy artifact had that effect. Even in their bedroom, under magical lock and key, the aura of the Web Gem felt so close. It was hard to get too worried about anything else, or even to think about anything else. Sometimes, Benji marveled at the fact they'd even managed to graduate high school. In addition to its raw power, the Web Gem was the first tangible link Benji had to the fairy heritage they had felt since they were old enough to have memories. Unfortunately, that heritage had not turned out to be linked to the cheerful Small Folk or the haughty Seelie Court, nor even to the brooding Wild Hunt or the outright evil Unseelie Court, but instead to the ancient and nightmarish spiderkin.

Be careful what you wish for, right?

Some things, once known, can never be unknown.

Benji hadn't slept properly for a week after learning that factoid.

It was all good, though. While Benji didn't feel particularly spidery, they still felt a deep, undeniable connection to the Fairy

Realm as a whole. Once they'd gotten over the initial shock, they'd had an easy enough time falling back into their usual bright attitude. The spiderkin were pretty cool, really. Very mysterious. And powerful, too.

Benji spent an awful lot of the last semester of senior year daydreaming about the silken quality of the light the Web Gem emitted when they held it and imagining the magic it took to create that kind of artifact. Some nights they would lie in bed and feel the essence of the artifact's magic flowing through them in the form of lucid dreams that would have them flying over Pattersonville.

Benji shook their head to clear it and made another circle under the oak tree. At least the crow had remained quiet this time rather than startling them out of their reverie. They didn't want to be caught with a brain full of cobwebs when Megan and Adrien came around.

Right on cue, the murmur of voices wafted from around the front of the house.

Benji couldn't make out the words, but they caught Megan's quick tone and the rumble of Adrien's laughter that followed.

Overhead, the crow let out a full-throated caw, then spread its heavy wings and flapped away. A pair of brown leaves trailed down from the branch where it had been perched.

Benji twisted their lips into a frown as the leaves twirled in ominous silence towards the ground. The odor of fire rose in the moment, then left. Benji gazed up to track the crow, but it was already gone.

"Hey, Benji. Thanks for letting us come over so soon," Megan said as she and Adrien appeared around the corner of the house. She had her phone in her hand, clearly in full journalist mode. Behind her, Adrien ambled along with his hands in the pockets of his Unicorns' windbreaker, his baseball glove tucked under one arm. He pulled the opposite hand out to give Benji a wave of greeting.

"Nice eyeliner today, Benj," he said.

"Thanks," Benji said, turning to smile at the two of them. The compliment smoothed away the ominous sensation the crow had left behind. It was always nice when someone noticed their efforts with makeup. "And it's no trouble at all. My folks are out having their anniversary dinner. I've got the place to myself."

"That's sweet," Megan said. Her smile softened the reporter hardness she normally carried herself with.

Benji smiled, too. "Yeah, it's nice. But that's not why you wanted to meet up, is it? Unless you're doing a human-interest piece on all the long-lasting relationships around town?"

Megan rolled her eyes and fiddled with something on her phone. "Hardly. Not to downplay those kinds of things, but we've got something more important to talk about."

"Matters that have to do with the Fairy Realm, I presume?"

Adrien shifted. Though the movement was slight, the change in his posture was instant. Where a moment ago he'd been casual, now he was practically military.

"We need to do something to ward Unicorn Field before the season starts, Benji. The idea of fairies— from any faction— running loose in Pattersonville..." He trailed off, staring into the middle distance for a heartbeat before snapping back to attention. "I'm not saying we shouldn't have agreed to play this new season with them, because even I couldn't deny the draw of the idea. But Emily was right to worry about the danger they present, and you and I both know it."

A surge of connection to the Web Gem swelled, and Benji's first reaction was to want to disagree. They loved the Fairy Realm just as much as they always had, and they'd long held the stance that Pattersonville deserved to know its connection to that fantastical place. More families here than just the Ambermans could trace their heritage back to the Realm. But after that intense game last spring, and after how close they and their friends had come to letting control of the Web Gem fall into the Seelie Court's hands forever, Benji couldn't deny the threat those connections held, too.

They blew out a sigh. "I do know it. But I don't know how I can help you with any kind of ward. My ability to use the Web Gem is still kind of limited. Really, I'm just trying to keep it safe."

Saying that aloud left a sour taste in Benji's mouth. Maybe they *were* supposed to just keep it safe, but Benji hadn't been able to resist trying to use it for something more. And they'd made progress since first receiving the artifact. At least Benji had been able to move back and forth between the realms. But they still weren't anywhere near as capable as Mr. McMasters had been, for example. McMasters' progress was probably because the Seelies themselves had coached him up, but the knowledge that a sleazy wannabe like him was able to do flashier things than Benji prickled underneath their skin.

Adrien shook his head. "We're not here to ask for help casting the ward itself."

"Then what are you—" Benji stopped. Understanding washed over them. "You're going to work the talisman magic again."

"Right," Adrien said.

Benji continued, halfway ruminating on the past. "Like you did to un-statue everyone after the spring game."

"Exactly," Megan confirmed. Her smile beamed.

Benji had been able to help Adrien, Emily DeWitt, and Callie back then, using the Web Gem to see through the tangle of magic the Unseelie Queen had cast with her stolen baseball magic, turning many of their friends into statues in her bid for control of the Fairy Realm. Benji helped the three of them realize they could use their separate talismans together to work bigger magic than they each could individually.

"That makes sense," Benji said. "Maybe the three bound together would make a difference."

"We know you've been going back and forth for a while now. Can you get us across to talk to Callie?"

"Sure. I think so, anyway. Making my way between the mortal world and the Fairy Realm is apparently my jam." A sense of relief let the back of Benji's neck relax and their eagerness to help flared. Benji had been practicing small jumps for months now. And, as the fairies had said, the magic had flowed easier as Samhain drew near. They'd been itching to try moving more than just themself when the fairy delegation had swooped in and presented them with just the opportunity they'd been hoping for. Excitement hummed through Benji. "This would be a good time to practice taking whole teams back and forth, too."

They glanced back and forth between Adrien and Megan, sensing something more here than met the eye. Benji read a sense of energy in Megan's presence that he was getting familiar with. Giving her a sideways stare, Benji followed that tingle of intuition.

"Adrien may be trying to cast a spell, but you're up to something else."

Megan returned Benji's stare with a look that sliced as coldly as the crisp autumn wind. "There have been more people who have fallen through that thing than just Adrien and Emily, Benji. I want to find them. Their story is what I'm chasing now. I'm going to expose the full extent of the danger that will come of that ring if it's left unwarded."

Benji stared at her with growing respect. Knowing she was tenacious was one thing, but being on the receiving end of that intensity was another thing altogether.

They cleared their throat. "All right, then. What about Emily? You need her baseball, right? Do we swing by her place and pick her up?"

An unexpected darkness fell over Adrien's eyes, and Megan glanced away.

"Emily's focused on what college she wants to go to," Adrien replied. Then he raised the glove he held in his hand enough that Benji saw the baseball inside its pocket. "She lent me her ball to work a ward, but that's it."

"Oh. I see." Benji shifted enough that their boots crunched more dry leaves. "Well. Yeah. That makes sense. She's been through a lot already."

That was true. From her first disappearance into the Fairy Realm to dealing with Fred McMasters and then getting put between a rock and a hard place with the Seelie King and the Web Gem last spring, Emily had been dealing with the Fairy Realm longer than anyone but Adrien. If she wanted to step away from it all, nobody had any right to stop her, Benji least of all. But it was also true that Adrien had even more cause to walk away, by Benji's thinking, anyway, and here he was, putting himself on the line for Pattersonville once again.

Comparing and contrasting their friends like that felt ugly, though. With a conscious effort, they made themself smile.

There was magic to be done here. It would be good to see the Fairy Realm in its Fall Season splendor.

"Well, she's missing out on all the fun, then, isn't she?"

Adrien gave a reserved sigh of success. "Great. Can we do it now?"

"I don't see why not," Benji said. "Come on, we'll go up to my room. That's where I've been keeping the Web Gem."

CHAPTER

FOUR

The artifact sat in the vastness of the fold, sensing.

As it always had, it touched the infinite tensions that ran along the infinite threads of existence as those same threads twined together to form the ancient realms of power and time, stretching and flowing into the forever fields of the Realms to mix with the churning masses of baseball magic, the awesome power of the fey, and the beautiful frailty that hums in every mortal existence.

But, for the first time in its existence, the artifact was now untethered.

Owned by no faction of the Fairy Realm.

If the Web Gem had been fully conscious perhaps it would have felt uncomfortable here in the realm of mortals, adrift since last season when factions within the Seelie Court had conspired to break the pact of the Fairy League and had ripped the artifact from the Small Folk who were its proper owner. It had tried to maintain the balance of power. Tried to right the wrong. But the strength and conniving of the Unseelie Queen and the intensity of her conflict with those same Seelies had broken the artifact's hold, and the bumbling mishandling by the mortal known as McMasters had ensured the Web Gem could not regain its sphere of influence. As such, the baseball magic had been polluted. So perhaps— if the Web Gem *had* been truly sentient— it would have felt anger. Or fear. Or deep sadness.

But the Web Gem was what it was. A great power, but one without the autonomy or the emotions that would have come from such conscience.

Instead, it pulsed in the forever confines of its physical form, sensing and waiting in the infinite moment of each passing second, folding events into the silken cocoons of its own power until the next season was won and the Keeper— known in the Mortal Realm as Benji Amberman— returned to set it back to its true task: regulating the flow of baseball magic throughout the realms like so many glistening drops of dew slithering along the threads of a spider's web.

Even in this untethered state, the Web Gem felt that flow, and within the flow, everything else. The Keeper and two others entering the house, a door opening somewhere in the moment, the fall of mortal footsteps crossing the carpeted bedroom to send dying vibrations through its base, and the new light filtering through its crystals to be cut into prismatic flares of power.

"Come in." The Keeper's voice flowed with golden flashes that calmed the roiling sea of all that has been, all that is now, and all that could ever be. Their touch gave the artifact a sense of stability.

One of the others was familiar, too.

Designated Hitter, the name flowed over threads. Adrien Thorn.

"Why are we here?" the other asked. She was tall and slight, and spoke into one of the devices that the Web Gem could sense all around them, a piece of unfeeling mortal magic. She was a reporter, the Web Gem recalled from her time at the last Big Game. Someone who records events for all history.

The artifact touched her aura and felt kinship.

"I've only gone through the gate by myself," Benji Amberman

said. "I think I'm going to need its help to take the two of you with me."

Hearing the Keeper express a proper understanding of the difficulties they faced sent shivers of confidence through the Web Gem, which it funneled back into the threads to create eddies of calm in the storm of power. The Keeper's spiderkin ancestry was too thin to allow unfettered access to the transfer spells. At least it was too thin to do so without considerably deeper learning and practice. The artifact could help, though. Its crystals flared with something that might have been comfort.

It was time, the artifact felt.

Time to introduce the Keeper to the full depths of the Fairy Realm.

The Keeper wrapped their fingers around the Web Gem's base, then draped a blanket over its wooden and crystal features before cradling it in the crook of one arm, similar and yet different from the way the Unseelie Queen had once cradled it. Spiderkin magic was its own thing. The Keeper had a different power about them.

"Let's go," the Keeper said. The Web Gem shivered in readiness.

The inherent power in the soil grew bolder as the Keeper, the Designated Hitter, and the reporter walked through a chilled afternoon to draw near Unicorn Field. The closeness of the Fairy Realm was strong here. The Web Gem read the pulse of drums and the screech of a Hunted creature in the vibrations. Power roiled in the currents. The threads throbbed with anticipation.

"Hold on tight," the Keeper said as they uncovered the Web Gem.

Sunlight burned through the artifact's crystals, and the warmth of three hands pressed against the Web Gem's base.

The Keeper's spell work filled the area. It was thin, yes, but pure, and properly done. It needed only a small boost to function properly.

And the Web Gem was happy to provide that boost— as happy

as it could be, anyway— to the first true student it had ever had. The Web Gem absorbed the Keeper's spell, then tied it first to a single thread connected to the Fairy Realm, and then another, multiplying them, letting the power run across the fairy ring's perimeter, and helping the one known as Benji Amberman find the proper timing.

A whirlwind picked up on the baseball field, carrying dust from the infield to swirl with drying leaves and blades of dead grass. Power rose to latch onto all three travelers. Their hairs blew in the wind, and the Web Gem could feel the trills of each of their three hearts beating in unison.

Then they were slipping through the portal in a way that no mortal soul had ever experienced.

Flying, one might call it. Gliding along the invisible threads spun between the Realms. Seeing a spider's-eye view of the land below. Living through a lucid dream, their mortal bodies extended into a realm that existed only in their own space.

The magic of the Fairy Realm lent a sweetness to the air that had the Web Gem humming in dim nostalgia.

With that flavor came a realization of freedom and a rediscovery of old power.

Now that no Denizen of the Realms, no Court or Lesser House, could claim ownership of it, the artifact was free as it hadn't been in eons. It felt that freedom now in the threads and powers of All Existence, heard the chatter of the factions, and sensed the raw thrill of excitement coming from every team in the Fairy League as they gossiped and prepared for the season ahead. This slate of games would be a free-for-all, everyone realized— the first to be played without an established owner of the Web Gem among the courts and houses since the first festival season so long ago.

The artifact carried the three mortals through the realm.

Past the River Kin lounging in their cavernous palace, splashing in cool springs, and discussing new strategies, watching their leader, Lady Marne, as she split off to rendezvous with Maddoc of the Small Folk. Around to the Small Folk practicing in the overgrown glade where Emily DeWitt had first brought them together, seeing the anxiety etched on manager Fennoc's face as the team bumbled through their jovial practices and boggling as Greeven, the rag-armed elf, patrolled third base and Essie the brownie cheered his every errant throw.

The artifact whisked them to the darkest part of the cobweb-laden forests to see the Hag Sisters concocting trick plays and plotting steps to exploit weaknesses in their opposition. It infiltrated the Seelie Court to find the King and members of the Court itself embroiled in subterfuge, knives at each other's backs as much as anyone else's. The Web Gem experienced a small vibration at the sight— those same roots of subterfuge had created the intrigue that resulted in the Web Gem's freedom to begin with.

Then, using the power flowing from the Keeper, the artifact followed the threads that led to the Unseelie Queen herself, cloistered in a cocoon of secrecy so dark and so hard that even the Web Gem's power could reveal only the land below.

It was not in the artifact's powers to understand mortal emotions, but it felt the humans each react to this tour— and especially this last node, which made the Designated Hitter grow sour and sallow, and wrap his gloved hand around the baseball that he carried with such force that the Web Gem felt the bones of his fingers come near the point they might shatter.

"There's no good can come from that," Adrien Thorn said into the warbling wind, and the reporter shivered.

The Web Gem scampered across one thread and then another, drinking in the power that the Keeper was still funneling into their spell work, pulling threads together to break their speed and bring the full corporeal essence of their bodies back together to land there in the woods that were the central practice fields of the Hunt.

They coalesced among the trees, hair windblown and eyes watering from the bluster, faces glowing with something that might otherwise have been a sunburn.

Benji Amberman, the Keeper, grasped the Web Gem with all their might, wobbled, then collapsed to one knee. A twinge of something like regret tugged at the Web Gem. Its student was spent far more so than they ought to be.

Adrien Thorn, gripping that magic-laden baseball inside the glove that also came tinged with power, glared through the trees as if preparing to cast a spell of his own.

And the reporter, wide-eyed and winded, but with a fresh sense of determination that the Web Gem could not miss, stared at her surroundings, cataloging every detail.

There, amid the pack of the Wild Hunt in mid-practice, stood another mortal soul. Callie McMasters. Complete with a bat that seeped power as certainly as the Designated Hitter's glove and ball.

CHAPTER
FIVE

Callie McMasters, one-time star player of the Marion Bulldogs and now contracted member of the Wild Hunt's baseball team, straddled the flat stone that served as the pitcher's rubber and sniffed at the air as the satyr batter came up to home plate. Pyrgin had become a friend as well as a valuable teammate as the Wild Hunt's preseason scrimmage series developed. With the power of the baseball magic proved during last year's screwy events, Pyrgin, along with many other of the Hunt's players, had decided to knuckle down and get serious this season.

That was good. Encouraging, even.

But today, as a batter, he was her prey.

She cast a honed glance at Thacker, the menacing little Red Cap who sat hunched behind the plate, and waited for him to crook his dirty talons in a signal for the pitch.

Two blood-caked nails descended.

Callie bit back her initial scoff. The curveball was usually one that Pyrgin would pounce on, but she knew Thacker better these days, and she'd come to trust his calls as her catcher. If he said this was the time to show Pyrgin the deuce, she should follow up on that trail.

The satyr *had* been boasting a bit during the Wild Hunt's run yesterday evening. She'd heard his sharp barks even from her place near the front with Trace.

And now, standing at the plate with the bat resting casually against his shoulder, he oozed so much cocky self-confidence it was practically dripping from the points of his curved horns.

Stifling a grin, Callie nodded to Thacker, then set her grip for the curve.

The other Wild Hunt players scattered about the practice field jeered and hollered as she wound up. Pyrgin twirled his bat, bared his teeth, and flashed knife-sharp talons in a display of threat. Callie let it all wash over her. After more than a year spent with the Hunt, their antics were becoming familiar to her now. Amongst fellow hunters, these displays were shows of affection or even signs of respect.

Naturally, that affection came with a healthy helping of good, old-fashioned trash-talk, too.

With a grunt, Callie let the curve fly. She'd put a special spin on it, something a bit twistier than the curves Pyrgin was most familiar with.

She caught a glimpse of the Leader of the Hunt where he stood at deceptive leisure in the umpire's spot. His golden wolf eyes sparkled with approval.

Pyrgin, oblivious to this instantaneous exchange, swung.

As Callie had intended, the ball waited until the bat was a hairs-breadth away before swerving sharply— not to the side, but upward to smash into Pyrgin's nose with a sharp crunch.

The satyr let out a decidedly un-cocky squeal, and the other players roared with laughter.

"A nose-breaker! She got 'im with a Hunt classic!"

Callie let her grin show now. Pyrgin wouldn't be seriously hurt, and even if he was, the Hunt wasn't without its own flavor of healing magic. As he glared at her with bright red blood slipping between the fingers he held to his nose, she gave a jaunty two-fingered salute.

"Strike one, yeah, Pyr?"

"Yeah, yeah. Enjoy id now, Mistress. Dere won'd be ady bore."

Wiping his bloody hand on his furred thigh, Pyrgin took up a more serious batter's stance. The sight made Callie glad.

"For the sake of our chances in the Fall Season, I hope not!"

She desperately wanted to win the upcoming Fairy League Season, but not for herself. True, her contract with the Hunt stipulated that she could not return home to the mortal world until the season was completed and the Web Gem was awarded. Also true, last season that clause had caused her to become something of a damsel in distress when the Web Gem went missing and thus was unable to be awarded to anyone.

But she'd come to appreciate the Wild Hunt in ways she never expected when she'd first signed on with them. She'd been in a low place back then, kicked off the Bulldogs, coming to grips with her newfound respect for her then-rival Emily DeWitt, and looking for someone, anyone, to play ball with.

It had been a rocky start, but the Wild Hunt, from the gentle Centaur Trace to the wild little gremlin-thing Thacker, was starting to feel like family.

It was a strange feeling. One she had never truly felt. She wanted to win this season for the Hunt itself.

Callie prepared to pitch again, but when the wind shifted it brought a strange new scent with it, one that had her perking up in concern.

Her hunting skills had improved during her time here, and though she still had room to improve further, she didn't think she'd misread the scent on the wind. She peered into the shadows of the forest that surrounded the Hunt's practice field, the scrimmage all but driven from her mind.

"Adrien?" she said. What was Adrien Thorn doing in the Fairy Realm when he was supposed to be in Pattersonville?

But it was, indeed, Adrien— crashing around in the foliage with no care for hiding his approach, which meant the whole of the Wild Hunt was keenly aware of him long before he finally emerged into view, strolling out of the forest as if it were as docile a place as any park in the mortal world, as well as Benji Amberman and the reporter girl Callie had met at that fateful spring game. Megan, she thought quickly. Megan Moore was the girl's name. Benji had the look of prey that's been run to its collapse point, their face so pale that their makeup, which was beginning to run a bit, stood out in sharp contrast. The reporter, meanwhile, with her dogged determination mingling with boundless energy, looked as though she'd be right at home amongst the hunting hounds.

Sharp annoyance crossed Callie's mind. Adrien of all people ought to know better than to treat any place in the Fairy Realm so casually. But the annoyance quickly faded in favor of her former concern. Adrien wasn't stupid. He had to have a reason for this visit.

"Halt scrimmage," she called, though it was hardly necessary now.

"Hope this isn't a bad time," Adrien said as he and his companions stepped up to the third base foul line. "We've got a favor to ask you."

CALLIE HAD AT FIRST INSISTED on having Trace and the rest of the Hunt with her as they talked. She and Trace made a good team, and the Wild Hunt was her family now. She owed them that much.

"That's good and all," Trace had said. "But let's have the scrimmage continue. Perhaps just you and I can converse with your mortal friends?"

And as soon as the Leader realized Benji carried the Web Gem, he'd made every effort to see to their comfort before, surprisingly, deferring to Benji's request that they be able to speak with Callie in private.

Now, they sat behind the dugout, just Callie, Trace, and their three visitors, while the Leader of the Hunt oversaw the continuing scrimmage. Benji was lolling against the back wall and trying desperately to look like they weren't about to fall asleep as Adrien and Megan laid out their story and their requests.

"Missing kids?" Trace said, his deep voice rumbling in mild confusion. "Human children?"

Megan nodded, so focused on the topic that she ignored the growing swarm of tiny glowing pixies they'd accumulated. "Human children. Nobody older than a senior in high school, anyway. There are at least seven of them, maybe more. But whatever, I intend to find them."

"Meanwhile," Adrien cut in, "*I* intend to keep any more from joining them. Will you help me work the warding magic, Callie?" He held up the talismans of his own glove and Emily's baseball, then cast a pointed glance at the magical bat lying in the grass beside Callie, the one she never went anywhere without, even when she was pitching rather than hitting. "If we get our pieces of baseball magic together, I think we can protect Pattersonville from the worst of it."

"It's a good idea," Callie said. "And I'm happy to help. But I don't think I can do anything until we play a game at Unicorn Field. My contract, you know," she added with a grimace. "I can't leave the Fairy Realm without a game."

Trace twisted his torso to look at her. He sat with his horse legs curled under himself in a pose Callie privately thought of as elegant. "Surely our Leader would allow a brief excursion if you asked."

"I could not if I wanted to," the Hunt Leader said. He'd stepped forward from the umpire's box and now examined the visitors with curious anxiety. The Hunt was quite disciplined in its way. Callie had been happy to see his focus on the season. "Her contract is clear."

"What if I said I wanted to go visit Dear Old Dad?"

As if that would ever happen. Callie had disowned her father, and if she ever saw him again, she might even tell him so.

Seelie suck-up.

The Leader narrowed his eyes, and Callie's blood ran cold in a way that felt strangely good.

"We both know that would be a lie."

Callie nodded, and after a deep breath turned to Adrien. "So, that's it," she said. "I'll help when we play our first game in the mortal realm." She turned to the reporter to see Megan's thumbs racing along the surface of her phone, madly typing a draft of her story.

Adrien frowned as he idly tore blades of grass from the dirt. "Per the schedule, the Wild Hunt doesn't play the Unicorns for a few games yet. I was hoping to get the field warded before the games began."

"I get it," Callie said. "But I don't think it's likely to be that much of an issue. The schedule only has the Unicorns hosting the River Kin before us, with their other games played on this side of the portal, at the Other Field. You can trust the River Kin, as much as you can trust any fairies, I think. Lady Marne's good."

"She certainly doesn't seem to have any interest in whisking away mortal souls," Adrien said. "You're probably right."

"Besides, you'll have both you and Emily there to stop any shenanigans, right?"

A dark look crossed Adrien's face, and Megan glanced away. Benji, still leaning against the back of the dugout, let out a grunt of discontent.

Callie didn't need Hunt skills to read between the lines. Something was wrong with Emily DeWitt.

"Never mind. Look, even though I can't get to Unicorn Field right now, I think I can be of more immediate help with tracking down those kids. I've learned a few tricks in my time here with the Hunt. How about Trace and I start following the trail of those kids, and when our game comes up, I'll report back what we've found. If you can hold on until then, you and I can work to cast the warding magic.

And… well, if you can get Emily to come around between now and then, that's all the better, yeah?"

"She'll come around," Benji said, their voice full of insistence despite the thready thinness of it.

Adrien sighed, but then nodded. "Yeah. I understand your deal. Fairy contracts are tricky and dangerous to fiddle with. So that seems like the best we can do. I'll talk to Emily again. Thanks for your help, Cal."

"No problem," Callie said.

As a group, they clambered to their feet, brushing dirt from their pants, and stretching cramped muscles. Trace flicked his tail and gave his pelt a quivering shake, sending twigs and leaves tumbling back to the ground. He watched intently as Benji struggled to stand.

"Do you need help, Keeper?" he asked gently, noting Benji's carefully precise movements.

"No, no, I'm totally fine." Benji stood up straight and beamed a forced smile at the group.

Adrien and Megan seemed to buy it, but Callie was unconvinced. Benji's color was still too pale under their makeup. Still, if they wanted to push themself, that was up to them.

"You guys should head on back. Don't want to lose track of time in the Fairy Realm, you know," Callie said.

Adrien squinted at her. "What about you, then? You've been here for over a year now. Are you all right?"

Callie scoffed and bent to scoop up her bat. The feel of its hefty weight against her shoulder sent a wave of confidence through her. "I'm not as fragile as some folk."

Adrien's squint became a smirk. "Careful, Cal. You and I haven't played against one another yet. You might eat those words."

Benji fumbled with the Web Gem, holding it before themself like it was a snared fox, still thrashing and capable of delivering a wicked bite. "Let's get going, okay?"

Adrien cast one last competitive look Callie's way, then went to stand beside Benji, placing his hand on the Web Gem, too. "C'mon, Megan."

The reporter, however, stood where she was, an intense expression on her face. Her fingers wrapped so tightly around her phone that her knuckles went white.

A sense of unease crept over Callie. That girl really did look as if she'd be right at home among the hounds.

Then, in one swift motion, Megan went to Adrien's side.

On her arrival, Benji screwed up their face and began the spell that would take the three of them home.

But as the spell work unfolded, instead of placing her hand on the Web Gem like the others, Megan cupped Adrien's cheek.

Adrien's eyes went comically wide as she pressed her lips to his.

He remained frozen in place as she stepped away.

"Sorry, Adrien. You go on and talk to Emily. But what kind of reporter would I be if I just sat back and let someone else do all my legwork for me? I've got to chase this story my own way."

She darted off into the depths of the forest, then, leaving behind a swirl of dead leaves and bobbing pixie lights.

A heartbeat later, Benji and Adrien disappeared, swept away by the power of the Web Gem.

SIX

With her fists shoved into her hoodie's pockets, Emily DeWitt took brisk strides across the sun-drenched sidewalk that ran from Bradford Street toward Pattersonville's downtown area. She lifted her clouded gaze and unscrunched the lips she had twisted into knots the moment before. The bill of her Cubs' hat—Mom's favorite team—shaded her eyes from the noontime sun that sat high in a partially cloudy sky. A hint of dry leaves flavored the breeze. Her right hand, her pitching hand, which usually wrapped around her mom's baseball when she walked this way, felt empty now. The other was just closed up in a tight fist. The absence of the ball made her mad at herself. She should never have lent it to Adrien.

Just one more crappy thing to add to the pile.

It was lunchtime. With Dad at work, she'd been all alone in the house and had been going crazy enough that she decided she was going to hit up Annie's for one of their awesome grilled cheese sandwiches, and an old-fashioned orange drink from the old-fashioned fountain Annie kept behind the counter. Annie's always reminded her of her mom because, while Dad had Victory Lasagna to his name,

Mom had taken her there many afternoons after heartbreak or when things were getting too depressing. *"An orange drink from an old-fashioned fountain has a special kind of magic in it, now, doesn't it?"* she'd say, sipping from a soggy paper straw.

Eventually, they would leave, and every time, Emily felt better about whatever it was that was bothering her.

She wasn't sure it was going to work this time, though.

Two days from now, the Unicorns were going to host the River Kin in the first game of the Fall Season, and Emily couldn't stop the anger from burning through her. When did it end? When did she get to move on with her life? When did she get to be a normal girl again, instead of the one everyone ran to whenever they had a fairy problem they needed to solve?

The bell hanging over Annie's front door clanked as she entered.

The diner was a throwback to the middle of last century. Emily stepped further in, feeling the heat of the busy room as a cacophony of voices in conversation welled up.

The place was warm after the autumn chill. It smelled of pizza and root beer.

The building was deeper than it was wide, and the padded edge of the counter ran along the far right-hand side. Being downtown adjacent, as Dad would say, Annie's was always a popular lunchtime place, but now its array of tables was even more jam-packed. *Tourists,* Emily thought with a scowl. Ever since the news stories about the Fairy Realm had started to leak out, it was like Pattersonville's population had doubled, and with them, the expectations on Emily. Couldn't they leave anything alone?

Leaving a space between herself and a guy and a girl who both wore long-sleeved shirts with the logo of the florist shop next door, Emily slid into an open barstool at the far end of the counter and grabbed a laminated menu, realizing she wanted it more to have something to play with than to decide what she wanted. She had the whole thing memorized, anyway. For a moment, remembering her mother again, she used it as a fan, feeling the breeze it made pick at random strands of her frazzled hair. From the back of the diner, the ancient player organ pushed against the far-away wall began to play "Take Me Out to the Ball Game."

Great.

"Hey, Emily," Dassandra Newton, the server behind the counter, said as she glided over. "Grilled cheese and an orange?"

"You know me too well."

"Well," Dassandra said, pausing to give Emily a mockingly grave expression. "I know that look, anyway. What's up, girl? State Championship got you down?"

Dassandra had been in the same year as Emily, which meant she'd graduated last year. If there was a poster child for optimism and bright faces, she was it.

Emily couldn't help but return a small smile, though it felt bitter across her face.

That was one more thing the arrival of the fairy lords had taken from her. She'd finally led her Mom's Unicorns to victory, finally fulfilled her promise, and then the invitation to play in the next Fairy League season had come in, and everyone had moved on to newer, more exciting things.

In a way, it even felt like that victory was only because the fairies had meddled in her life. She'd gotten to repeat senior year because she'd spent too much of her first go-around playing with the Small Folk, after all.

"Life's supposed to get easier after you graduate, isn't it?" Emily said.

"Ha ha ha, ha ha ha ha!" Dassandra sang, her head tottering right and left to punctuate each syllable. "Sure thing. No more homework, but more bills. And I didn't even go to college like you lot are planning on."

As she sang, the two florists had slipped out of their seats, and in their places it was like Emily's teammates Jake Nesbitt, Patsy Pell, and Jamal Douglass just materialized in a row beside her.

Her ex-teammates, anyway. State Champions or not, they'd all graduated now.

They were all free agents.

Dassandra swept the florists' empty plates away with a cheery smile, leaving the baseball players alone.

"What do you have to worry about?" Patsy said in that way she had. She'd obviously heard Emily complaining. "Must be great to get to choose out of all the offers you got piling in. I got squat." As usual, Patsy's outfit was black from her boots and jeans to the dyed denim jacket she wore over her Unicorns championship T-shirt. Her makeup was, as always, impeccable, and included a quite fashionable black outlined lip paint that transitioned to bone gray over the plump of her lip. Her dark hair had been recently cut, and fell perfectly over her forehead and around her cheekbones.

Who would have thought that just a few days ago she'd clobbered a fat fastball into the left field stands to tie up the final game?

"You'll be fine," Emily said. "You know you can do anything you put your mind to."

"Says the one with fifteen gazillion offers from fifteen gazillion schools."

"Yeah. Well. You look really cute today by the way. Very Halloween chic."

"Thanks."

"I wish I had your way with things."

Seeing Patsy's perfect get-up made Emily imagine her friend peering into her vanity mirror and working to get that effect on her lips. That thought made Emily flash on her time in the Fairy Realm when Mellica and Jessebel had doted on her to pretty her up. It had worked, kind of. But only because the pixies had the same special kind of magic that seemed to reside in Patsy. They could all see things Emily couldn't.

Maybe that was why Patsy, as well as the others, were so excited about playing this extra season with the fairies, despite the dangers. Emily knew she ought to be excited about the opportunity to play with the baseball magic again, but she was just so tired. She wanted to focus on choosing a college, but even that decision was more difficult than she'd hoped. Patsy was right. She did have too many offers.

She ground her teeth to keep from complaining further. How many of those offers had come in simply because of what the fairies had made of her life and her baseball style?

Unconsciously, the fingers of her pitching hand twitched as if to close around her Mom's ball.

"You're going to be fine, too," Jake said to Emily. "I mean, I've got three schools wanting me to play with them, so I get it. Admittedly, they're only partial scholarships, but it's still tough to choose."

Jamal patted Jake on the back. "Don't worry, wherever you go it won't be long before you play them into a full ride."

"Maybe. Still, though. We gotta give Emily some space. It's not like she's making a decision that will change everything about her life now, is it?"

Everyone laughed.

"Hey! You're the Unicorn players, right? The ones who are going to play against real live fairies?" It was an older woman with three kids by her side. They had all eaten and were leaving. She was already pointing her camera at them. "Can I get a picture of my kids with you? You're all they can talk about now!"

"What are the fairies like?" the older boy said before anyone could answer. His face was glowing.

"Sure," Jamal said, motioning the four of them to scrunch in together, and for the kids to come closer.

A moment later, with picture taken and gawkers moved on, the four of them were again alone.

"Better get used to it," Jake said, seeing the expression on Emily's face. "You're a celebrity now."

"Great," Emily replied. She blew out a deep breath. It was like her skin was going to split. "Can the world just stop for a second already?"

Patsy put her hand on Emily's shoulder. "At least with the

Unicorns playing in the Fairy Realm League we get to play one more season together, right? That means the college decision can wait."

There it was. The pointed question she'd been dreading since the moment the Unicorns had accepted the offer to play in the Fall Season. Emily knew absolutely everyone had made their assumptions about her. She'd already set Adrien straight on his ideas, but she'd let the others hang.

She hated making her friends upset, either her human Unicorns friends or her fairy Small Folk ones. And both teams were hoping she'd play for them, of course.

"Hmm," Emily said, taking advantage of the arrival of her grilled cheese and orange drink to avoid answering a moment longer.

Which friends do you choose?

Which do you offend?

Or, she thought again, what if she *didn't* decide to put off her college ambitions for yet another year and play in this fantastical, once-in-a-lifetime collaboration between mortal and fairy?

"I don't think I'm going to play at all," Emily said. She took a bite of the sandwich, and despite her stress and anger, the cheesy goodness of it all calmed her down a notch. A sip of fizzy orange fountain drink made it even better.

"What?" Patsy said.

Emily shook her head, and before she could reply another voice came in.

"There you are!" Adrien, coming into the diner and making his way to the quartet, called out. Heads turned in his wake, but Adrien ignored the attention. He wore a tight expression of determination. "I've been looking all over for you. Here," he said, handing Emily her mother's baseball.

Emily took it and immediately felt more grounded. She reached up and adjusted her cap, feeling the brim rub comfortingly against her scalp. She was making the right decision.

"What's up?" Patsy said to Adrien. "Tell me you're here to talk some sense into Emily. Our girl says she's not going to play the Fairy Realm season."

Adrien stood over them silently, the muscles in his clenched jaw standing out boldly. That gave her pause. She hated the way the urge to help him rose up inside her. He was the one who had decided to keep messing with the fairies. She'd lent him her ball, hadn't she? But Adrien didn't get angry easily. Something must have happened.

Adrien drew a deep breath, and his glance bounced around them all before finally landing on Emily. The shadows in his eyes made her feel the full weight of the hundred years he'd lived in the Fairy Realm. "I need to talk to you," he said. "Alone if possible."

An awkward moment later, Jake spoke up. "That's cool. We'll see ya later."

It was clearly not what the others wanted to hear, but they got the message. Jake had grown into a true leader, Emily realized with no little delight. It was great to see a friend do that.

Emily finished off the first half of her sandwich as the three slid off their seats and made it out of the diner. Adrien sat beside her. She offered him a sip of her orange, but he declined it.

"What's going on, Adrien?"

"I need you to play in the Fall Season, Em. Unicorns, Small Folk, heck, join the Seelies if you want. I don't care. But you have to play."

"We've been over this," Emily said, frowning into her orange drink to avoid his heavy gaze. "I'm going to college."

Adrien shifted on his stool, making the leather covering squeak. "It's not just about you. The mayor's idea is a cute one, but people are going to be in danger if we don't put something in place to keep them safe."

"Yeah. I'm the one who spoke against accepting this invitation if you remember correctly." Emily couldn't stop the bitter tone from entering her voice. "But I'm hardly the only one who can help you, am I? Talk to Benji. Talk to Callie. They're the ones with magic to spare and who apparently can't get enough of the fairies despite everything else."

Adrien let out a sound that might have been a growl. "I've talked to both already. Benji wants to help but can't handle the power of the Web Gem without getting wiped out, even if they don't want to admit it. Callie says she'll help ward the field, but her contract won't let her do it until the Wild Hunt visits."

"I see."

She took another sip of her orange drink, enjoying the carbonation that made her taste buds come alive, and feeling the strength of her mother in the baseball she now gripped in her hand.

She understood Adrien's frustration. But frustration didn't account for the tightness of his jaw or the way he sat on the edge of his stool, ready to leap into action at the word go.

"There's something more, isn't there?"

Adrien stared at his own fist, clenching and unclenching against the top of the bar.

"Megan went to visit Callie with me. She stayed behind," Adrien said. "At the last minute, she stepped out of Benji's magic."

Emily couldn't help herself. She literally laughed, though the sound came tinged with a bitterness that tended toward fear. "Well, of course she did. She's got a story to chase down. Just like always."

"It's not funny, Em. I'm terrified for her. If the Queen gets her hooks in Megan, I'll—"

Emily put a hand on Adrien's elbow and felt the shivering tension running through him. "Hey, I'm sorry. You're right. She's in trouble no matter what she thinks she can handle."

Adrien's nod was morose. "I hope the Fairy Realm doesn't eat her up. But she's chasing that story she was working on before, about the lost kids. At first, she saw it as her scoop, but it's way beyond that now. She's so determined to right that wrong, Em, she's so certain she can find those kids and get them back. I need to find a way to keep her safe while she does it."

Emily sighed, feeling the weight of expectation descending on her once again.

"Adrien," she said with an effort. "You can't protect everyone.

That's what I've been trying to say this whole time. I've tried to keep people safe. I've done the heroic rescue thing and the putting-it-all-on-the-line thing. And it's worked. But then the people I rescue turn right around and go back to the fairies anyway. Callie. Benji. Even you, and you used to be so gung-ho about keeping a safe distance."

Adrien shook his head. "It's the baseball magic. It draws you in. You feel it, too, even if you're turning your back on it."

"Of course I do. And I'm not turning my back on it. I'm just letting it flow where it wants. It'll always be there, whether I'm playing in the Fairy League or on a college team."

"So, that's it, then? Your new philosophy is 'live and let live' no matter who gets hurt?"

Emily resented the disappointment radiating from him. "You know you have to let her do her own thing."

"I know." He nodded. "But that doesn't mean I have to act like I'm helpless when she's in danger."

He shoved himself out of the stool hard enough to set the seat spinning on its axis. Then he stared down at her, his eyes like chips of ice.

"You'd better pick a college to play for quick, Em. Players who don't play don't create magic."

Then he stormed away, leaving a swath of turned heads in his wake.

Emily pursed her lips. Then she took a final bite of her grilled cheese. It had grown cold, though. It tasted like glue and cardboard.

She felt the truth of Adrien's parting shot in her veins.

She was going to need to make a choice, and she still didn't know what to do.

CHAPTER

SEVEN

Today, three days after Benji had taken Adrien and Megan into the Fairy Realm, was the first game of the Fall Season. Unicorns vs. the River Kin. Now it was up to Benji to transport the fairy team across the portal, and then to play as the Unicorns' third baseperson. They stood over Unicorn Field's third base, letting the morning chill seep into their skin through their Unicorns uniform and thinking calming thoughts.

Clasped tightly in both hands, the Web Gem vibrated with swelling waves of energy that set the deep parts of Benji resonating in time with them. The third base bag seemed to provide an extra boost of powerful rightness, mixing with the autumnal taste of Samhain to promise smooth sailing.

But Benji was worried.

They'd crossed the portal by themselves several times before, but that last time— carrying only Adrien and Megan along— had taken all three days to recover from. And that was only two passengers. The memory of bone-wearying fatigue intruded on their attempts to psych themself up, so Benji had come here early in the day, well before the game was to start, and well before anyone else would arrive at Unicorn Field, hoping to use the empty field as a kind of meditation circle. It turned out that the decision only made things worse. The wind whipping around an empty baseball park simply served to make it more obvious that soon enough, others would be arriving. First the Unicorns, eager and ready for an exciting game tinged with magic, and then the spectators from Pattersonville and, if the mayor got her wish, beyond. And while the ballpark atmosphere usually made Benji happy, right now the solitude served as a reminder that time was growing short.

It made them want to just go home.

The Web Gem hummed soothingly against their palms.

Benji let an anxious breath whoosh out of their lungs, realizing it was all just an exercise in procrastination. When Benji was younger, they had dreamed of moments like this. Had simply *known* that their family line was connected to the Fairy Realm and had yearned to have something like the Web Gem at their service. And now, with it bequeathed to their control, Benji had been eager to work with the Web Gem.

But the anxiety gnawing at them made them feel embarrassed.

So they'd fallen off the horse last time? That only meant they had to get back on its back.

Besides, if they left now, they could drink in the sweet, magical air of the Fairy Realm until they got their strength back. That always made them feel better.

"Don't let one bad experience sour things," they muttered. It was a phrase Grandma Agness had always said when she did something that didn't work out.

With a burst of confidence backed up by the reassuring vibrations of the Web Gem, Benji reached deep down within themself and worked the transfer spell. The air swirled and grew crisper, the scent of spice and fall decay heightened into full flavors, and the light took on a silken quality. The blare of a horn and the scent of blood came through the distance.

Benji prepared to experience the airy, swooping sensation of flight that had happened last time.

Then, with a jolt instead, they stood on the other side, in the Other Field, right over third base, where a River Kin selkie was in the midst of trying to catch a warmup throw.

"Oops!" Benji said, stumbling aside just in time to avoid getting beaned.

The selkie they'd nearly tried to occupy the same space with cast a startled look at them, and the ball sailed away uncaught.

"Sorry," Benji said.

The selkie gave a seal-like bark of a laugh and grinned. Her long white whiskers perked up, and she clapped her hands together with her glove. Several times. "No harm no foul ball!" the selkie barked, then laughed even harder at her own joke.

Benji grinned back.

That playfulness was infectious, and it helped that Benji felt fine after the trip. More than fine, really. Practically brimming with energy after that transfer. Sure, it had been only themself this time, but it was still a good sign that the previous trip had been a fluke.

Lady Marne's voice rippled like sunlight on a clear pool as she strode across the field to greet Benji. "Web Gem Keeper! Come to enjoy our warmups?" She, too, wore a wide smile, and though it did show off her sharp teeth, it held no hint of evil intent, only readiness for a good game of baseball. Callie was right about trusting the River Kin.

Benji tucked the Web Gem under one arm. "I didn't mean to get in the way, and I didn't realize you were already warming up. I only wanted to get some fresh air before taking your team across the portal."

Lady Marne laughed at their distress. "You've no need to apologize. I wouldn't accuse you of all people of spying on us prior to our game. You care about the baseball magic too much to cheat. Come, sit in the dugout with me."

Benji followed her into the cool shade of the dugout and sat on the bench beside her, placing the Web Gem between their feet. For a moment, the two of them simply sat and watched the River Kin cavorting on the field. Balls flew through the air, sending waves of silvery sparkles trailing behind them. The crack of a bat in the batting cage popped rhythmically over the barks of the selkies and the soft whinnies of the kelpies. A siren stood on the first base foul line, running through scales.

Benji breathed in deeply, savoring the watery tang the River Kin's magic added to the sharpness of Samhain.

"You seem to be doing well enough today," said Lady Marne. "Mistress Cal made mention of your previous exhaustion."

Benji winced. "Uh. She's here?" The last thing they needed was Callie McMasters popping up to give that look she'd laid on them last time, the one that was part pity and fully assessing. Her scrutiny always felt like she was examining a fly caught in a spider's web. Maybe it was just because Benji knew who her father was.

"She was here earlier, yes. She and her special Centaur. But they had Hunt business to pursue, so they didn't stick around."

The trail of the missing kids, Benji thought.

They spared a moment to wonder how that was turning out. Then they wondered how Megan was faring, all alone in the Fairy Realm as far as Benji knew. Adrien was worried about her, of course. But Benji had a feeling Megan could manage herself here, even without a trace of fairy blood in her veins. She was a breed apart, as far as full-blooded mortals went.

"Ah, well, you know the Hunt. Always focused on the details, but only the ones that matter to their current chase. I'm fine, though. Thank you for asking."

Lady Marne nodded. "The spiderkin would not have chosen one to watch over their artifact who could not accomplish the job."

Her matter-of-fact tone set Benji's insides to tingling. She was right. They could handle this. They hoped.

Keeping contact with the Web Gem allowed Benji to see along its many threads, which meant they could keep tabs on the time passing in the mortal world even as the River Kin's warmups continued here. Brushing a thumb over a crystal facet showed them a glimpse of the Unicorns arriving for their own warmups. Curling their fingers around a golden arm let Benji watch the stands begin to fill with spectators.

Handy device, Benji thought as they regained focus.

"Thank you again, Lady. But I think it's officially time for us to go."

"Indeed, Gem Keeper. I agree it is."

With that, Lady Marne beckoned her team to join them.

Bursting with confidence and fairy magic, Benji stood and made their way to the pitching mound. Swift as the incoming tide, the River Kin surged around them. Baseball magic filled the air.

Lady Marne placed one delicate hand on Benji's shoulder. Benji looked around the group to ensure everyone was touching one another, completing the chain that would allow everyone to cross over.

Then they began the spell work.

Easy, they told themself. Just like this morning.

The strain of additional passengers made the work harder, though. The magic couldn't come as smoothly as when they were alone, and the threads of it shivered under the extra weight. Gritting their teeth, Benji pushed harder.

Then the Web Gem hummed, and the pulling sensation of fairy magic came over Benji again, just as it had when they'd taken Adrien and Megan across. The flow of magic was draining too fast, Benji thought, fighting it this time. But no matter what they tried they could not control the currents as they hemorrhaged out.

Vaguely, Benji was aware of the sensation of flight happening once again, of visions of Pattersonville flicking by as if the town were far below them. They heard the awed utterings of the River Kin as they, too, saw these visions.

Then they were on Unicorn Field, and the last of Benji's energy gushed out of them, leaving them to fall, panting, to all fours. The Web Gem fell from their hands to bury itself in the infield dirt.

Adrien Thorn came forward, hands outstretched to help them up.

But before he could touch them, Benji blacked out.

EIGHT

Like everyone else in Pattersonville, Emily went to the game. She hadn't really wanted to, because she knew how much just showing her face at a Unicorns game would amp up the pressure to play, and she knew that wasn't happening. Every face in the crowd would look at her and the pressure would build. And that was even before the ones who would openly judge her put on their snide expressions, or worse get up in her face to make her feel bad about herself. As Dad said, people could be idiots. The older she got, the more she understood just what that meant. But, in the end, both the Unicorns and the River Kin were her friends. She couldn't stay away.

She couldn't wait to see Lady Marne again, and she wondered if Maddoc, her faun boyfriend and the Small Folk's first baseman, would come with her. She'd already planned to ask him to join her in the bleachers if he did. But, alas, the River Kin were without their Small Folk contingent. Probably because he had a game of his own to play.

She wasn't surprised to feel crushed at the faun's absence.

She missed the way his gruff exterior covered up his powderpuff personality.

Now it was a crisp evening, and as the sun set over the horizon, the stadium lights kicked on. As Mayor Culpepper— who had volunteered to be the PA speaker for all the games at Unicorn Field— prattled on, relentlessly extolling the many amazing features of Pattersonville over the loudspeakers, the attendees from the city oohed and aahed as the team from the Fairy Realm finished their warmups. Pure white baseballs left streaks of silver under the lights as the River Kin lined up to play catch. The chatter of infield drills kicked up invisible tendrils of the baseball magic that every attendee could feel even if they couldn't see them like Emily could.

Because to be sure, Emily did see the baseball magic.

Wafting in the air along with the buttery aroma of ballpark popcorn.

Lingering with a wild scent of a spice that was sometimes sweet but would then turn sour and dry.

Coriander, she thought at one point. Rye. Then sage, and the clean scent of a field of goldenrod.

Each turn of the baseball magic reminded her of the danger that lay buried under this field and sent her gaze flickering around the periphery. Even though the River Kin were her friends, she did not trust the Fairy Realm itself to play fair— which she suddenly realized was why she was here to begin with. Playing baseball or not, there would always be a part of her that wanted to stand guard for the innocent people of Pattersonville.

She clenched her teeth against that feeling.

For their part, the players played up the moment. Selkies balanced their infield ground balls on the tips of their noses before tossing them to first. A water nymph taking batting practice let herself drain into the dirt around the batter's box as the pitcher wound up, then reformed in enough time to crack a solid line drive. Then there was Lady Marne herself. Already achingly beautiful in the way of the fey, the iridescent scales that coated her human legs flared with her every step as she coached her team.

Emily could already imagine the posts coming after the game.

Every man, woman, and everything in between was going to be crushing on the River Kin's mermaid leader.

Unicorn Field itself was in rare form.

Pristine and beautiful in its old-timey nature already, Unicorn Field displayed the special steps Adrien had taken to make it feel like the Other Field across the portal. He'd bordered the foul lines with daisies and draped the left and right field fences with loops of holly that had been donated by local businesses. He had ensured that the stadium light system had been freshly cleaned to the point that their beams dazzled with clear silver streams. Her friend was a true wizard when it came to his eye for what made a ballpark special, and Emily didn't think it possible that there could be a better place than Unicorn Field for the first official game ever between teams from the fairy and mortal realms.

"I can't believe this is happening," her dad said from beside her, his hand wrapped around a travel mug of hot cocoa.

"They're just incredible," Elaine, who was sitting opposite her father, added as she watched the River Kin. "So cute!"

The two looked good together, Emily decided. The chill of the evening "forced" them to sit close together, and while Dad's black-piped White Sox cap gave him a jovial appearance, Elaine's toboggan cap was the right shade of red to match her cheeks' blush. It was good to see Dad happy again, and the warm sense that came from Mom's baseball made Emily feel good about it, too. They'd been together for six months now. Elaine had even stopped tiptoeing around the topic of Emily's mom with her. "I know I can't replace her," Elaine had told her just last week. "But I know you're going through a lot, and if you ever want to talk about anything, I'd love to help if you want it."

Sitting on the bleacher seats and feeling the pressures build, Emily rolled her mom's baseball around inside the pocket of her hoodie and actually thought about talking to Elaine. Not that it was going to happen. She would deal with this on her own. But the idea that Elaine wanted to help clicked a button inside her. It made her feel better for Dad.

To be honest, she wasn't concentrating on either them or the River Kin right now. Or even the Unicorns for that matter.

Instead, Emily's gaze kept going to Benji, who— even though they'd executed the crossing several hours before— still sat slumped over in the dugout. Adrien, who had already warmed up, sat beside Benji now, whispering something into their ear that didn't seem to be helping much at all. Benji hadn't even come out to third base when Coach Amabe was hitting the Unicorns' infield practice.

Their lethargy brought true fear to her heart.

She'd worried about Benji ever since the spiderkin had burdened them with the keeping of the Web Gem, and she couldn't help but note the ancient artifact was on the bench beside them.

If Benji couldn't pull themself together in time, the Unicorns might find themselves a player down.

Another player down, that was.

"Why aren't you out there, Emily?" a man Dad's age said, leaning back from a row below her. "You should be playing!"

Emily startled, then collected herself.

"They'll do great without me," she said, gritting her teeth to stifle a grimace. It was a response she'd given a dozen times if she'd given it once.

Emily didn't recall seeing the man in the stands when they were playing over the summer, but admittedly there had been so many people coming to the games it wouldn't have been hard to miss him. The man was wearing a Unicorn's jacket and cap, though, and seemed to be having a great time getting into the Unicorn Chant.

"Ladies and gentlemen," the mayor called on the PA system. "Welcome to Opening Day at Unicorn Field, the most beautiful little baseball park you'll ever visit, where you can *always* get the best baseball food, and where tonight the River Kin team from the Fairy

Realm will face our own State Champion Pattersonville West Unicorns!"

Voices rose in a throaty cheer.

"And now your starting lineups... batting first for the visiting River Kin, and playing shortstop..."

Emily took a deep breath and scanned the field where all the players were heading to their dugouts. Despite everything that was wrong with this situation, despite the danger to the city and the confusion she had about letting one set of her friends or the other down, the urge to play welled inside her. Excitement in the mayor's voice hit all her buttons. That ice-cold sense of anticipation that lived in the moments before the first pitch filled her, and it was impossible to deny she loved the game itself.

Yet, as the game called her, the nature of the Fairy Realm scoured like sandpaper against her skin. The scent of the Realm's magical fabric seeped from the ground, and as the Unicorns took the field to start the game, a certain sense of panic flowed into her veins.

Her gaze locked onto the Web Gem. Then, nervously, she tried to take in the entire crowd at once.

Could the Unseelie Queen be lurking here?

Could the realm swallow any of her teammates like it had swallowed her?

And could she really just sit here and let it happen, thinking only of how unfair this new call to action was on her?

A wave of fear crashed over her. The press of faces made her heart clench, and for a moment she fought to breathe. It was too much. All she could think of was how the Web Gem was sitting here, unprotected and out in the open. How anyone could come and snatch it right out from under Benji's practically comatose form.

Then she saw him.

Down at the field level, shoulders hunched under an old silk jacket that she knew would have the *Ball and Glove* logo stitched high on its left breast.

Mr. McMasters.

"Play ball!" the umpire called, and as Jamal unleashed the first pitch of the season, the game started.

In that moment, Emily, her eyes trained on McMasters' shadowy form, knew Adrien was one hundred percent right. It didn't matter which team she chose, but she'd regret it forever if she didn't play. And not only because it was a once-in-a-lifetime opportunity.

Down on the field, McMasters slunk closer to the Unicorns' dugout.

Emily stood.

"Be back in a minute," she mumbled in answer to Dad's and Elaine's questioning looks.

Then she made her way out of the stands and around the back towards the dugout.

It might be too late for her to join in this game, but that didn't mean she couldn't defend her team off the field.

Once a Unicorn, always a Unicorn, after all.

NINE

The only way Benji made it through the game at all, even riding the bench for most of it, was with the subtle splashes of power Lady Marne kept giving them. Adrien had helped, too, with gentle nudges from his magic glove each time he returned to the dugout. In the seventh inning, Benji had finally managed to scrounge up enough energy to stand at third base.

The River Kin had scored two runs during that inning.

Luckily, Adrien and Patsy had pulled off a spectacular double play that kept their opponents from scoring again, and at the bottom of the inning, Jake had pelted a home run to win the game before Benji even came up in the batting order.

Then, amidst the celebrations, Benji had to take the River Kin back across the portal.

The next day, Benji woke up filled with the remnants of a migraine headache.

They'd slept past noon and were still feeling sluggish as they made their way down Main Street now. Their new boots *thunked* hollowly against the sidewalk. Their pleated skirt rustled limply in the cool fall breeze.

They felt like a jack-o-lantern hollowed out, then left out to rot.

So much for Samhain making things easier.

They really should be back in bed, resting up and conserving their strength. But if they did that, this problem would only get worse. They needed a solution, and they needed it now. The Web Gem couldn't be left in the keeping of someone who couldn't use it without wiping themself out, now, could it?

A swell of determination rose in them. Benji pulled their shoulders back as they passed under a hand-painted banner someone had strung up in celebration of the Unicorns' magical victory yesterday. The town of Pattersonville was coming to embrace their heritage, just as Benji was. They needed Benji to work this magic, to make the transfers that made this incredible Fall Season possible.

Benji wouldn't give up, no matter how exhausted the effort left them.

But they'd rather not be exhausted if they could help it. Which was why they were out now, following the lingering vibrations of the Web Gem.

Something had to be done, after all. And Benji had no idea how to deal with this problem. But all through their long, deep sleep, Benji had dreamed about the artifact. It had talked all night, or rather had sung and hummed and presented itself in an endless stream of colors, numbers, and sensations that might have been taste or smell or might have been something beyond.

The artifact wanted to help them, Benji could tell.

And though they'd left it behind in their bedroom today, they could still feel a connection that fed them bits of information they could follow to a place where they might find answers. It felt so Hansel and Gretel, but with nothing else to try, and knowing in their soul that they couldn't keep going like this forever, Benji followed those crumbs without error, hoping this story didn't come complete with a flock of dream crows to eat up those bits.

Sensing a turn, Benji took a left off Main Street and into a little alleyway.

It wasn't dark and cramped, or even dirty, but it still gave off a subtle sensation of *keep away* that Benji had to struggle against. Clearly fairy magic, or the residue of it, anyway. The effort of pushing past that slight barrier left them breathless for a moment, and suddenly the open, airy nature of the alleyway left Benji feeling exposed and vulnerable.

Catching their breath again, they recognized the place— sort of. Or, rather, they realized what the building had once been.

McMasters' Ball and Glove.

The place was abandoned now— not totally empty, as Benji could still make out racks of sporting goods through the grimy back windows, but silent and still. McMasters hadn't been evicted or anything. He'd just made himself scarce after last spring's events.

But the place was quiet now as if waiting for him to return.

An eerie sense of anticipation hung in the air.

On the left side of the alleyway was the back entrance to the unit.

As they looked on, a furtive motion in the window caught their eye. Maybe the place wasn't as abandoned as they'd thought.

McMasters had been at the game last night, after all. Benji hadn't even needed the Web Gem's help to pick up on his slimy presence. Even despite their utter exhaustion. The businessman hadn't done anything more than lurk, but the fact he'd been there at all still made Benji's skin crawl.

Across the distance, Benji felt the Web Gem shudder, too. It remembered McMasters' touch.

Not here, the connection whispered through the threads, dropping more bits of encouragement. A soft nudge turned Benji's head to the other side of the alleyway. Toward another door that stood on that side, nestled cozily at the top of a short flight of gray stone stairs, tucked slightly inward between walls of red brick.

An old-fashioned lantern hung to the right of the door, and the warm yellow light it emitted flickered as if a large moth were caught in the glass bulb. The foundation concrete was cracked with an old, spidery fissure. As Benji approached, a fuzzy, papery smell wafted from the entrance.

Benji didn't recognize this door.

Though they wracked their brain trying to remember what lay on the street side, nothing came to mind.

The moment they touched the door handle, the door swung open, and a familiar swirl of fairy magic greeted them.

Benji breathed it in and let its tingling sensation sweep through them. It left a freshness in their limbs, and as they stepped over the threshold, their energy levels surged. The headache was gone.

The aroma was better than any bakery, they thought. Better than any perfume counter ever devised.

It was a bookstore.

Or, as Benji glanced around shelves crammed full of books and found no counter with a cash register, a library.

A fairy library, obviously. The sense of gratitude washed over them.

A fairy library, hidden away in a pocket of the mortal world, waiting for someone like Benji to have need of the knowledge it held in safekeeping.

If any place was going to have a solution to their problem, this was it.

They had no clue where to start looking, though, and the Web Gem was unresponsive when they checked. So, with fingers trailing along the spines of the books, Benji wandered, letting whatever aspect of the Web Gem connection had brought them here continue to have its head.

They needed to be extra careful.

Benji had read the fables. This was exactly the sort of place someone could lose whole years of their life in if they weren't paying attention.

The promise of arcane knowledge was as alluring as the imme-diacy of baseball magic, and the utter silence of the space was an extra temptation. *Come, enjoy the quiet, open a tome. Even if this one doesn't hold the answers you seek, surely you'll learn something interesting anyway. And the next book might be the one you were looking for...*

Benji held back from opening any of the books they passed, flashing on the image of Adrien Thorn locked away for a century in the Fairy Realm. They had enough experience with their own meager fairy magic from before they'd gotten possession of the Web Gem to avoid sticking their head in a maze designed to lead them astray. Instead, they touched each spine with a tiny spark of their fairy glow, just enough to glimpse the subject contained within and determine it wasn't what they sought. Book after book they examined and discarded like this, but they didn't lose hope, and book after book they felt the connection with the Web Gem twist and turn with new ideas and new directions.

There were innumerable shelves to work through. So many that their dusty, cobweb-encased multitudes disappeared into the shadowy darkness of the deeper library. The space held inside this alleyway building was far larger than the building could possibly contain. Knowing that, and seeing it, made Benji happy because it made them feel competent. It was good to feel like they understood something about their ancestral world.

The cobwebs felt like a sign, too.

Benji was searching for guidance on using a spiderkin artifact. Perhaps they ought to ask the spiders for directions. They headed into the inky shadows, squinting to see, and turned a corner to find a small bank of reading desks.

Benji was surprised to see one of the desks was occupied.

The occupant was a woman with obsidian dark hair, surrounded by stacks of dusty books, head bent over a pile of loose leaves of notes as she scratched furiously away at them. A small flame, barely more than a single candle's worth, floated in the air beside her head, illuminating only the scant space where she worked and setting sparks like embers among that obsidian-black hair. In the power of the room, Benji felt her breathing pattern, calm and in control. Her midnight-colored dress draped like a solid shadow over her figure.

Her eyes as she looked up to see who had intruded upon her solitude pierced like spears of starlight.

The Unseelie Queen.

Benji managed to keep from taking a step back under her fierce gaze.

For a single, unending moment, the two of them stared at one another. The very air remained as still as the grave, waiting.

Benji swallowed against a sense of betrayal.

Had the Web Gem truly led them here, to her? Surely not. It had recoiled from McMasters' presence, after all. It knew evil when it felt it. But then again, McMasters was a bumbling, ignorant idiot. The Unseelie Queen had held the Web Gem for over a century. If anyone knew how it worked...

Benji swallowed again, forcing the lump of discomfort from where it had lodged in their throat.

Then, with a nearly audible breath, the queen relaxed and turned back to her notes.

"You needn't fear me, Web Gem Keeper," she said. Her voice was a whisper, and yet Benji felt it rattle through their bones as strongly as if she'd shouted. "I've withdrawn my team from the proceedings this Fall Season, after all."

"Everyone is wondering why you aren't playing," they said, recovering. "They're afraid you've got some trick up your sleeve."

The Unseelie Queen scoffed, flipped a page in one of her books, and scratched a new note on her worksheet. "Let the fools play their season. I am capable of learning my lesson. I know my place in the hierarchy, and I know the debt I owe your clan, young spiderkin. The least I can do is spend my time researching the trail of the lost arachnid artifacts instead of frittering it away on squabbles over your measly baseball magic."

Suspicion gnawed at Benji. This was a trap. A fairy trick pulled by the tricksiest fairy of all. Only an idiot would trust the Unseelie Queen.

But the books she had spread over her desk were the very ones

Benji needed. As if to highlight that need, the energy the library had poured into Benji seeped away, just a little. Just enough to leave them leaning against the shelf for support.

Just enough for the Unseelie Queen to notice.

But she did not smirk in triumph at her foe's weakness or take the opportunity to pull Benji's soul from their body. Nor did she sweeten the deal by offering to reinvigorate Benji with her dark magic. She simply acknowledged it, then kept on with her patient and relentless research.

Benji watched her, wariness warring with a desire to pull up a chair and join her.

"Tell me about these spiderkin artifacts," they said.

The queen let out an exasperated sigh. "Wouldn't you rather go play your baseball, and enjoy your merging of the worlds?"

Her tone carried a very human irritation at being interrupted by one who didn't properly respect the vigor of academia, and that, more than anything, let Benji approach her in earnest. They pulled a musty chair from the next desk over and sat in it.

"I've always wanted to know everything about my heritage. That hasn't changed now that I know one piece of it. If you've been studying the spiderkin I would like you to teach me what you've learned. If I understand more, I might be better able to use the magic of the Web Gem. And maybe we can use that knowledge to make the baseball magic available to everyone like it's supposed to be."

A flash of longing crossed the Unseelie Queen's face, and Benji knew she wasn't as flippant about cutting herself off from that source of power as she had acted earlier. She was a woman serving a self-inflicted penance, even if no one believed her capable of such sacrifice.

"Very well," she said after a long moment. "Perhaps that is the best way after all. If I can deliver even one of the lost artifacts into the hands of a scion of the House of Arachnids, mayhap I will have atoned for my part in the events of the spring, and I will finally be able to clear the cobwebs from my dreams."

"Have you got any leads?" Benji asked, shifting forward in their chair.

The Unseelie Queen turned the top sheet of her notes so Benji could make out her cramped handwriting. There was much crossing out and blotting of ink across the page, but one name was listed boldly and circled thrice.

"I've found one, little spiderling, or I think I have." She raised her gaze to lock on Benji's, and once again there was an endless moment. "Have you heard of a piece called the Octagon?"

TEN

Perfect timing.

Megan slid onto the polished wood of one of the ancient tree stumps that served as seats at the Other Field and pressed record on her phone just in time to capture the singsong chant that came from spectators who were here to celebrate the Hag Sisters of the Wood's first batter of the season.

"Double me, double me, double me, get the pitcher in trouble, ye!" the first verse went.

The seat was surprisingly comfortable. It was like the wood conformed to her jean-clad bottom, which was a far sight better than she could say for any seat in Unicorn Field's bleachers.

Megan wanted to get all the fanfare she could. Wanted to capture pictures of the fancied-up lords standing in their personal spaces, and wanted to memorize the smells of the park as the baseball magic wafted over it. She needed to get the essence of Opening Day into the first article she was going to write when she got back across to Pattersonville. Her readers would eat that up, and while other reporters would certainly capture the event at Unicorn Field, the games in the Fairy Realm were all hers. So, she marveled at the amazing array of spectators in the seats, noting everything from the regal, cerulean uniforms of the courts to the tattered and gummed-up, often threadbare outfits worn by followers of the Small Folk. The less said about the reek that came from the Wild Hunt, the better, but after spending these past few days with Callie and Trace— her trusty Centaur bloodhound— following up on decades-old trails of those missing kids, Megan had grown something close to comfortable with that smell.

That said, even though it was the official opening Fairy Realm game of the Fairy League season, Megan had ducked out of watching the Wild Hunt face the Seelie Court earlier because it had been the only way to pursue a lead without either Callie or Trace getting in the way.

Adrien would have been furious at her trekking through the Fairy Realm alone like she had, but what he didn't know wouldn't hurt him.

The treks the three of them had gone together on so far had proved fruitless, after all. But Megan didn't have the reservations her hosts seemed to foster regarding the dangers of the deep forest.

This place was weird as all get out, but she could handle herself.

She'd used the three hours it took the Wild Hunt to defeat the Seelies to explore a section of the woods that Trace had seemed particularly uncomfortable with her seeing yesterday. After a hard struggle through the overgrown thickets that included wriggling through a knothole in a long-dead tree, avoiding a thin trip wire, and using her phone's flashlight to blind the attack of a swooping owl, she had found herself standing in a small, open glade.

Floating in the middle of that glade was a well-tended collection of brush and shrubbery that had been clearly magicked into the shape of a globe. Additional branches, desiccated and segmented, stuck this way and that from its strange surface, and its orb sparked with static charges every time she moved.

As she circled it, staring in wonder, the whole construction tilted and turned to follow her motions.

What was it?

Some creature's hidden stockpile of forest magic? A mystical compass pointing the way to treasure? A map?

Whatever.

Standing in that glade had given Megan the feeling that she could reach out and touch anything else in the world, though she had no idea how. Fairy creatures seemed like they could jump from place to place whenever they wanted. Could it be a nexus?

She didn't know.

All she could say for certain was that the glade gave her the heebie-jeebies and that the power vibrating in the air made her stomach so queasy she nearly barfed.

She felt like she didn't belong there.

Regardless, Megan knew a lead when she ran across one.

Something was going on there, and she was going to find out what that something was.

With luck, it might help her find the lost kids.

But despite her most terrier-like tenacity, the odd, leafy globe refused to give up its secrets to her. After an hour and a half of poking at, prodding, tugging, and even thrusting her phone inside the woven branches to try and get some photographic evidence, all she had to show for her efforts was a lot of scratches on her arms and a sticky coating of greenish sap on her fingers.

Luckily, Megan didn't frustrate easily. She used the new energy burning through her to fuel her rush back to the Other Field.

Whatever that place was, she was happy for both the free time to explore it and for the fact that she'd somehow managed to make it back in one piece. She was also happy that she made it back to the Other Field in just enough time to see the first pitch of the matchup between the Small Folk and the Hag Sisters of the Wood.

Now, as she sat on the surprisingly comfortable stump bench, deliberately slowed her breathing, and got herself back into the headspace of covering an exciting show of baseball, the game started.

Twy, the lithe pixie pitcher for the Small Folk, sang a thin arpeggio before delivering her pitch to the Hag Sister who stood at the plate with a gnarled branch of a broomstick as her bat.

The Hag swung and connected to squib a grounder to the elf at third base, who pounced on the ball and tossed a corkscrewing throw over to Maddoc at first base for the out.

From the Small Folk bench, a squeaky voice gave out a big cheer. *"That's my Greeven!"*

Megan laughed to herself.

She wanted to talk to whoever that was.

She also wanted to talk to Fennoc, the manager of the Small Folk. The two had met when the faun came across to lead the collective team of humans and fairy lords against the Seelie Courters in the game that set the precedent for this entire season.

He was down on the field now, shouting encouragement to his team and consulting a slab of bark that served as a clipboard. Even from this distance, the cleanliness of his uniform stood out. The Small Folk might be a rough-and-tumble bunch, but Fennoc ran a tight ship. It was a big part of how they'd done so well in the past seasons.

The thought sent a little tingle through her. One of those intuitions she'd learned not to ignore. Sometimes she thought of it as her Spidey-sense.

Spider-Man had nothing on her, though.

After her time in that strange little glen, the idea of getting to talk to Fennoc between innings slotted into place like a piece in a jigsaw puzzle.

The weird bush thing had made her think of portals, she realized now with sudden clarity. She'd spoken with Emily DeWitt about the experience of being pulled across the portal in Unicorn Field. And though Emily hadn't outright said who was responsible, Megan's years of investigative reporting had given her the ability to read between various lines. Megan was sure Fennoc, along with his first baseman brother, Maddoc, were, in some fashion, responsible for having first kidnapped Emily DeWitt.

She'd like to know just how responsible.

Since she had also met Maddoc (after Adrien, Emily, and Callie had combined the baseball magic with the Web Gem to save Maddoc from being a statue forever), she felt like both of them would be comfortable talking with her.

Suddenly Megan was hungry.

She flagged down a gnarled little gnome that was carrying a tray of assorted fruits and nuts as well as a tub of some kind of bloody broth that smelled horrific. Ignoring the broth, she grabbed a handful of the nuts and a fruit that looked roughly like a pear.

"Beware what you ingest in the Fairy Realm, tall and gangly human," the gnome said with an unsettling smile. "It may not satisfy as you'd wish."

Pausing with her hand halfway to her mouth, Megan grimaced. She'd forgotten that part of fairy lore.

Still, she'd been eating plenty with Callie and the Hunt, and she didn't *feel* like she was tethered to the Realm for six months or whatever. Maybe there was something different about non-Hunt food?

Her stomach growled. The nuts smelled heavenly.

With a sigh, Megan slipped the food into her pockets and, phone still recording, stepped down the aisle toward the open dugout areas.

By the time she made it to the field level, Twy had struck out the second batter, and the third had hit a rainbow-arced pop fly to another pixie in center field. After catching the ball, the fielder executed a dazzling cartwheel run of flips and twists on his way back to the dugout that would have made an Olympic gymnast cry.

"Good job, kiddoes!" Fennoc's voice boomed from the dugout, and he clapped his hands as the Small Folk clambered in. As he stepped out to greet his center fielder, Megan saw his brown and white uniform was spotless and perfectly creased, and his furred goat legs had been brushed until they gleamed in the afternoon sunlight. A long reed drooped from the corner of his lip. "Great play out there, Izusa!" Fennoc continued.

Megan leaned over the brick and wood railing. "Hi, Fennoc!"

The faun turned to take her in, then gave a shuddering double-take and blinked his glistening black eyes twice. "Lady Reporter? What are you doing here in the Fairy Realm?"

"I'm getting the story of the season down," Megan said, perhaps too quickly. "Can I interview you while the game goes on? I know the humans on the other side would love to hear what you've got to say."

Fennoc stared at her like a goat in the headlights, but his brother joined him with casual ease and a wide grin.

"Any friend of Miss Em's is a friend of ours," Maddoc said. "Come on down."

Not wasting any time, Megan slid over the barrier and onto the field, then stepped into the dugout to find a rambunctious gathering of what she might otherwise have thought of as super-cute little fairy creatures.

The whole crew buzzed with excitement the moment Megan stepped into the dugout.

The elf who had made the first play of the game came to shake her hand. "I'm Greeven, and this is Essie, our biggest fan," he said, pointing to the tiny brownie who had climbed into a pocket in his shirt.

"Go, Small Folk!" Essie said, both minuscule fists clenched and outstretched over her head.

In turn, Megan met them all. Delananey, the second base elf. Shady Marie, the dryad shortstop. Nash, the dirt-covered gnome who embodied all the traits of the perfect catcher. Then came the pixies Shayla, Twy, Jessebel, and Mellica, and, of course, the acro-batic Izusa.

The entire group bombarded Megan with questions.

"How is Miss Em? Is she well? Has she made any spectacular pitches over in the mortal world?"

"She's great," Megan replied, not knowing what else to say. "Her team won the State Championship."

Everyone brightened.

"We heard! We heard!" called Essie. "Go, Miss Em!"

Out on the field, the game started again, and Nash, who was leading off, grabbed a bat and went to the plate to take his squat, walk-inducing stance.

"Everyone here misses Miss Em," Fennoc said to Megan as the team's attention was drawn to the game.

"I'm sure she misses you, too," Megan said.

Fennoc smiled. "She's given us all so much. But we all understand where her heart is at. If she needs to play with her Unicorns, we're all happy for her. At least we'll get to see her when we play them."

"I'm sure she'd be happy to hear that, but I don't think Emi—" Megan stopped herself. Full and true names were off the record here in the Fairy Realm, and even though she was fairly sure Fennoc knew Emily's, she felt it better not to share it so publicly. "—um, Miss Em is planning to play the Fall Season at all."

"What? Whyever not?"

Megan shrugged. "You'll have to ask her. But I'll warn you, she can be a hard nut to crack. Speaking of which, are these okay for me to eat here?" Megan pulled some of the nuts out of her pocket.

Fennoc huffed through open nostrils, looking so exceptionally goat-like that Megan had to stifle a giggle. But his nod of approval was serious. "They should be fine. No need to starve yourself among the Small Folk."

Too hungry to be polite, Megan gratefully shoved the handful of nuts into her mouth. The flavor settled on her tongue in a soft, earthy wash, and she barely kept herself from moaning in happiness.

On the field, Nash ambled to first base after four pitches.

"Attaboy, Nashy!" Essie called.

That brought Greeven to the plate.

With a neat swing, he blooped one of the Hag Sister's enspelled pitches into right field for a hit. Nash trundled his way to second and wisely stopped there. He was not fast for a gnome, and gnomes were not speedy at all to begin with.

Maddoc stepped to the plate next, armed with a massive piece of lumber that, to Megan's eye, was nothing more refined than a full section out of the trunk of a young sugar maple.

"You said you wanted to interview me," Fennoc said. His voice was calm, but the fur around his neck had fluffed up a bit, betraying his bashfulness. "What do you think your readers want to hear from us?" Fennoc said as his brother took his warmup swings.

Megan held her phone forward. "I'm sure the people of Pattersonville would be most interested in stories about how you and Miss Em got together in the first place. Like, I know about the fairy ring, obviously. But how did it all come about? And how did you and your brother pull it off? I understand the Small Folk didn't control the Web Gem at all at that time."

Fennoc's nose grew an embarrassed pink. "Oh that. I'm sure no one cares to hear about that kind of silliness. I'm actually quite sorry we got Miss Em and everyone else into such a pickle. If she and her friend hadn't come to our aid, though, things could have been so much worse."

"I was wondering about the baseball parks, you know?" Megan said, pushing on as if he hadn't just tried to rebuff her.

"What about them?"

"Well, obviously there's a link from the Other Field to Unicorn Field. And, as I understand, that was a big part of the first time Miss Em came to the Fairy Realm. And I know that there are at least three other fields here, right? There's a practice field, and the place where the Wild Hunt scrimmage, and, what is it, Unseelie Court?"

"Unseelie Pitch!" Little Essie chimed in from the side, shivering as she said it. "That's a horrible place!"

"Ah, yes, Unseelie Pitch. That's what Miss Em called it." Megan jotted a note into her phone. "How does all that work? Do you think there could be links between each of those fields and other fields in the mortal realm?"

Megan's brain was going a hundred miles a minute now, finally putting ideas her subconscious had been working on for days together in new ways. The lost kids had to have come here somehow, and while her research in the mortal realm had confirmed four of them had likely been at or near the grounds of Unicorn Field, she couldn't say that about all of them. But it was coming on to Samhain, as she heard over and over. And the walls were thinnest here and now. She was beginning to wonder how many places the two realms might have in common.

"It all depends on if you are a lord or not," Fennoc said.

Megan nodded, remembering the first big game she'd covered. "Like how the Seelie King could bring his whole team from anywhere?"

"Yes, indeed. With enough of the baseball magic, a true fairy lord is unchained to the realities the rest of us suffer under."

"Meaning you needed the fairy ring."

"Of course. As well as the right circumstances." He was speaking almost jovially now, as if he'd gotten comfortable with her and they were just chatting.

Fennoc explained how Adrien— the Designated Hitter— wanting to free himself of his bindings, had arranged to help Essie take the Web Gem from the Unseelie Queen to begin with, and then how, once Fennoc and his brother had realized what they had, they used it to wish Miss Em across the portal.

"I guess we got a little too big for our britches, as they say." Fennoc gave a little bray.

"It's that easy?"

"Ha! Easy!"

"You make it sound that way."

Fennoc twisted his lips, and the reed he kept between them swayed back and forth.

From the field, Maddoc's bat gave out a great crack, jarring

Megan's attention back to the game. The ball he'd smashed rose high into the air. In an attempt to reel in the hit, one of the Hag Sisters twined a blood-red thread over the silver thimble she wore in place of a fielding glove, but Maddoc's power was too great, and the ball sailed over the fence and into the tangled mass of the woods in deepest center field.

As the Small Folk dugout erupted in cheers, and as his brother trotted around the base paths, Fennoc leaned in so that his goatish face filled Megan's field of view. His voice came low and strong. The smell of his breath was rich and earthy.

"Nothing comes easy in the Fairy Realm, Lady Reporter. And there is always a price for power. Do not confuse yourself on this point."

"I see." Megan swallowed to compose herself, then, feeling that sense of determination that kept her always on the trail, went back in. "Could there be other places where fairy magic works with base-ball magic like that?" *Could there be other places where a nefarious fairy lord might have stolen more kids?*

Megan flashed on the little glade and its mysterious, floating globe of leaves.

Fennoc shivered as if the autumnal breeze blustering through the dugout chilled him, and he ruffled his neck fur deliberately this time. "If there are, it's not for me to know about them. Nor is it for a mortal like you, no matter how driven."

Megan heard his warning and filed it away for future reference. She had no intention of heeding it, but it could prove a useful piece of information on its own.

She shook her head and finished with the interview.

Then she talked to Essie for a puff piece on what it was like to be the biggest baseball fan in the Fairy Realm, and to Mellica and Jessebel about the time they dressed Miss Em for the festival ball, and how much they wished they could do that for the Samhain cele-bration at the end of this season.

When she got a moment with Maddoc, she revisited the topic of

Emily DeWitt's initial kidnapping in a gentle unassuming fashion, and then concluded with a quick, triangulating question.

"I guess I'm wondering, assuming there are linkages to other baseball parks, if it would be possible to tinker with them," she said.

"For the average people, you mean?" Maddoc said, preparing to go back out to the field.

"Sure. Could anyone figure out how to use them?"

"Unlikely."

"But anything's possible?"

Maddoc's whiskers twitched. "It's the Fairy Realm, Lady Reporter. Anything is possible. If you're willing to pay the price."

By the time the game was over, the Small Folk had won by the score of six runs to three. She had talked to everyone on the Small Folk team, and she was drained.

She needed sleep but knew it was going to be hard to get any.

As she put her phone away and began her trip to rejoin Callie and Trace in the home woods of the Hunt, she let her surface thinking begin composing the Opening Day story in her head. But it was a simple tale, one she could spout off almost without effort.

The real thinking was going on underneath.

She needed to investigate the other ballparks here in the Realm. The practice park might yield some interesting revelations, for example. But she knew in her gut that Unseelie Pitch was where the true scoop lay. To find out what tricks the queen had worked up there, Megan would have to pull out all her best snooping skills.

And she needed to understand what the orb in that glade in the woods might mean.

Megan loved it when a story was coming together.

CHAPTER

ELEVEN

After having spent so much time in the heart of the Wild Hunt, Callie had come to realize there was no better way to celebrate a victory on the baseball field than with a good, hard run through the forest. The wind whipping through her hair and the scent of prey drawing her ever onward ignited her veins like nothing else. Even the feel of the supple bow against her palms and the melodic twang of its string served as a lovely finish to a full set of innings slamming pitches with her magical bat.

They had beaten the Seelies, too, making this victory dash even that much sweeter.

Seeing the Seelie King's exasperated expression as she clouted her walk-off homer was pretty great, but making the post-game run with her most special friend at her side was the icing on the cake.

Sometimes, like now, she rode astride Trace's back. Being a rider didn't lessen the fire in her muscles, only shifted it to different ones. And it left her focus free to better scan the ground for hints of where their quarry had darted off to.

She'd missed this over the break between seasons.

A run after scrimmage didn't carry the same headiness as one after a true game played against a properly motivated opponent.

Of course, these last few days, they'd been joined by a third, which Callie found annoying. Megan was nice enough and all, a smart girl, and a keen hunter in her own right. But she did kind of spoil the mood. Luckily, when Callie had gone looking for her earlier, the reporter had been quite wrapped up in covering the next game, or whatever had pulled at the journalist's attention. That was the main thing Callie found so bothersome about Megan. The girl had a one-track brain when it came to being on point with a story. As unnerving as residents of the Fairy Realm's pursuit of certain achievements could be at times, they held no advantage in that category over Megan Moore. The upside was that Callie had taken the opportunity to leave Megan behind, just this once.

Leaning forward, Callie pressed her uniform-clad chest against the firm muscles of Trace's human back. She breathed in a lungful that tasted of decaying leaves, damp ground, and warm horsehair. A spicy hint of the little rabbit they were chasing tickled at her nose, too.

"That way," she said, nudging Trace with her knees.

Indulgent, the Centaur leapt over the tangle of brambles that bordered the trail, and the pair thundered off into the shadowy depths of the forest.

This part of the forest used to frighten Callie, and even now it could still send shivers running over her skin if she ventured out into it alone. But with Trace's sturdiness accompanying her, she could let the wariness slide away and enjoy the many splendors the place had to offer. This was Trace's home turf. He knew it backward and forward.

So she didn't worry about the babbling brook that ran with black water and made you sleepy if you listened to it too closely. Or the hunched and gnarled tree that, even in the high winds of autumn, stood so still that you'd swear it was made of stone. Or the way solitary needles of sunlight penetrated the canopy in certain places, illuminating the moss-covered rock formations lying just beneath the haze of mist that laced the ground. Many of the formations looked like faces, and while that was unsettling, most of the faces wore expressions of strange comfort.

Maybe the living creatures they'd once been had listened to the brook too closely.

This place made the baseball bat she wore strapped across her back resonate with shared memory. Trace had told her the wood he'd carved it from had come from the heart of one of the fallen trees here, and Callie liked the idea that it was getting to experience life again in its new form. It was humming against her back now. But as they moved through the shadows, the hum shifted from gentle buzzing to insistent pulsing.

Callie looked over her shoulder.

"Trace," she said, her voice little more than a whisper.

Trace stopped at once, his head cocked to listen intently. "The rabbit went the other way," he said. His tone was dismissive, though, as if he'd already half-forgotten the prey they'd been on the cusp of catching.

Callie ignored him. She squinted into the thickets, instead, and unsheathed her bat, wrapping her fingers around the handle to better feel the energy shift within it. "Something's in there," she said. She saw nothing, though. Despite peering deeply into the woods, she couldn't make out the source of her discomfort. Whatever it was, though, its lure was like a siren's song or the enticing bobbing of a will-o'-the-wisp. There was a sharper sensation underneath that draw, too. Something that hissed at her to keep far, far away. The bat, though. It wouldn't let go. There was a connection there. Something so connected with the baseball magic that she could not deny its draw. *Sacrifice,* it whispered in the ethereal netherlight of the moment.

"What is it?" Trace replied, equally dumbfounded.

"I don't know. But it's... baseball-y."

She gave an involuntary shrug of her shoulders, letting the bat reposition itself against her spine. Its vibrations now were more like jolts rattling through her bones to the point of pain. But she used that pain to heighten her senses as she peered harder into the darkness before them. Though the darkness didn't dissipate any, Callie's efforts didn't go unrewarded. She held her bat in her hands like a great sword now, her bow slung back over her shoulder instead.

The pings of baseball magic she'd picked up were coming to her stronger now. It was older than the style of baseball magic she was used to, but maybe not quite so old as what she often picked up from Adrien Thorn.

"Those kids," she murmured, a realization dawning. The sensation coming through the bat was distant and diluted by fear and anger, but it brought her the adrenaline she felt when she played baseball and it made her memory flash to Megan Moore and her quest to find those lost kids.

Trace gave a nervous chuff and shifted beneath her in unease. "I'm sorry, Callie," he said, suddenly alert again. "This is my fault. I was too caught up in the Hunt with you to be aware. But this place... it's the one I've always avoided because it feels so... well... never mind now. I'm surprised we even made it this far in. But no matter. We aren't equipped to track any deeper into the woods right now. We should have turned back some time ago. Don't you see how late it's become? The Huntmaster will have my hide now, and rightly so."

Callie blinked with a start.

Midnight had caught her all unawares. The darkness of the forest was more than the simple shadows of the canopy now. Those needles of sunlight she'd admired earlier had disappeared entirely. Anger flared. She hated when the Fairy Realm managed to pull its tricks on her. She'd gotten the hang of recognizing most of those tricks before they happened, but the wonky flow of time was one that still managed to snare her regularly. She wrapped her fists around the hard handle of her bat and waggled it before her. "No," she said through gritted teeth. "Don't patronize me like that, Trace. It's not like I'm some clueless first-year here. If we're late, it's *our* fault, not just yours. And the Huntmaster will have to fight me before he takes your hide."

Trace took his reprimand in silence.

So like a boy.

She'd meant for them to be back at the Wild Hunt's standing stones before sunset. They had their first game at Unicorn Field tomorrow, and she wanted a good night's rest before crossing through the fairy ring.

She glared out at the source of the strange signal. Still unable to sense anything solid, she gave a huff of irritation and replaced the bat across her back.

"All right. We turn back now. But let's mark this place. I want to come back first thing after the game. I'd bet a bag of fairy gold there's a lead on those missing kids here."

Trace was already trotting back the way they'd come. Callie fought against every fiber of her being to keep from twisting around to look at the receding spot.

Trace's voice helped her center herself. "I suspect you're right. We should come back. But I don't think we ought to tell your reporter friend. She's a tough one, but even so, a mortal like her would be in grave danger in a place like that."

Callie gave his shoulder a playful swat. She thought for an instant on how glad she was that Megan wasn't here, but she couldn't let him get away with that. "'A mortal like her,' huh? And what am I? Cannon fodder?"

Trace made a graceful leap over an inky blackness— a fallen tree trunk— and then glanced back at her with a soft smile. "Oh, no, my sweet. You are half-fairy already. And I don't mean because of that drop of Seelie blood running through your veins. Feeling the pounding of your heart and your grip on my shoulders as we pursue the Hunt is all I need to know you're one of us."

A wave of fierce pride swept over her, and she leaned into the wind as he increased his pace to a gallop on the open trail.

· · ·

THE NEXT MORNING, Callie awoke not exactly well-rested.

She was still buzzing with the strange energy of that place in the deep woods and the sense of playing baseball that came with it. From the distance of the morning after, she found the memory carried a deep sadness that clung to her every moment. She wondered if she was imagining it. Making it up. If that place was a link to the missing kids that Megan was looking for, she didn't know what it meant. But it was clear that place was dangerous in the way that all fairy magic was dangerous, and that feeling just added to her sense of uncertainty and confusion. With a willfulness honed over years of living up to Dear Old Dad's expectations, she forced the thoughts of that place into the back of her head. Her team had a game to play today. They needed her at full strength.

It was hard at first, but when she didn't give up, the clinging memories and churning suspicions let go of their hold. Really, what could hold a candle to baseball?

At Unicorn Field, too.

How cool was this going to be?

Rolling her shoulders to loosen her muscles, Callie drew in a deep breath scented with the familiar musk of the Wild Hunt's camping grounds. The fresh autumn breeze wafting over it perked her up. Then she joined her wild teammates as they prepared for their first game in the mortal world.

They made their way to the Other Field at the appointed time.

The whole of the Hunt had come along to wish them good hunting on the playing field, though they knew they would not be able to come across to spectate. It made for nearly as raucous a procession as a true full run of the Wild Hunt, and the Other Field rang with their yips, howls, barks, and growls of jubilation. Callie was a little surprised that Megan Moore didn't make an appearance. But then, the reporter was prone to poking around on her own despite Callie and Trace's attempts to warn her of the dangers that exposed her to, and, to be honest Callie was glad she didn't have to confront her while the memory of that place was still fresh in her mind. Callie suspected Megan had decided to take advantage of the fact that her babysitters were going to be a world away today, and that was good.

Benji Amberman was already waiting at third base, the Web Gem glinting in their hands and the wind tousling their loose hair around their pensive face. They wore their Unicorns uniform, the cap tilted back to let the morning sunlight fall on their cheeks.

Callie appraised Benji as she approached. They didn't look as tired as they had the last time she'd seen them. They were standing without any assistance, at least. But there was something about Benji's posture that set off Callie's growing hunter's sense. Something she couldn't quite catch hold of to look at properly, but she felt inside nonetheless.

"Hey," Benji called as she came closer. The pensive expression melted into a bright smile that made her surprisingly happy. They definitely didn't look as though they were about to pass out this time, and she realized she was happy for that little bit of normalcy amid this period where so much was just weird and worrisome.

"Good day for a game, isn't it?" Benji said.

"It is here, anyway. What's the weather like in Pattersonville?"

"Pretty much the same, just a touch less magical. But that's changing, you know."

"Yeah," she replied. "I know." Callie wondered if that was a good thing. There would always be people like her dad looking to exploit any power that fell into their hands.

The back of her mind was getting rather cramped.

Baseball, her bat whispered to calm her. Its eagerness seeped into her.

On the field around them, her teammates were moving through their warmups. The pop of bat on ball, the slap of ball into glove, the grunt of effort, and the scrape of hoof or claw or hard leather shoe on dirt set up a rhythm of anticipation in Callie's heart. The rest of the Wild Hunt had thronged the stands and were setting up their favorite eerie chants, howling at the moon despite the fact it was now midmorning and the moon was nowhere in sight. The sound still made the hairs on the back of her neck prickle in the most exquisite way.

Pride filled her. This was her team, and they were ready.

With a grin she knew was nearly as wolfish as the Leader's own, she turned back to Benji. "You Unicorns had better be ready for a good scrap."

"Oh, they are."

"They are?" Callie asked, noting the pensive look that had returned to Benji's face. "Aren't you playing, too? Or are you, uh, taking it easy after the transfers?" She winced at the awkward question. Speaking just for herself, Callie always hated being too hurt or sick to play and despised when people mentioned it.

Seeming unruffled, Benji gave a casual shrug. "I'd love to play, and I think I'll be okay. But the truth is, I've got a lead on some research I've been doing on my spiderkin heritage, and I've got an opportunity to follow up on it today. So, once I get you and your horde of lovable mongrels across the ring, I'm sticking around here to get some work done."

That sounded reasonable enough, and though Callie still had the niggling feeling that something wasn't quite right, she couldn't find anything to pull on. Benji was even more fairy than she was. If anyone could deal with weirdness in the Realm, it was them.

The Leader of the Hunt approached, moving more like he was stalking prey rather than coming to have a friendly conversation. As usual, an essence of fairy magic had his tattered cloak billowing around him far more than the gentle breeze could account for, and his golden wolf eyes glowed with a keen light that set Callie's blood pumping. At first, that effect had made her feel like sighted prey; now, it made her anticipate a good, hard run, and the reward of fresh meat at the end of it.

"We are ready," he said in a low growl. "Work your magic, Web Gem Keeper."

He lifted one arm, fist clenched in signal, and the rest of the team arrayed themselves in rows behind him. Callie did not move to take her place, but only because they had agreed ahead of time that her role was to be ready to assist Benji if necessary.

But not only did Benji not look a bit like the wilting flower they'd resembled the last few times, they also had another surprise up their sleeve.

"Bring your supporters down. I can carry them across, too. It's only fair for you to have a cheering section the same as the Unicorns."

Callie frowned. "Are you sure? Don't overtax yourself."

"It's all good. I've found some things that help."

That was as evasive an answer as she'd ever heard, but this wasn't the time to do more than narrow her eyes in suspicion.

The Leader's sharp gaze bounced between them for a moment, then he shrugged and lifted his arm again, this time letting two snaps echo across the field.

Instantly, their excitement level growing palpable, the Hunt members in the stands rushed into the field. Callie's own excitement was ramping up, despite her lingering worry for what Benji was about to attempt.

"I hope you know what you're doing, kiddo," she said as Benji hefted the Web Gem.

Benji flashed another grin, and the Web Gem let out a flare of prismatic light.

The world around Callie shimmered, and then, in a blink, she was on Unicorn Field once again, surrounded by her wildling team-mates and their excitable supporters. Their animalistic sounds mingled with the cheers of the humans already filling the stands.

The usual tricks of time were in play, as midmorning in the Realm had become early evening in Pattersonville. The sky overhead was colored with the pinks and purples of sunset. The smell of mundane ballpark food filled the air— popcorn, hot dogs, soda pop — and on the field around them, the Unicorns finished up their own warmups and turned to greet their rivals for the day with smiles of challenge.

Callie scanned the area, taking in all these details as if preparing for a chase as, across the way, Adrien Thorn emerged from the dugout, wearing a clouded expression and making a beeline for her.

Benji Amberman, she noted, had stayed behind, just as they'd promised.

CHAPTER

TWELVE

After safely crossing the Wild Hunt over to Unicorn Field, Benji, attempting to project a casual air by tucking the Web Gem under one arm and cramming their hands into the pockets of their uniform pants, made their way out of the Other Field.

The Unseelie Queen's barrier was working.

Benji hadn't been sure it would.

Given her history, the queen was not exactly trustworthy. And Benji hadn't fallen off the fairy truck just yesterday. But their discussion in the library betwixt the worlds the other day had shown Benji how recalcitrant their former enemy had become. The queen had spoken of her work seeking the spiderkin artifacts with genuine feeling. And, Benji had to admit, the information she'd shared about the one called the Octagon was intriguing, to say the least. According to the histories she'd read, it had the power to bring a community together for a common purpose. Seemed like it would play nicely with the Web Gem's power, anyway.

But the queen's search for the artifacts took second place to her promise to help Benji learn to use the Web Gem properly. It was a

92

simple fact that she had the most experience with the artifact, and the chance to learn from a master was too good to pass up. And when Benji had allowed her to place her dark shield around them, the Web Gem had given a twinge of something akin to relief. Benji couldn't deny the spell was doing its job, at the very least. The crippling exhaustion Benji ought to be feeling after pushing so many fairies across the portal licked ineffectually at the edges of the Unseelie Queen's magic shield, flickering around them instead, flaring against the shield's power like flames desperate to burn an encircled building to ash.

The sense of relief was real.

The queen had passed the test. Maybe she was truly trustworthy now?

Just the thought brought Benji images of Emily's rolling eyes and Adrien's lips pursing as shadows cloaked their expressions.

Luckily, no fairies other than those that belonged to the Wild Hunt had come to the Other Field yet. The River Kin and the Seelie Court would play a game later today. But for now, the Other Field was tranquil and empty of all but the tiniest of pixies, winking like fireflies over the outfield grass.

That made it easier to slink away for the next steps in their plans.

Benji left the field and slipped towards the darkened horizon— the Unseelie Queen's lands.

The real test would come as soon as they arrived at Her Majesty's chambers today. Her reaction to such temptation as Benji physically bearing the Web Gem would be telling, that was for sure. Benji had no intention of letting her get close enough to lay a sharp-taloned finger on the trophy, though. With the barrier in place, they had enough strength left now to skip back into the mortal world if she tried anything stupid.

One step at a time.

And the first step was making it to the Unseelie Court unscathed.

I don't want to have to figure out how to use the Web Gem on my own if I don't have to, Benji thought, mostly as a bit of a pep talk. Given their luck thus far in trying to get the Web Gem to work well, the thought was more than a bit melancholy. It would still be easy to give up and go home.

Another scan of the darkly vined forests ahead made Benji swallow against a dry throat.

Making the trip alone weighed like the idea of a root canal.

Then, before they could force themself past their trepidation, it got worse.

As Benji stepped out of the shadow of the Other Field's charming wooden grandstands, a distant rattling sound from beyond the surrounding hillocks set their teeth to clench. The desire to run was strong, but their feet felt like they'd been frozen in place. Another moment, and a huge black shape appeared from around the stadium's corner, trundling along the faint trail that led off toward the woods. A pair of pitch-black horses formed from the shadows, trotting in step, and pulling a carriage draped in enough black that Benji wondered if it had been fitted out for mourning. Despite the midmorning sunlight, a pair of dingy lanterns hung from the carriage front like old-fashioned headlights. Impenetrable shadows cloaked the coachman perched on the box, but an eerie blue light shone from the depths of his hood.

At least the coachman was not headless, or Benji might have lost their proverbial shit right there.

As it was, as the horrific transport clattered closer, Benji still recoiled from the grave stench that preceded it. For a brief moment, they hoped, wished, and prayed that the dank carriage would simply pass by, but it swung around on the pathway, stopping so the carriage doors stood exactly in front of Benji.

Then the coachman leaned from his high perch and hissed a strange whisper from within the hood. There were no words, as such, but Benji got the gist anyway.

My mistress bids thee ride with me.

Unable to help themself, Benji lifted their eyes to meet the coachman's gaze. No head sat within the folds of his hood, only a lone blue flame, floating above the ragged edges of a bloody neck stump.

So much for that.

Just as Benji managed to tear their gaze away, the carriage doors clapped open of their own accord.

Delightful.

Benji's stomach soured. Did they dare step foot inside? Or would it be even more dangerous to refuse the ride their new partner had sent?

The Web Gem shivered from the crook of their arm, and the furious, incessant waves of exhaustion pressed against their protective dark magic barrier once again.

In for a penny, Benji thought with a sigh.

Clutching the grimy bronze handrail, they hoisted themself into the carriage.

The stink inside was even worse, but it was too late now; the doors snapped shut behind them, and before Benji had a chance to settle on the velvet-covered bench, the carriage was already rattling away.

***

"You had a pleasant ride, I trust?"

The Unseelie Queen's tone was soft in welcome as Benji entered her study. The chamber was dark, of course, with guttering torches along the stone walls serving only to break up the gathered shadows rather than truly light the room. A large bank of mullioned windows took up one wall entirely, opening out to look over the gloomy prospects of the Unseelie Court. Another wall featured built-in shelving overflowing with tomes, each one looking as though it contained knowledge better left unlearned between its grisly covers. The furniture, while plushly upholstered, still exuded a forbidding air, with its dark coloring and carved claw and ball feet. Still, the chamber wasn't entirely off-putting. The queen had a tray of tea set up on the worktable, and the warm scent of it told Benji it was genuinely wholesome— a plain old Earl Gray with a lovely porcelain creamer and sugar bowl accompanying the pot. A plate of small, triangular sandwiches sat beside the tea things, orange jam spilling from the insides.

Benji's stomach growled despite the scent of death that still clung to their Unicorns uniform after the carriage ride.

"I guess I can't complain," they said.

The queen made a small noise, and Benji realized she was amused at their feeble attempt at diplomacy. "Your mortal blood abhors the grimmer aspects of our fair Realm?"

"I wouldn't call that hearse *fair,* exactly. But it was a smooth ride, despite the, uh, aroma. I barely felt any bumps in the road."

"My personal carriage is very well sprung," the queen said with a growing smile.

Benji smothered the urge to fidget under that knowing gaze. They clamped their arm tighter around the Web Gem, making the trophy dig painfully into their side.

The queen took mercy on them. With a titter of laughter, she waved one pale hand at the worktable and the tea things waiting there. "Come, child. Have some refreshment. I am eager to see how my little spell worked for you. You seem no worse for wear after transporting the Hunt, at least."

Any protest Benji might have made was undercut by the loud rumble their stomach let free. Sheepishly, yet gratefully, they approached the table and reached for one of the jam sandwiches.

The sweet, tangy flavor of the orange burst upon their tongue brighter than anything Benji had ever tasted in the mortal world. The bread, too, tasted sweet, and still slightly warm, as if it had been cut from a freshly baked loaf mere minutes earlier. The replenishing rush of pure energy flooded their body. In no time, Benji had polished off two of the little sandwiches, and the pounding waves of their exhaustion had finally receded fully from the queen's barrier.

The Unseelie Queen, watching with keen eyes, poured two cups of tea. Without asking, she doctored one of the cups precisely the way Benji liked it— two lumps of sugar and a tiny drop of cream— and slid it daintily across the table. Then she sat back with her black tea cradled in her long, spindly fingers.

Benji nodded thanks and took a sip. The temperature was perfect, of course. They drank half the cup in one go.

Feeling suddenly rude with their gorging, Benji forced themself to lower the cup back to the saucer. "I've never tasted *anything* so…"

They trailed off, unable to articulate the immense pleasure of eating fey food.

The queen, to her credit, looked pleased and even a little bashful at the praise. "I am glad you find it satisfactory. I want you to feel comfortable with me, Benji. I believe we can help one another, and I know that requires trust on both sides."

Her dark eyes flicked towards the Web Gem, sitting by Benji's elbow as they ate. She took a deep breath through her nostrils, then quietly released it through her black-painted lips before bringing her gaze back to Benji.

"I'd like to start with another lesson for you, if you would accept it. Perhaps after that we can discuss what I've found out about the Octagon."

Benji, resisting the urge to reach for another sandwich, gave a slow nod, trying not to think of themself as a failure. Working with the Web Gem should have been easier, shouldn't it? Especially given their alignment with the spiderkin makers. It stung that they were still having such trouble using an artifact that was— supposedly— their birthright. Just being here was a positive sign, though. At least determination was in Benji's favor.

"Your barrier has helped a lot, but I know I need to be able to control the Web Gem's power myself. So another lesson would be good. As for the Octagon…" They shrugged, then smiled self-deprecatingly. "I'll help if I can, but unfortunately, I feel like our relationship is going to be a bit one-sided for a while."

The queen lifted one hand as if intending to reach out to pat

Benji's arm, but she hesitated in the gesture, then lowered her hand back to her lap.

"Let us see how you fare after my lesson," she said instead.

Benji sat up straighter, then, as if their strictest teacher— Mrs. Harmon, Geometry, 10th grade— were suddenly in residence. The queen's voice had become harder than it had been previously. A trickle of unease ran down Benji's spine. They'd struggled hard in that class, spending night after night cursing Mrs. Harmon's name as well as whoever had invented trigonometry.

But they'd finished the semester with an A+.

This felt the same, if not a bit more dangerous. Okay, a lot more dangerous.

Picking up their teacup, Benji met the Unseelie Queen's eye straight on.

"Bring it on," they said. "I'll even do the extra credit."

The queen's smile showed her gleaming alabaster teeth, then she drained her cup.

THIRTEEN

"Where's Benji?" Adrien said from several steps away as he hustled across the outfield to where the Wild Hunt had just begun to warm up. The way his dark eyes glittered in the early evening gloam over Unicorn Field said he was worried.

"Good to see you, too," Callie quipped.

The bat in her hand still buzzed with the same level of anticipation and excitement it had given off from the first moment Callie's cleats had hit the grass here. Glancing around Unicorn Field was a mesmerizing experience now. Adrien was a true artist with a baseball diamond. He'd even threaded strings of soft, purple-white fairy lights into the hedgework along the left and right field lines and laid a series of jack-o'-lanterns spaced out at their base. Paired with the fresh October breeze coming off the oak and sycamore trees and what promised to be a full-packed house of excited fans, this might be the most perfect baseball field ever designed.

Adrien stopped in front of her, chest heaving under the teal button-down Unicorns baseball shirt he wore. Callie had heard Jackson's Sports, a local shop that had always been a little brother kind of competitor to her dad's Ball and Glove, had donated these most perfectly old-fashioned uniforms for the Fairy Season. Throwback uniforms for a throwback event.

"I'm sorry, Cal," Adrien said. "It's great to see you again and all that. But, seriously, where's Benji? Are they all right?"

"They stayed in the Fairy Realm," Trace replied, coming to stand first defensively beside Callie, then putting one hoof between her and Adrien.

She put her hand on Trace's well-muscled shoulder. "Stand down, Trace. You know Adrien's good with me."

Adrien took a half step back, though. "So?" he said, focusing the question again.

"Benji's fine," Callie replied. "Said they had something to look into, and that we should go on and play the game."

Adrien's face clouded even further, and his lips twisted into something uncertain. "They weren't dead tired?"

"I was surprised at that, too, but they seemed okay enough. Why?"

He lifted his cap off his head and reseated it while taking a deep breath and avoiding her gaze. "I don't know. Probably nothing."

"Now you've got me worried."

"Yeah. I know. It's just that using the Web Gem to transport teams has been knocking Benji down pretty good. I guess being stronger should be a good thing."

"But?" Callie said.

"I don't trust anything about the realm."

"That I understand."

Adrien hesitated another moment, then cast a faintly hopeless look at Callie. "Did Megan...?"

Callie gave him a wry smile. "You know her. Always off chasing stories. I think she wanted to stick around and watch the River Kin play the Seelies today."

Adrien deflated. "Right. She's got her exclusive scoop on the Fairy Realm side of this season. Any leads on those kids?"

The memory of that strange hint of baseball magic in the deep woods flared in Callie's mind, and she suppressed a shudder. "Nothing more than some faint traces to follow up on."

Adrien pulled his shoulders back again, his confidence returning. "If anyone can follow up on faint traces, it's Megan."

Callie liked the proud tone of his voice as he praised the reporter. Maybe Megan was a little young for him— Adrien being, in fact, one hundred and eighteen years old— but Callie was happy to see him getting attached to someone, anyway.

Adrien lifted his glove. "All right, though. We've got a game to play. Are you still good afterward?"

Callie raised her bat to say she was ready to do her part in the warding spell. "Where's Emily?"

"She says she thinks she wants to play, but still hasn't picked a team yet. She's here, though, and she's ready to help." Adrien pointed to the stands behind home plate where Emily DeWitt was sitting with her dad again.

Callie looked more closely and saw Emily was wearing both her Small Folk cap and her favorite Unicorns jacket, with both fists pushed into its pockets. One, certainly the right hand, would be carrying her mom's baseball, which had helped Emily use dollops of the baseball magic ever since she'd been abducted to the Fairy Realm.

"What's she waiting for?"

"I don't know," Adrien said. "It's annoying. But at least I can see she's in a tougher place than you or me. She's got friends on both sides. Whoever she chooses leaves someone out."

"Ah. I hadn't thought about it that way." Callie grinned at Adrien. "So, anyway. At least the gang's all here, then. So, let's have some fun, eh?"

For the first time tonight, Adrien beamed a full smile. "Good luck!" he called.

As he jogged back to his teammates, the old-timey #13 embroidered on the back of his uniform blazed in the stadium lights.

Those uniforms, Callie thought, were totally sick.

A HALF HOUR later the game started, and it was the exact kind of rollicking affair that Callie had anticipated.

In the stands, the people of Pattersonville showed their home-town pride, cheering and clapping for the home team and booing the visiting team's best players— or rather barking and yapping at them — with that perfect mix of angst and respect that said there wasn't anything personal in their desire to see the Wild Hunt choke on a bone. On the PA, Mayor Culpepper was in rare form. She'd obviously been taking stand-up comedy lessons or at least been paying attention to the tourists coming into town.

"Visit the Parkland Gardens before our next game with the Seelie Court. But first be sure to visit the Jones' Apothecary to stock up on those allergy pills. No sneezing or scratching is allowed as the pitch comes in! Unless, of course, it helps the Unicorns!" she quipped once between innings.

She introduced each Unicorn at the plate as "State Champion Pattersonville West's great shortstop," or "happiest catcher," or "most spectacular purveyor of the hit and run."

The fans ate it up, repeating her introduction in a joyous chant.

"Hap-piest catcher!"

"Hit. And run!"

On the field, the game was *also* everything it was meant to be.

With one out in the first inning, Trace cracked a ringing double off the wall in left-center field but got thrown out thundering to third in a poorly conceived attempt to stretch his double to a triple.

Then, in the bottom of the inning, Callie hung a first-pitch curve-ball to Jake Nesbitt, and he walloped it high and deep. But, as the crowd hushed in that most beautiful sound of group anticipation, the Leader, who tended to play a shallow center field, saved her by slipping into his wolf form, racing backward, and giving one of the most acrobatic leaps Callie had ever seen, nabbing the ball in his jaws, and racing it back to the infield before dropping it into her open hand.

Slobbery, yes.

But still an out.

The fans of Pattersonville, to their credit, gave the Leader a standing ovation as he trotted back to his position, though several took their lives into their own hands by catcalling the Leader with a collection of "Who's a good boy! Who's a good boy!"

The Leader's gaze narrowed into a sharp stare and the edge of his lip drew back to expose the sharp canines within.

"It's all good, Huntmaster. Just shut them up with the bat next inning!" Callie called, and when the Leader put his head down and kept trotting out to his position, she breathed a sigh of relief.

She circled the mound, rubbing the ball dry for an extra moment to give him a chance to catch his breath.

Ever since the spiderkin ancients had given Benji stewardship of the Web Gem and declared a fresh championship season, Callie had seen something special happening in the Leader. He seemed focused now. He still leaned on the ways of the Hunt, but there had been a contemplative day when she'd talked to him alone and found that he'd seemed excited for the game, rather than viewing it simply as a lottery ticket to be played whenever the whim struck.

"The hunting field is finally level for all the houses and all the courts, now," he'd said.

It took seeing the Leader turn down a chase right now for her to fully understand.

If there was anything Callie had learned about her Huntsfolk teammates it was how much they revered fairness and clarity. For them, life was the chase, and the chase was all about cause and effect. Chase prey, catch prey. Or, if the prey is more worthy than the Hunt that day, it gets away. In their world, the playing field was level. Every time. But the fight for control of the baseball magic in the Fairy Realm, no matter how vital, hadn't been level.

Until now.

Understanding her leader's newfound approach made her even more determined.

As she stood in the middle of the field, Callie felt two things as certainly as she'd ever felt them.

First was the welling of the purest baseball magic she'd ever imagined.

And second was the speck of darkness huddled under a tree just beyond the right field fence.

Her dad.

Fred McMasters, hiding away. Her first sensation was simply anger that he'd had the gall to show his face. But, of course, that was wrong. He wasn't showing his face. Instead, her father was huddling in the shadows of the park, his anger probably growing even more caustic as he took in the amazing things Adrien had done with the very ballpark that he had once tried to turn into a monstrosity of modern capitalism. Eventually, though, as she finally stalked her way back to the pitching rubber, Callie's anger faded to a new emotion. Sadness. And loss. Her father had lost so much, all due to his own hubris and the oblivious nature that surrounded his actions. Her dad didn't care about the world, or about any teammates. He didn't care about anyone, it seemed, anyone but himself, anyway. And that was sad.

"Ladies and gentlemen," the mayor called over the PA. *"Batting for our State Champion Unicorns, the slickest left fielder in the game, and everyone's coolest centenarian, Adrien Thorn!"*

"Coolest centenari-an!" the crowd chanted back.

Callie took a clearing breath as Adrien used his back foot to dig into the batter's box, then swiped a couple practice swings. Feeling her dad there, cowering in the shadows to watch and almost certainly trying to concoct another scheme to come out on top, brought her a fresh flavor of anger.

How annoying he was.

There was nothing to do for it, though, she thought as she peered into the catcher and caught the one blood-ringed fingertip that called for a fastball.

Nothing but to strike out Adrien Thorn, anyway.

Which she did, after an epic twelve-pitch battle that was good enough to draw such appreciative cheers from the crowd that Callie tipped her cap as she left the field to prepare to bat.

It went that way for seven more innings, Jamal Douglass matching Callie's pitching toss-for-toss, each team threatening to score often, but the defense pulling some amazing play to keep it from happening.

Then, with an out in the top of the ninth inning, Callie hit a lucky double that bounced just fair. When she stole third a pitch later, it left the Hunt Leader at the plate with one out and the lead run on third. A hit to win. Callie watched him dial in. His practice swings were intense. If there was anything on that one-track mind it was hunting down one of Jamal's pitches and pouncing on it with all his might.

And, yet.

When Jamal wound up and threw...

She saw the tell that no one else would— a twitch of his whiskers as the ball flew. With an instinctive certainty, she broke for the plate, and with the wind of her racing footsteps echoing inside her helmet, and as voices rose in excited fervor, instead of taking the mightiest of swings, the Hunt Leader instead turned to lay down the most perfect sacrifice bunt Callie had ever seen.

Patsy at first fielded it and, seeing she had no play on Callie, threw to Pash Kulpari covering first base for the only out she could get.

Callie leapt for joy.

1-0!

The Hunt were ahead!

"I can't believe you sacrificed yourself," Callie said, hugging the Leader despite herself as he returned to the dugout.

"A good Huntmaster does what it takes to make the chase

successful," the Leader replied, obviously feeling awkward with her praise.

They both knew such self-sacrifice was not in the Hunt's makeup.

But, after Callie retired the Unicorns in order in the bottom of the inning, the game was over, and the Hunt's chase had, indeed, been successful. The team — from Red Caps to Centaurs to Satyrs to even Callie herself — celebrated with a furious race around the entire field, yipping and yapping, and howling at the approaching Samhain moon.

It was, perhaps, the best win of Callie McMasters' career.

And, it was made better by that presence she still felt in the distance out beyond right field. That sad, bitter presence of her father, who would never know how it felt to be part of a true team.

Later.

Unicorn Field stood empty now.

Its banks of lights had shut down, leaving only Adrien's fairy lights, the glowering jack-o'-lanterns, and the dim light of the scorer's cabin behind home plate as illumination. Callie joined with Adrien and, finally, Emily DeWitt as she stepped onto the field.

Her Wild Hunt teammates were huddled in their dugout, the Huntmaster having agreed to give Callie this moment alone with her friends.

They had to move fast, though. Even as Emily emerged from the darkness, Callie could feel the restless nature of her Huntmates as they chomped at the bit. The Hunt would be long and raucous when they returned to the Fairy Realm. She could already smell blood in her nostrils, and if she were honest with herself, she, too, wanted to run free, wanted to feel Trace's muscles flow as he carried her along and to feel the air burning her cheeks as he leapt from gully to gully.

Victory brought a need for release, and her Hunt would celebrate this victory long and hard.

"Hey there," Emily said as she drew close. Her hand held her mother's baseball in a four-seam grip.

"Hey," Adrien said, proffering his mitt.

The bat in Callie's grip buzzed with the energy that came from the three together, reminding her of the spell they'd cast that had freed Trace and the others from their statue prisons the last time they were all together. It made her happy.

"I missed beating the Unicorns without their best player," Callie said with a grin.

"Sorry." Emily gave a defensive shrug.

"Hey. I didn't mean anything by that, you know. Just busting your chops."

"I know. It's just..."

Callie felt her friend's sense of discomfort. "Yeah. I know. It's all right. It'll come when it comes."

Emily's expression relaxed but she didn't seem any more relieved. "All right," she said, holding the ball out in the palm of her hand. "Let's see if we can set this ward and get on with things."

Circling home plate, they each knelt on the infield dirt.

Adrien held his opened glove over home plate. Emily put the ball into it, maintaining contact. Then Callie laid her bat over the ball.

As one, they took a deep breath and exchanged flickering glances before pressing the collection onto home plate.

"*Strike thrice the bone white plate...*" Adrien recited the phrase he'd learned during his long servitude in the Realm.

Together, they lifted, then pressed down again. Flames from the jack-o'-lanterns drew toward the infield.

"*...and bring about...*" Callie added her bit, and the fairy lights around the field pulsed a slow beat as they lifted a third time. The odor of wood smoke seeped up from the dirt.

"*...a shielded gate,*" Emily said, finishing the chant they'd agreed upon earlier.

The ball, glove, and bat all hit home plate for the third time.

The plate flared a golden pulse, and a tang of incense merged with that of the woodsmoke. Owl call echoed from the woods, perhaps from outside Unicorn Field or perhaps from some place or time far away. The fairy lights flared again, *whoomp*ing in the cold autumn darkness, flickering in a bright twine of purple and white. A strong wind blasted Callie's cap from her head and sent it tumbling to the outfield, and a roaring wave of power brought tears to her eyes.

This was nothing like what had happened when they'd broken the statue spell.

Callie's ears rang with the overflow of magic. Her veins throbbed. Her skin crackled as if on the verge of bursting into flame.

Then everything went silent.

Except...

There came a single yip from a Red Cap. A grating groan from Grangle, the team's tiny rock troll scorekeeper, filled the lower register. Then came a howl. The Leader this time.

"What's...," Emily said. "What's wrong?"

Callie glanced from Emily to Adrien, feeling the wrongness, too, as her Wild Hunt compatriots began to stir wildly. A horrible, claustrophobic sensation crawled over Callie's entire body.

Trapped. She felt trapped, cut off from a vital resource, blocked away from her home. From the place she belonged.

Adrien's face was gaunt and pale, carrying an expression of something between terror and pure horror. He clutched his glove to his chest. Emily's ball dropped to the hard ground with a thud.

"I don't know," he said. "I don't know. The spell was supposed to put a bubble around the whole field, just to ward it, to keep the fairies from leaving the ballpark and getting up to mischief in the town. But this..."

Callie stared in growing numbness at the baseball diamond, trying to sense the connection that had caused so much trouble as her bat lay like dead weight in her grip. She could read what lay between its bright white lines as easily as any trail.

Unicorn Field, a place that had always hummed with the faint undercurrent of its connection to the Fairy Realm, now felt as mundane and empty as any other ballpark.

The portal wasn't warded. It was sealed.

"I screwed it up," Emily said, bursting into tears. "I should have picked a team! I should have! And now I've gone and messed it all up! The baseball magic… it didn't work for me like it usually does. You feel it, don't you? The fairy ring? It's locked!"

Callie, too caught up in her own fear, didn't answer.

Adrien stood in silence, too, staring at home plate as if he could shatter it with his gaze.

With a cry of dismay, Emily ran off into the darkness.

Behind Callie, the sound of the Hunt grew ever more restless. *Prey,* they whispered. *Blood and prey!*

Benji, Callie thought.

Emily was right. The portal between the Fairy Realm and the Real World was closed.

And Benji, the only one with any chance of opening it, was on the other side.

CHAPTER

FOURTEEN

Benji floated, suspended in a solution of magics.

Their spirit burned with excitement.

The pure, golden light of the Web Gem's power was all around them, within reach for any purpose they might dream of, threaded through with a century of the Unseelie Queen's black touch. Though Benji felt she had enough power here to wrest control of the trophy for herself, she did no such thing.

The temptation must be tremendous, though.

See how the light flows, she said into Benji's mind as the lesson continued. *Feel how it moves swift as a stream running through the forest. Deep as an ocean keeping its secrets.*

I feel it, Benji replied.

With a thick tendril of liquid darkness, she took hold of Benji's consciousness and turned it inward. *You must find the place within yourself that reflects these same qualities.*

The queen pointed.

Benji fought the need to struggle against the queen's forceful hold. She meant them no harm, they felt. Here in this place where their mingling magics left all exposed, Benji could read the Unseelie

Queen's heart as easily as their own. Obediently, Benji looked to that place within. True to her word, it glowed and thrummed with fey power not unlike the Web Gem's. But this wasn't new. Benji had known about this place within themself all their life. Disappointment dragged at their incorporeal spirit.

Look deeper, the queen said, irritated now. Her dark tendrils locked down before Benji could squirm away, keeping their attention where she wanted it.

Light swirled, golden and flecked with rainbow hues that shimmered faintly as if from a very far distance.

Sweat beaded on Benji's brow.

Then, they saw it. A flicker at first. Not something they would have noticed if the queen weren't forcing them to examine things so closely, but it was there. A flash of something more lay within the folds of Benji's innate magic.

With ethereal fingers, Benji dug past the surface level of it until they brushed up against the silken material lying within. Strands. Connections. Passages— though to where they led Benji could not say. The material tangled around Benji's grip, and Benji marveled at the energetic burn of its touch.

The light of the Web Gem flooded them, warm and spicy.

More, Benji thought as they reached further.

The queen jerked back on her tendrils so hard it knocked Benji, breathless, back into their physical body.

They startled abruptly to find themself hunched over their cup of tea, gasping.

Benji rubbed their chest. It felt like they'd been kicked by one of the queen's horrible horses.

"What was that for?" Benji said, unable to keep bitterness from their voice. "I was only doing what you told me."

The queen, utterly unruffled, refilled her teacup. "You reached too far, Spider Child. That place is the source of your power, but it is also the source of *yourself.* You need to learn of your limits before delving into it. Better sorcerers than you have thought to utilize their deepest energies, and then have suffered the consequences. Unless you would enjoy turning yourself quite inside out?"

She lifted her cup and took a demure sip.

Benji shuddered at the image her quiet threat conjured. "Then... how do I use it? The Web Gem responded when I touched it."

"You don't *use* it. You open yourself up to it, you let it fill you with power, and then you direct that power to your desire. It is quite simple."

Benji reached for the teapot, trying to keep their hands from shaking too much as they poured. They recalled the sense of connection that had been so strong within, then shuddered as they realized the paths inside had been even more tangled than any trail through the queen's dark woodlands. "Simple doesn't mean easy, does it?"

The queen made no reply, but her eyes glittered over the rim of her cup.

Benji sighed. "No. It doesn't." They took a fortifying drink of tea — still hot, despite the time they'd spent on the lesson. If the new slant of the light filtering in through the mullioned windows meant anything, that time they'd been in the netherworld of their own essence had been longer than Benji had first thought. Where the grounds outside Unseelie Castle had previously been gloomy with daytime darkness, now the horizon had been stained bloody by the setting sun.

The games of the day must be long over with, Benji realized with a start.

"Oh, crap," Benji said as a bolt of stress shot through them. "I'm late."

Both the game here between the River Kin and the Seelies, and the one on the other side of the portal. The Wild Hunt must have been waiting for their assistance in returning home for ages.

With a grimace, they set their cup back on its saucer, then levered up from the plush chair they'd been sitting in. Benji's muscles ached the same as if they'd spent the entire day running fielding drills. They were almost surprised to see their uniform still pristine and completely without the many grass stains they'd have picked up during practice.

"We'll have to continue this next time, Your Majesty. I think I'm terribly late getting back to the Other Field."

Benji had to admit, the idea of shutting down today's lesson appealed in more ways than one. Not only did their muscles have that dead-weight feeling, the atmosphere of the Unseelie Court had frazzled their nerves. The queen may be staying on her best behavior, but there was only so much dark magic Benji could take on at once.

The queen's lips twitched, only the tightness at the corners speaking of her displeasure at the interruption. But her midnight skirts swirled around her like a storm cloud as she, too, rose from her chair. "I shall order my carriage for you."

"Thanks." A certain sense of desperation covered Benji at the idea of a second odiferous ride, but a single thought of traipsing alone through her tangled forest made their fatigue well into a wall of despair. There were worse things than a smelly ride.

"When you return, perhaps we can devote more time to untangling the history of the Octagon. I have reason to believe time may be of the essence in its discovery."

Benji gave a noncommittal shrug. They reached for the Web Gem, though not with the protective urgency that had colored the start of this meeting. The Unseelie Queen had had many chances to take it and had passed on each one. "I hope I can help. But I think we need to focus on my progress with the magic, first. And the Fairy League Season has to take priority. I'm sure you understand that."

"Do not delay too long, Spider Child. I understand that nothing will change in the Fairy Realm if the Web Gem is allowed to be awarded as it has been for eons."

Benji flashed her a grin, but as they stepped away from the table a blast of power hit so hard and so sudden that they nearly dropped the Web Gem in their haste to grab the table's edge. A wave of dizziness flashed over them. It was a stabbing pain, Benji thought. Or a pounding one. The bruising sense of having a door of stone slammed in one's face.

The wave subsided though, and Benji saw their fingers were white where they clutched the table.

Panicked, they looked up, and taking a deep breath, blinked away the watery veil of tears that had sprung from their clenched eyes. "I'm sorry," they said, ashamed of their weakness. "The lesson must have taken more from me than I thought."

But when Benji regained full control, they saw the queen, too, had stumbled, and that wild strands of stray hair now filtered down from her forehead.

She stood firmly rigid now, glaring out the window, her face a mix of anger and confusion. "What...?"

A sense of something utterly wrong fell upon the room.

Inside Benji, that new, deep place gave a single painful throb.

Instinctively, Benji ignored the protests of aching muscles to stretch their inner self towards the Web Gem. Their grasp met with the Unseelie Queen's, and together, they tapped into the power of the artifact to see what it could show them.

Unicorn Field, Benji saw.

Covered in the pitch-black darkness of night.

Full of the trilling howls of the Wild Hunt echoing like the shrill cries of caged animals.

There was a force here, too. A wall, thick and unmovable.

Baseball magic, Benji knew.

It laced the air in a dense, impenetrable lattice. And beyond that barrier, Benji's friends stood in aghast horror, their talismans glowing in their hands, hot and smoking from recent use.

"The *fools*," the queen spat. "Utter imbeciles! What did they think would happen?"

Benji knew what Adrien, Emily, and Callie had thought they were doing. Warding the field. Protecting their city. But what they'd wrought was entirely different.

Benji, still immersed in the Web Gem, felt the ramifications of their friends' actions ripple across the entirety of the Fairy Realm.

The fairy ring linking the Other Field and Unicorn Field had been closed, and with it, the power of anyone in the Fairy Realm, from the lowest Small Folk pixie to the highest Lord of the Courts, to cross between the worlds had evaporated like morning mist over the grass.

Benji met the queen's gaze.

Their heart raced with quicksilver fear as the queen's anger rose.

Benji was trapped, now. Locked down on this side of the gate, and at the mercy of the hospitality of the Unseelie Queen.

CHAPTER

FIFTEEN

"Unless you want to sacrifice your firstborn, you have to cross here," Essie said to Megan, pointing a tiny finger to where the rounded humps of three stones poked up from the surface of the bubbling creek that wound through the darkening woods. Megan and the little brownie— on their way to Unseelie Pitch— had been hiking along this forest trail for longer than Megan thought was prudent. After having overheard Megan's conversation with Fennoc in the Small Folk dugout, the little brownie had approached Megan and offered herself as a guide. Or to be more appropriate, Essie had demanded Megan take her along because— as Essie had said— *I'll feel terribly horrible if you die out there.* At first, Megan had denied any intention of going to Unseelie Pitch. But Essie had given her a look— one eyebrow raised, minuscule arms crossed over her chest, toe even tapping in impatience— and Megan had admitted the truth. She'd even brought Essie in on her real quest, telling her all about the missing kids she was searching for.

Now Essie clutched the collar of Megan's Red Sox shirt to keep from sliding too far off her shoulder. Megan was happy for the guid-

116

ance, but she was growing a bit weary of Essie's high-pitched chatter right in her ear.

She was getting tired already, too, and there was still the return trip to make.

"Your firstborn? That seems a bit much to pay just to cross a little stream," Megan said.

"Well, it's a metaphor, anyway," Essie said.

"You mean it's an idiom."

"Whatever. This is the only place where the river fairies can't ask a boon for passage. Or put you to sleep and take your living breath. Or... well... spirits like theirs can be quite inventive when they want to be."

"That's interesting," Megan said, unable to keep from indulging her reporter's mindset and asking questions. "How did that come about? The river fairies?"

Essie shrugged. "It's always been that way, but I guess I never thought about it. The spirits don't field teams, so I don't know much about them except that you don't want to be looking the other way when they show up. Cross here, though, and things work out."

"That's good enough for me," Megan said. "I appreciate the warning."

If there was one thing *Megan* could say for sure after the past few hours it was that without Essie's help, she truly wouldn't have made it out of the woods. Everything here was twisty and turny, and the vines that hung down from the trees writhed and rasped with a steady hiss that made it easy to lose track of everything. The brownie knew the lay of the land, though. She had kept them out of two swamps, avoided a mud troll's lair, and skirted a slithering field of those snaky vines, though one had still managed to wrap around Megan's ankle before she slipped away. Essie had even helped her get her sneaker back by tossing in a gnarled lump of dead wood to distract the vines. Which was good. The idea of hobbling around in the wilds of the Fairy Realm on one shoe made Megan go squishy inside.

Terrier attitude or not, she was learning that a Fairy Realm woodland always had more inside than met the eye. And she was also gaining a more than healthy respect for the little brownie.

The breeze from upstream was full of fluff from cattails, but Megan ignored the way the stuff made her nose itch. Instead, she focused on the exposed, rocky stones that made a path to the other side. The current gurgled with an enticing sound, and river moss drooped from tree limbs toward the water's surface as if trying to hide the exposed stones.

It made sense if this really was the only place someone could cross without giving up their future child.

With a fortifying breath, Megan jumped from stone to stone. Though it was only three little leaps, by the time she landed on the other side, her lungs were heaving as if she'd run the gauntlet on the latest Ninja Warrior show.

So much for even this place being free of charge to cross.

"How much farther?" she asked.

"We're close now. Just up that mound and around a pass. But you'll want to keep to the shadows."

Megan gave Essie the side-eye. "Because?"

"The Unseelie Queen's dryad grounds crew are unpleasant creatures."

"How so?"

"The less said, the better."

Megan sighed, knowing she wasn't going to get anything else. Likable or not, the brownie could be entirely frustrating.

She followed Essie's directions, though, climbing a grassy mound full of pink and purple wildflowers and then slipping into the shadowed side of the pass that led to an open pasture ringed with a dark, eccentric structure that could only be a Fairy Realm grandstand.

"Is that it?" Megan whispered.

"It is," Essie shot back in a clipped voice that said she wasn't happy for the conversation.

With the sun heading toward the horizon, a cold shadow fell

across the enclosed field. Even from the distance, Megan could tell the thick hedge that ringed the outfield fences was full of prickly thorns. She'd heard stories about Unseelie magic, and having met the dark queen herself, understood the truth of them. The tales made her skin crawl as she edged further down the tree-lined path.

"And what have we here?" The words came from behind her like a chilled breath against the back of Megan's neck.

She whirled, then stepped backward, raising her hands.

"I told you not to draw attention!" Essie snapped, gathering up the fabric of Megan's Red Sox shirt to keep from falling.

It was a dark thing— a man of sorts— awkward in its bearing as it leaned forward, tall and whiplike, and smelling so strongly of ancient oak that it brought Megan to the brink of sneezing. Its face was so deeply lined it might have been made of bark. Its deep black eyes glimmered with a purple malevolence that made Megan's heart freeze.

It took a deep breath.

"Mortal blood," it drawled with a satisfied moan as it reached its dry, bonelike fingers out as if to caress Megan's cheek. "Very good for wetting of infields."

"I think not," Megan said, ducking away.

A sharp screech came from the dark recesses of the shadowed tree line. Then another. A moment later, two more of the creatures stepped onto the path, their knees cracking like a house settling.

Essie twisted at Megan's collar like it was a horse's rein and she was riding at the Kentucky Derby. "We need to be going."

The creature craned its willowy neck to stare at the brownie. "It's too late for that, my little morsel. And I'm afraid you know that all too well." Its voice grated, and as its glare grew sharper a wind gusted up, creating a cloud filled with mossy peat and the smells of leaves and grass and wild weeds. Bright lights tinged in red and orange sparked inside the cloud, and an ethereal aroma thick with woodsmoke grew all around them. "Baseball or not this season," the thing said, "the queen's decree says we have a field to tend, and uninvited intruders make the best seed fodder."

"You're the dryad grounds crew?" Megan said, understanding dawning. Her mind churned. Then, pasting a bright smile on her face, she said, "Just the people we came to interview!"

"What?" said the dryad.

"What?" said Essie.

Megan didn't let her smile falter. She was grasping at straws, but the alternative at this point seemed completely unattractive. She needed time to think.

"You *are* the dark dryad grounds crew my friend promised we'd find here, right?"

"Yes, but..." The dryad creaked its knuckles as it moved to wrap them around her neck. "Nobody comes to ask the opinions of the likes of us."

The second dryad leaned into Megan's face and let go an all-encompassing screech.

"Don't be dense," Megan said, edging back slightly. "My friend and I have traipsed all this way through this morass of godforsaken woods just to get the inside scoop on Fairy Realm ballpark mainte-nance, and now you're going to threaten to grind us into mulch?" Megan stood straighter, happy that for once her gawky teenaged height was an advantage. "I guess you haven't heard of journalistic immunity?"

"Journalistic immunity?" the dark groundskeeper said. "There is no such thing."

"Of course there is," Megan snapped back, feeling suddenly better about being on the offensive. "It's right there in the First Amendment. Freedom of the Press. We can write whatever is the truth and no one in the government can retaliate."

"The government?" the dryad said, bending backward as Megan stepped further forward.

She was on a roll. "Since the Fairy Realm invited us to play base-ball, it provides me just that. Journalistic immunity, So, you see, if you were to grind us into ballpark fertilizer, you'd be creating a cross-worlds incident bigger than you can imagine, and no one wants that, now, do we? Mortal Realm and Fairy Realm at war?"

Sensing the tide turning, Essie piped in. "Think how upset the Unseelie Queen would be!"

"Right," Megan added. "How bad would it look if all that trouble started because an innocent reporter came out to learn how the best grounds crew in the worlds keeps their park so…um…" Megan motioned to the grotesque park below them. "…so beautiful, and that grounds crew mashed them into pulp?"

Essie let go of her stranglehold on Megan's shirt and crossed her little arms defiantly. "I really wouldn't want to be you then!"

The head groundskeeper's expression grew puzzled. He scratched his gnarled brow, then bent backward. The two other dryads slunk back into the shadows far enough that, while Megan could still see them, they were out of the picture. "Journalistic immunity. I see how that could work."

"That's good. Because I was wondering if you could give me a bit of a tour and explain to me how the Unseelies do such a marvelous job of keeping their ballpark so… um… magical."

"A tour? To show the worlds our life's work?" The dark dryad's gaze bounced between Essie and Megan. The first glimmerings of vanity sparked in the depths of his beady black eyes. "Yes. I'm sure the queen would approve of that, though I'm certain she'll want to keep the *magical* part of it under wraps."

"Oh. No worries. No one thinks you'd give away any trade secrets." Megan pulled out her phone and prepared to take notes, then proceeded with a breathless tone. "Maybe we could start with those amazing hedges. Are those thorns really as deadly as they look like they'd be?"

"Even more so, Lady Journalist. The wailings of those ensnared in their piercing grip serve as a vital part of our game-day atmosphere." He drew himself up taller, pride evident in his tone. "Their ability to extract the deepest scream of pain just as the opposition is batting is both a work of art and a large part of our home-field advantage."

"Amazing. Please do lead on, then!"

The head groundskeeper nodded, then headed down the now even darker path that led toward the baseball field, where, below, fairy lights had begun to dance, and the glinting red shades of the evening sunset were edging everything in fire.

Trying to appear relaxed, Megan drew a deep breath and followed the groundskeeper, clearing her mind for the questions she knew she needed to ask while also trying to ignore the fact that the groundskeeper's two dryad thugs followed closely behind.

The groundskeeper took her through the dugouts, the home team's crafted of the finest warm-hewn wood, and the visitors' lined with benches cut from hard limestone that still showed the marks of the axes and picks used to mine it. Seeing those marks of labor, Essie's face darkened, and Megan didn't need to be a great scholar of Fairy Realm history to know her guide was thinking of the Small Folk who had likely given their blood and toil to excavate and install those benches.

The dark dryad let her stand on the pitcher's mound, too, which felt tall and dominating, and smelled of superiority. The dirt here was tinged purple, too. "Aged from a century of the queen's presence," he said proudly. "We make every effort to ensure no player walks off with even a single flake of its dust on their person."

She saw home plate, too, a matted sheet of bone and teeth held together with a frame of magic so strong that even a wholly mortal Megan could feel it.

She understood that time moved in mysterious ways in the Fairy Realm, but as best as she could tell an hour had passed by the time she'd seen the outfield hedgerows (with their curved, talon-y thorns thankfully currently empty of victims), the blood-soil outfields that reeked of earthy richness, and the basepaths of slithery vines, which Essie noted would slip and slide in ways that supported the home team whenever the Unseelie Queen desired.

"Indeed," the groundskeeper sighed with a savory sense of wistfulness. "They are my favorite pets."

"It's all so amazing," she said when the tour finished. She let her gaze run over the rounded arc of the spectators' benches and the royal chambers where the courts had reserved seating. "I can feel the magic of everything here," she said. "I can see why they call your crew the greatest groundskeepers of all time."

Even in the darkness, now cut only by the dancing fairy light of outfield pixies, Megan could see the dryad blush. "We certainly do our best."

"I imagine this place has to be connected to something fabulous," Megan said, trying not to put too much energy into the comment.

"What do you mean, Miss Taker of Notes?"

"Well, I'm sure you're aware the Other Field is connected with a fairy ring to Unicorn Field, right?"

"I did not simply sprout yesterday. Of course, I'm aware of that."

"And it seems that the practice field is similarly connected to another field in the Real World. She raised a brow."

"Harumpf."

Megan turned her gaze back to the stands and then around to the outfield, the foul lines, and everything in between. As revulsive as much of it was, she made her expression seem delighted. "Given both of those fields have connections, I can't imagine a place as amazing as this wouldn't have at least some kind of connection someplace."

"Oh, believe me, Miss. You don't want to know how the queen can use this field."

Megan's eyebrows rose, but she didn't want to press the groundskeeper. "I'm sure I don't."

Which, of course, was a lie.

She'd gotten what she came for, however, and given Essie's tiny gasp at the dryad's answer, she knew even the brownie had just become even more certain that the queen had something to say about the missing kids. It was just a lead, though. An opening story in a full set of investigations. But it made her itch to find a way into the castle itself. To dig around the queen.

But that was something for another day.

"Thank you for the tour, head groundskeeper," Megan said. "We'll have to be getting along now or it will be well past the darkest hour when we get home."

"Indeed," the groundskeeper said. "It's been my boon to serve. Please do show the queen's generosity when you write your journalistic story."

"I sure will," Megan responded, shoving her phone into her pocket. "Are you ready, Essie?"

The little brownie nodded. But as Megan made a show of waving to the other dryads and tramping back up the path they'd arrived on, Essie leaned over to whisper in her ear.

"Don't tell me we're going home already?"

Megan grinned. "After a lead like that? You'd better believe we're sticking around. I can't imagine those tree guys working too late into the night. You up for some covert investigations, Ess?"

"Ready as I am to cheer on a Small Folk victory!"

Megan nodded, full of energy once more.

The return trip could wait. It was an excellent night for doing journalism.

CHAPTER

SIXTEEN

The Wild Hunt's restlessness was already edging towards panic.

After Emily dashed off, Callie knew she had to leave, too, despite the look of desperate horror Adrien turned toward her. She knew what her Huntmates were capable of on a normal night in the Fairy Realm, but this was neither the Fairy Realm nor a normal night.

This was Pattersonville two nights before Halloween— Samhain. The moon overhead was nearly full, its pale light settling over Unicorn Field like a layer of silvery snow. Its cold touch set Callie's skin twitching and her legs quivering with a need to run, to chase, to tear into the flesh of her prey, to breathe in the crisp air of the night and cry out her ecstasy alongside her packmates.

Emily shouldn't have run like that. Such prey behavior made everything worse.

And if someone— *Callie*— didn't step in to soothe them, disaster was inevitable.

So, casting an apologetic look at Adrien, Callie had done a dash of her own— straight to the dugout where the Hunt Leader was pacing and growling up at the moon.

He was shifting partway between his human and wolf forms. The change rippled over his corded muscles like disturbed water. He alternately snuffled at the ground to seek scents and raised himself to full height to cast a piercing glare at the team arrayed in the dugout behind him, as if preparing to bark an order at them. The rest of the Wild Hunt, which had come to take in the game, filled the section of the stands directly above the dugout. While the team remained relatively disciplined, sitting on the bench with their claws wrapped around their baseball bats, the spectators were building themselves into a frenzy.

A scent hovered on the wind. One Callie hadn't smelled among the Hunt before, though she'd picked it up plenty of times from their prey during runs through the Realm. Sharp and salty. If it lingered much longer, it would turn sour and heavy like a stagnant ocean pond. It stung her nostrils and made her shoulders hunch about her ears automatically.

Fear.

She felt it rattling around inside herself, too. It bounced around that space where, at times, she could feel the magic that hummed through the fairy ring. Even the draw of her bat felt remote now. The jagged edges of the fear made it impossible to ignore this new, hollow lack.

Ignore it anyway, she admonished herself, feeling the burn of anger as she called on long-ago advice from her father. *Don't let them see you sweat, or they'll never calm down.*

Her footsteps crunched in the dirt at the edge of the dugout.

The Leader spun to face her. His lips pulled back from his lupine snout, and a low growl rumbled in his throat. His golden eyes shone with bright accusation. "Girl," he said through clenched teeth. "What have you done?"

Callie forced her shoulders to stay down, relaxed. "We miscalculated," she said. Her voice held a quaver she hoped he'd miss.

His golden eyes narrowed, and she bit back a scoff at herself. Who was she kidding?

"Look," she said, taking a step closer. "I—"

The Hunt Leader shifted deeper into his wolf form and bared his teeth fully. Behind him, the hunters in the stands jeered at her.

Callie reversed her step. Her throat was so tight she couldn't even make a squeak of terror. She'd never had the keen attention of the Wild Hunt turned on her in this way.

For the first time, she felt what it would be like to be truly chased, caught, and torn limb from limb. A red haze of anticipated pain edged her vision. She was aware that she was trembling, that her breath was coming in rapid gasps. She was suffocating. Her heart would burst any second now.

The moonlight fell on her like a spotlight she couldn't escape.

A shadow bolted across the meager space between her and the Leader, and suddenly, Callie was no longer alone in that spotlight. Trace stood beside her.

"Calm yourself, Huntmaster. You know perfectly well that what has occurred was an accident," he said. His gravelly voice remained even, and his calmness washed over Callie, cutting through her tight-wound fear enough that her nerveless fingers regained some feeling. The familiar, comforting weight of her magical bat registered once more, calming her further.

She wasn't powerless here, or defenseless. The bat still tingled with a little magic— not the deep magic of the Fairy Realm, which had been cut off the moment the spell went awry, but baseball magic, pure and simple.

Hefting the bat, she stepped forward once more. "Please don't give in to the panic, my lord. The Wild Hunt needs you to be strong now. In the meantime, I will figure out how to fix this so we can get back home. We still have the baseball magic, and—"

"The baseball magic!" the Leader said. He let out a bark of laughter that turned into a long, high howl to the moon. Behind him, the stands rang with the yips and yowls of the rest of the Hunt joining him.

Callie tightened her grip on her bat as the hair on the back of her neck stood up. She drew comfort from the fact that a few of the baseball players sitting uneasily in the dugout did not join in.

The Leader cut off his howl abruptly. His eyes danced with a maddening fever. "The baseball magic is nothing! A pretty lie the Courts dangle before us lowly houses to make us dance to their whims. More fool me, for believing it. We thought the playing field was level this season, but look at us now. Trapped here among these pitiful mortals. How the Lords of the Courts must be laughing tonight!"

Behind him, the baseball players shifted uneasily. Pyrgin shared a dubious glance with Grangle. Thacker clicked his blood-stained talons together in a nervous tic.

Callie dared to take another step forward. She held her bat out before her like a great sword. "You know that's not true. We've done amazing things with the baseball magic. The Seelie Court has trembled before our power while we wielded it. But we have to work together for it to work. We can't give in to our baser instincts here."

She let a pulse of baseball magic flare out from her bat. It was weak, yes, without the power of the Fairy Realm to back it up. But it was still there. She watched the reactions of the Wild Hunt as its feather-light touch brushed each of them, a soft reminder.

Here and there, some of the hunters stilled. They blinked in wonder not up at the moon that called them to run, but down at the pristine beauty of Unicorn Field.

Perhaps it helped that a cloud drifted across the moon at that moment. As its light dimmed, even the Leader shook himself, a dog flinging droplets of moonlight from his pelt. When he stilled, he looked more human. His cloak lay limp against his body without the magic of the Realm to keep it billowing mysteriously.

Slowly, contemplatively, he pulled a baseball from the folds of the cloak. He held it up with one hand, peering at it in a way that made Callie expect he'd be addressing it as Yorick any moment now.

A length of silence stretched out over the field.

In the distance, the wind moaned, and the trees roared, their dead leaves crashing together like waves on the beach.

The bit of cloud drifted away from the moon once again. As its light brightened, a hint of wild blood drifted on the cold breeze. Callie's heart sank.

"No," she whispered. "Please, don't."

The Leader grimaced at the baseball in his hand. His change came over him again, slowly and yet all at once, and he clenched his fist to dig his talons into the soft leather casing. The strained creak and pop of the ball's destruction echoed across the field like a gunshot. When he let the mutilated carcass fall to the ground, he dropped to all fours.

He was fully wolf when he turned his golden eyes on Callie for the last time. He said nothing. Words were for those who had a shred of humanity to them.

The wind swirled into a hard gust that lifted dirt and dust in a buffeting cloud.

Callie tried to stop him. She dashed forward this time, bat outstretched. The baseball magic flared along its length with promises of solid plays, bases stolen, and runs won. Trace galloped beside her, shouting a Centaur song at the top of his lungs, his tone rising above the swirling gale to enhance the images with his own innate magic.

But Trace's magic was just as weakened by the loss of the fairy ring as Callie's bat, and the hunters, caught up in the ancient moon madness of their kindred, paid them no mind.

In a clash of two against hundreds, they stood no chance.

The Hunt Leader's howl of triumph pulled at Callie, demanding that she join the hunt.

Callie fought it with everything she had. She knew what the prey would be tonight— not rabbits or deer, but people, humans she might even have known all her life. She refused to be a part of such a hunt, no matter how insistently her blood yearned to join in.

Something inside her tore as she forcefully pulled herself away from the call of the Leader and his Wild Hunt.

She shifted her stance, holding the bat diagonally across her chest. The baseball magic flowed around her new grip, and she fashioned it into a crude barrier. It was too small, too weak, too flimsy to accomplish anything, she knew. But she had to try to stop them.

The force of the horde breaking past her feeble hold sent Callie to her knees. She breathed in great gulps of night air, her lungs burning with failure as the Wild Hunt thundered by. Satyrs laughed, Red Caps screeched, and Centaurs bellowed. The hounds yipped and howled as they twined among the legs of their masters.

Trace sank down beside her, his chin dropping to his bare chest. He, too, was sucking in great breaths through his nose. At first, Callie thought he was struggling against the same exhaustion and anger that she was.

Then she caught a glimpse of his face in the harsh moonlight.

His black eyes glittered with the same instinctive light she'd seen in the Leader's.

She noticed now that the dugout was empty. The players who had seemed to be holding onto the baseball magic had succumbed to the Leader's call.

If Trace left now, she'd be all alone.

"Trace!" she said, not caring how desperation made her voice crack. "Fight it. You're stronger than the Leader. Think of the baseball magic!"

"Callie," he said. He rose from his kneel and tipped his head back to stare at the moon. "The Hunt calls."

He pivoted on his back hoof, then reared to paw at the air as he let out a cry. Great clods of dirt flew as he galloped after his packmates.

Callie's vision blurred the moment he disappeared into the trees beyond Unicorn Field. Her tears fell as she pounded her fist in the dirt. Her throat ached as if she'd been screaming, but she couldn't hear anything over the roaring in her ears.

When she had been kicked off the Bulldogs, she'd felt wronged. Jilted. But back then, she hadn't felt like she truly *belonged* with that team. She hadn't thought of them as *family* as she had come to see the Hunt. She thought she'd found a place here, though. She thought she'd made the Hunt think of her as one of their pack. But tonight they'd all looked at her like she was a stranger as they'd raced past.

Even Trace.

She supposed that was better than being their prey, but that thought didn't numb the pain that filled her now.

I'm alone, she thought.

It was, perhaps, the worst thing she'd ever felt.

And then a soft sound broke the stillness of the empty field. A footstep, scraping through the infield dirt.

Hope welled painfully in the hollow places inside her, and she looked up.

Her father emerged from the shadows under the stands and came to kneel beside her. His hand as he placed it on her shoulder was warm.

"Oh, Callie. My little girl. Come here, now. They hurt you, didn't they? I knew they would."

Callie drew a shuddering breath, and as more tears splashed to the ground by her fists, she didn't pull away from his embrace.

CHAPTER

SEVENTEEN

Emily dashed through the trees beyond Unicorn Field, barely noticing the way the rough branches and wet leaves slapped at her. The raw grip of panic wrapped around her throat, and the scent of damp soil turned dark and rancid as she ran.

She felt trapped.

Afraid in a way that took her back to when she'd been alone in the darkest woods of the Fairy Realm. In the far reaches of her hearing, the growing howls of the Wild Hunt warbled through the darkness. The ring was closed. The spell she, Adrien, and Callie had planned in so much detail had bombed. And the Wild Hunt, now whipped into a furious need to feast after their victory, was free to run. Free to have their way in the whole of Pattersonville.

The knowledge sent an ice-cold chill into Emily's bones that was worse than anything she'd felt since she had watched her mom go into the hospital that last time.

Because this was her fault.

She should have chosen a team. If she had just picked one of them, either the Unicorns or the Small Folk, the spell would have worked, and the city would be safe. Instead, the Wild Hunt had been unleashed, on point and ready for red meat, onto Pattersonville's streets.

This was a complete disaster.

And it was all her fault.

A protruding tree root caught her foot, and, with a cry, she crashed hard to the muddy ground. She didn't get up again. It seemed right that she simply lay there and let the pain radiate through her body. She deserved that.

Hot tears burned her cheeks, and cold shame pricked at her spine.

Why hadn't she picked a team? What was wrong with her? She loved baseball. *Loved* it. Why had she passed on the chance to play one more season with her friends?

For college?

Or was it fear?

Nobody who could play like she could wanted to become the person who stuck around at home instead of moving on to bigger and better things. Nobody wanted to be the one who squandered their talent like that. She'd thought she was better than all her friends. Plain and simple.

She really did belong down here in this mud puddle.

Something crashed through the underbrush behind her, but she didn't stir. It was probably just the Wild Hunt coming to crunch her into pulp.

"Emily!"

It was Adrien. Emily curled in on herself and considered crawling to a better hiding spot.

"Get up, Emily!"

Too late. He knelt over her, his Unicorns uniform glowing in the faint moonlight. "You've got to snap out of it! We've got to get the ring open again!"

"I... I can't," Emily said.

"I know you better than that. Emily DeWitt does *not* quit!"

The solid presence of his hands grasped her from behind and

craned her suddenly upward. She had no choice but to have her legs lock underneath her, and a moment later she was standing again, turning to face Adrien. Her shame spiked at the sight of the mud streaking his uniform now.

"I did this, Adrien! I'm so sorry!"

"Snap out of it. The city needs you now."

"I..."

"Benji needs you, Emily. Megan needs you. They're locked on the other side, right? Benji and Megan..." Adrien's voice cracked then, and he looked hard into Emily's eyes. "I need you, too, Em. I let Megan go. I can't..."

The moment crystallized for her, and Emily found herself breathing again.

Adrien was as distraught as she was. Seeing it helped her get hold of her own whirling emotions. And, after a few deep breaths, she knew he was right.

She bent to scoop up her mom's baseball from where it had fallen in her tumble and was relieved to still feel a sense of power there beyond anything she could define. The baseball magic was still here, despite the closed ring. It felt a little different now, kind of echo-y in the absence of pure fairy magic. But it was still there.

She knew something else, too. Her dad had always said it was never too late to do the right thing, and at that moment, a sense of certainty pulsed through her.

She couldn't give up.

Colleges could wait. She was playing baseball this year, and it was going to be for the Small Folk team.

Joy surged through her at the decision. Her certainty brushed away all the stinging pain from her scraped hands and knees and banished the cold slickness of the mud still clinging to her skin.

Truly, how had she gone this long resisting the call to play?

With a flick of her wrist, she tossed the ball upwards and caught it again. The slap of the leather casing against her palm was deeply satisfying. Nodding to Adrien, she turned back towards Unicorn Field and walked with purpose in her stride.

Adrien fell in beside her.

As they walked, an idea flared. "Dark Field," she said.

"What?"

"We both know that we're not going to be able to fix Unicorn Field all by ourselves. But what about that old field where we played against the Seelies? Do you think we could open a gate there?"

Adrien's lips pursed. "Hope Ballpark," he said.

Emily tilted her head, confused.

"That's what I'm going to call it when I fix it up," he said with a tone that said he expected her to scoff. "That's what I'm going to do."

"Great," Emily growled. "But what about it now? Do you think we could open a gate there?"

"I don't know. I don't... think so. Not without Callie, anyway."

Emily shook her head as another truth dawned. "We've already proved that the three of us can't do it that way, so I don't think Callie can help."

"Yeah, we'd probably just lock that place down, too," Adrien said remorsefully. Then he shook himself. "But I don't know. I still feel the baseball magic in my glove. What about your ball? We're two of the best baseball players Pattersonville's ever fielded. There's got to be something we can do."

They stepped back onto Unicorn Field just as the big stadium lights went out, and Emily felt suddenly displaced.

The smell of the park was still bold and strong.

The strands of fairy lights and the glow of off-kilter lanterns still marked the boundaries of the field. It all reminded her of the moment she'd first fallen through the portal to meet the Small Folk.

No.

Not to meet the Small Folk.

To meet Fennoc. The faun manager of the Small Folk.

She heard the sound of his voice deep inside her and recalled the image of him standing in his pristinely fastidious uniform, a long blade of dry reed dangling loosely from the corner of his thin lips.

The grit of the soil shifted below her feet, and the memory of the great power that he had used to bring her across filled her head so fully she was suddenly dizzy. He had been aided, of course. The Web Gem had provided the baseball magic to pull her across the portal.

But there had been something else there. She remembered that now.

A fair price.

The memory made her heart lurch.

It's never too late to do the right thing, she heard her dad's voice as if he were right here with her. But he was not. It was only her, the remote feel of Adrien's presence, and the sensation of baseball magic flowing from her mom's baseball into her body. The thin braying of the Hunt filled a space somewhere far away in her mind. The power of friendship she'd felt with her Small Folk teammates stood her up even more boldly.

Her baseball talent.

That was what it was going to cost her to open the portal again. To save Benji, and Megan. To save the whole city of Pattersonville.

CHAPTER

EIGHTEEN

"This is an opportunity," Callie's father said, stroking her back as nonchalantly as if he'd spent his entire fatherhood comforting his child. Only Callie's memories stood as proof against such an image of parental affection. "It's a chance for us McMasterses to pull our name out of the gutter."

"There is no us," Callie said, hackles finally rising.

With a harsh movement, she shrugged his hand away. Then she reached to where her bat had tumbled into the dirt.

"Callie!" her father said.

The second her fingers closed around the bat handle, a warm trickle of baseball magic suffused her. It wasn't much, but it made her feel just enough better. She clambered to her feet and turned a furious glare on her father.

"Don't you dare try to use your sleazy charm on me, *Dad*. Whatever you're planning, I don't want any part of it. It stinks of Seelie magic, anyway."

Her father remained on one knee before her and spread his hands along with a wide grin that said *what can you do?* "The Seelies were very good to me for a while, but in the end even they didn't under-

137

stand the value of a good deal. I'm talking about *us,* Callie girl. I'm talking about the kind of things we can do when we stick together, the way it's been ever since your deadbeat mother ran out on us. Back then, you and I both knew it was the two of us against the world."

Callie flinched against the memories. That sense of abandonment had echoed through her tiny kid body, not fading, but building into the ferocious competitiveness that had made her the star player of the Marion High Bulldogs. Of course, she knew her father had played his part in that, coaching and guiding her, encouraging extra hours of practice, and steering her away from those who would reach out in friendship. Callie McMasters didn't need friends. Not back then.

That old hardness stirred within her now. What did it matter if the Wild Hunt ran off? Who cared if Trace had left her, too? She wasn't one of them, because she wasn't one of anything except the duo of Fred McMasters and Daughter.

Blinking past the memories, she stared down at her dad now. The moonlight limned him in silver highlights that made him look ethereal, not wild like the hunters, but aloof and mysterious. Like the Seelies. He might not be working with them now, but she knew he'd still use that leverage if he thought he could get away with it.

Her own drop of Seelie blood thrummed within her, a whispered promise. She ignored it the same as she'd ignored the Seelie Duke's offer of a place on their baseball team.

Because deep down, she knew blood wasn't the deciding factor in her fate.

Practice made perfect, after all. And she'd spent too long honing her competitiveness, her doggedness, and her drive to chase victory at all costs.

Part of the pack or not, in her heart, Callie McMasters had always been a Huntress.

The night wind brought a plethora of scents to her well-trained nose. The trees beyond Unicorn Field teemed with mice, chipmunks, and squirrels, all rushing through the underbrush to new hiding places now that the horrific procession of the Wild Hunt had passed through. Somewhere further off, someone had lit a bonfire, sending sweet hickory smoke wafting through the moonlight. In the distant night, the sound of tires screeching blared like a trumpet peal. Her blood boiled, feeling Fairy rising. And deep in the Earth, worms toiled, churning the newly fallen dead leaves into the soil, sending renewed richness back up to the surface.

She smelled her father's sweat, and with it, his nervousness. He wasn't certain of her obedience, even though he acted like he was. One of his best tricks, she knew. He'd coached her on keeping her game face on.

Her smile felt wolf-like stretching across her face. "What kind of deal did you have in mind, *Dad*?"

She clocked the relief flickering across his face the same as she'd trace a pigeon racing across a clouded sky.

Her father rose, then brushed the infield dirt from his pant knee. "Everyone will be desperate for the ring under this field to open up again. We can use that desperation to get them to put Unicorn Field under my name again."

"What would that accomplish? The ring is closed." Callie didn't let herself shudder at the reminder. That feeling of hollowness at her error still stung. "And you don't have the Web Gem in your hands this time."

"No, and that will make it tricky. But you don't really think I spent all those weeks among the Seelies not ferreting out the secrets of their innate magic, do you? I'm a McMasters, and a descendant of the Court. Whatever they can do, I can do."

He lifted one hand and made a fist. White light bloomed forth around his closed fingers. The effort made him sweat more. Callie sniffed against the salty tang of it.

"Very impressive," she deadpanned.

Now her dad scowled at her. "No need for your sarcasm. If the field was still in my name, my power over it would increase tenfold.

Besides, I said it was the two of us, didn't I? My Seelie magic and your wild bat there. Put them together and we make the ring, and with it everyone else, our servants. Just think of it! We could charge a crossing fee. We'll make so much goddamned money off this."

Now the moonlight glinting in his eyes matched the look the Hunt Leader had sported earlier. Manic and instinctive. Her father would always be driven by money.

So long as their joint venture made him capital gains, she'd have a place at his side.

It made her sad, actually. This man standing before her, his hand outstretched and beckoning, was such a slave to his need to be important that nothing she tried would ever touch him, not really. His instincts were too ingrained to be overridden.

Still, she was grateful for this little encounter. It had helped clear her head of the emotions the Wild Hunt had left her with.

She might not be able to reach the man who had made her what she was, but she could reach the ones who had mostly accepted her as one of their own.

She was a McMasters, after all. A McMasters didn't give up just when things got hard.

And a hunter didn't let her prey escape after the first dive into the underbrush.

"Thanks, but no thanks," she said.

"You're turning me down?" The anger was back, hidden behind the salesman facade she was so used to. "That's a mistake you'll regret, Callie girl."

But Callie was already focused on the little forest, and on the town of Pattersonville that lay beyond it. "I wish you luck in your latest venture, Dad."

She didn't specify what kind of luck.

She slung her bat across her back and drew in a deep breath.

As she loped off into the trees, the distant sound of a siren rose to twine with the cacophony of howls, hoots, and high-pitched barks coming from downtown.

CHAPTER

NINETEEN

Trapped.

No way home.

The Samhain moon, large and bold as it stands in the dark sky, is the only thing that still makes sense, though it is early.

And so he runs.

The lights of this mortal town center flare and try to drown out the insistent light of the moon. Overhead, banners declaring "Happy Halloween!" flap and snap in the rising wind. The stench of the chemicals mortals use to power their mechanical horrors digs at his nostrils. The unnatural pavement the mortals use to build their roads tears at his paws. The pain only adds to his frenzy. It drives him to snarl at the prey he has cornered.

Show them his teeth. Make them scream.

The sounds are wrong for a Samhain run. Screams, yes. Panting and crying as energy depletes and fear replaces it, yes. The frequent patter of sweat droplets landing on the trail, even better on this artificial road.

But there is no sweetness of soily peat, no wisping of owl feather on dark skies, no dampness of misty fog rising from forest pools here. And the high wailing of the large, wheeled machines hurts his ears. Makes his head throb. Echoes off buildings that rise like canyon walls. Grows larger. Confounds his ability to trace its origin or determine how many assailants he faces. And the woman standing at the top of the wide stone steps of the downtown building, shouting into her handheld machine to make her voice loud and harsh, sets his bones vibrating uncomfortably.

"Emergency responders, hold your fire. Hunters! Hunters! Stand down. I repeat, stand down!"

Another sound: pop-pop-pop. *Behind him, a satyr yips and falls to the hard black ground, blood seeping from a sudden wound on his flank. A keening cry tells him one of the hounds has met a similar fate.*

"I said hold your fire!"

A restless stirring among his ranks. The scent of blood growing thick in the air. Red Caps leaving their post to turn hungry eyes on their fallen comrades.

Whirl around. Bare teeth at followers. Reinstate control.

But let the prey get away. Smell their fear-sweat growing distant. Fight the need to run, to chase, to recapture the prey. Keeping command is more important.

A sliver of satisfaction as the Red Caps slink back to their places.

A ripple of fury as more defectors shake off his hold.

A Centaur— black hair, gravelly voice— turns away from the procession and calls out to the others. The word "baseball" falls from his hated lips.

This one has tested his tethers before.

Run. Leap. Claws hooked, tear into horseflesh and manflesh. Teach a lesson that will stick.

It feels good to have blood well around his paws again.

The Centaur pants, and pain makes his eyes go glassy. He lifts one arm, weak, an ineffective attempt to push his rightful master away.

His rightful master shoves his snout into that rebellious face, shows all of his teeth. "I command. We hunt."

The others who would follow the rebel shift in uncertainty. He feels their dilemma, their wish that the baseball magic could feed them, their need to give in to the moonlight and join in the run as is right.

He digs his claws deeper. The Centaur moans. None challenge his command.

"Let him go!"

Girl. The one who runs with his Wild Hunt. The one who did not heed the call of the Samhain moon. The Host had left her behind as a crumpled carcass on the baseball field she loves so much, but now she stands on the road, hands hanging loose at her sides. The bat slung over her shoulder gives off a pale radiance that rivals the silver glow of the moon and the clashing colors of the town lights. The scent that rolls off her is savory determination.

She stares directly at him and does not break eye contact as she waves the bat before her.

A challenge.

With a growl, he pulls his claws from the Centaur and turns to face her fully.

"Girl," he says.

Then he leaps.

CHAPTER

TWENTY

As the Huntmaster leapt, Callie swung her bat in a backhanded arc. It hummed through the air, catching the Leader's shoulder.

His feral yelp sliced through the night.

She turned on him, stance balanced to keep herself between him and Trace's fallen form.

Three strikes and he's out, the bat crooned through their connection. The woodgrain gleamed with an ethereal glow in the dark, jack-o'-lantern-lined street. The smell of autumn grass and hard asphalt cooling in the October chill was as sharp as the sound of the pack's incessant baying. Her hands, moist with sweat, flexed over the grip. Its calming energy steadied her as the Leader's gaze glowed silver in a sudden calm. He circled her now, slavering jaws glistening, muscles bunched as if ready to spring again. His very presence taunted her. The deep rumble of his growl brought ire to the pit of her stomach.

"I said," Callie said, gripping the bat tighter. "Stay away from him."

Behind her, Trace managed to drag himself off the ground.

His shoulder ran crimson from the Huntmaster's attack, which brought howls of hunger from the pack. The damage was slight, though. If she'd been a moment later, Callie didn't want to know what the Leader would have done.

Callie presented the bat boldly, doing her best to ignore the fiery luminescence of the pack's eyes as they churned with deadly impatience in the darkness outside their circle.

"You know this is wrong, Hunt Leader. So, prove your position and control your host."

The leader snarled. "Prove my position?"

"You understand me."

"The Hunt hunts, mistress. Even you understand that much."

"Yes," she said. "But I also understand it hunts only with purpose."

Before her, almost imperceptibly, the Leader's eyes narrowed. She was right, and he knew it. The Hunt had a reason to exist in the Fairy Realm. A purpose to their task. The Wild Hunt provided meat and information at a premium, and it was that meat or that information that gave them reign to scour the lands as they did. Yet now...

"V-v-vengeance!" a hunchbacked wood troll yipped, clacking its long nails of bloodied bark against the hard pavement of Bradford Street.

"They trapped us!" screamed another howling member of the Hunt. Callie was too focused on the Huntmaster to identify him, though.

The gathering joined in unison. *"Punish the mortals! Punish the mortals!"*

Through it, Callie didn't let go of the Leader's gaze.

"You know what I'm saying, don't you?" Her bat moaned as she waved it again, and in the Leader's gaze, Callie saw that he did, indeed, understand her position. "There is no target here, is there, Leader?" she said, almost too rapidly. "There is no true prey in Pattersonville. No meat that's needed in the Fairy Realm. And you have no portent to bring, either. No word of war or famine to worry the masses over. All you've got here are innocent people cowering in their living rooms. But you know that if you unleash your violence on them, the Hunt will violate everything that has been built between the Fairy Realm and the mortal world."

The Leader growled.

Above, the fullness of the moon flared.

In unison, the pack's howling doubled itself as a chorus of voices that sent hard shivers up Callie's spine.

The leader puffed the fur at his chest and stood firm.

"You misread the signals, Mistress Cal, young swinger of bats. There *is* portent here. There *will be war*. When the courts and houses of the Fairy Realm find your friends have destroyed their portal, they will be distraught, and when they learn that they have locked away the very Hunt that fuels the innards of the Fairy Realm's existence —" The Leader caught her gaze fully. "—they will be furious."

She swallowed to bite back her confusion.

"Have you ever seen a Fairy Lord in his full fury, Mistress Cal? It is no sight for the uninitiated."

Doom closed over Callie. A sense of despair prickled her skin.

"Have you ever seen a human packing a gun in *their* full fury?" Callie replied, motioning toward the injured satyr in the pack, and still fighting anxiety that grew more certain every moment.

The Leader wasn't going to stop this. Instead, he was going to personally drive his host to its destruction.

"Do this and the Hunt will die," Callie said.

It was too late, though.

The Leader chuckled at first, then laid his head back and gave a long, stuttering howl.

The pack joined, pacing now in the darkness, their forms molding together into a dark morass of energy that churned in the shadows.

"Our blood is up, Mistress," he said when the calls died. "There's prey in the city. Stop us if you think you can!"

From the pack, three Red Caps cackled and raced away, yipping and ululating as their split nails gouged concrete until they ran up into a yard toward a suddenly darkened porch.

"Callie," Trace said gently from behind. In the baseball magic of her bat, she felt the Centaur's heart beating strong and pure. Trace was a member of the hunt, yes. But he understood order. He understood purpose. "I follow your lead. You know what you need to do."

And she did.

Magic from the bat welled inside her, strong still despite being separated from the Realm of its making. It spoke to her in an arcane tongue, whispering, humming, almost singing as the tone floated in a cloud around her. And there, in the middle of Bradford Street and surrounded by the frothing mass of the Hunt, the realization of what Callie McMasters needed to do clawed at her throat.

"I'm not done with you!" She glared at the Leader. He let out a snicker, then gave a triumphant howl that said he thought she'd abandoned her challenge.

"Come on." She urged Trace forward. "We've got to stop them before someone gets killed!"

Pivoting, she grabbed Trace's undamaged shoulder and, as the Centaur shot toward the house the Red Caps were swarming, swung her weight upward to come to rest on his back. He pounded forward, hooves thundering as he covered ground in huge, galloping strides.

Then there was just her and the bat, its magic flowing over the ground, radiating waves of warmth and an aroma of leather and grass. The distant sound of an organ played in her mind. Trace neared the closest Red Cap, and the baseball magic lifted them both into the air. She waved the bat, and a bolt of green fire spewed from its barrel, engulfing the raiding Hunt member. With a screech, the Red Cap tumbled forward into an unconscious ball, crashed into a second marauder, and forced him to slam hard into a picket fence.

Callie grabbed the bat barrel in her free hand and swung it around again, sending the green wave to engulf the third and final Red Cap just as its hard-scrabbled knuckles reached for the front door. It thudded against the screen door to collapse in a heap on the patio.

The rest of the Hunt had already begun to clamber through the streets, though. They split into two groups, circling the area like Callie had seen them do while chasing deer and elk in the wilding woods of the Fairy Realm. Sounds of traffic screeching to a halt ripped through the nighttime air. Heavy thuds of garbage cans being upturned clattered in the streets. The howls of beasts rang out.

"We'll never stop them all this way," Trace said through his exertion.

He was right.

There was another way, though. Seelie blood, weak as it was, roared through her, and her full Fairy Realm ancestry pulsed in tandem with the baseball magic that thrummed through the lumber Trace had so carefully worked into its perfect balance. As the Centaur carried her into battle now, its raw power folded and refolded inside her. She felt the thrill of seeing a fat fastball down the middle of the plate, and in the eddies of the baseball magic, Callie swung hard. A raw dose of the mystical sensation that came when she made perfect contact filled her. That magical, effortless moment when bat strikes ball and the perfect line drive is born into existence.

Trace raced at full gallop through Pattersonville's streets, turning corners like he was circling the bases.

Callie waved the bat and improvised spell work, laying down protection by summoning electric barriers, cold baselines from someplace ancient and perfect sparked with danger. Magic flowed. Power burst over her, and Callie found herself singing snippets of every baseball song she'd ever heard. "Glory Days" came to her. "Centerfield." "Ichiro's Theme," and then "Take Me Out to the Ball Game." She didn't know all the words, but somehow none of that mattered. As she sang her spell work, she felt the sound of baseballs on leather gloves and the heat of a fastball up and in. *The soul of the game*, she thought, as her baseball bat of fairy wood focused her power across the city— a city she suddenly knew she loved.

When she was finished Callie slumped forward, so spent that the only reason she managed to hold her place on Trace's back was because the Centaur adjusted to keep her safe.

She was done, though.

The spell was cast. The city was safe.

Holding him close, Callie felt Trace's entire body tremble as he tried to catch his breath.

Recalling the tension in Trace's posture as he had run off, Callie felt his pain like it was her own. He had fought the Call of the Hunt for her. Had tried to break the chain that was his very nature. And he had almost done it. The ugly sensation of her father's embrace rattled through her, in sync with Trace's trembling. How different were they, really? She had nearly fallen into her dad's enchantments, and they would be no match for what Trace had to endure.

In the distance, the Hunt still yelped and howled, but now their calls carried tones of longing and despair rather than action and vengeance.

Her head swam.

"You did it," she said, her tongue thick with fatigue.

"No," he gasped. "*We* did it. We made it."

The Hunt would still cause problems, she knew, but both the people and the Hunt would be safe, bound by the lines she'd laid down.

For now, anyway.

Callie wasn't such a bozo as to think her magic would last forever. Various howlings in the distance gave credence to reports that said the Hunt had parts of the city under lockdown. But as long as no one got caught outdoors, and as long as her baseball magic *did* last, the city would survive.

Of course, she still had to deal with the Huntmaster. Contrary to his belief, she hadn't dropped her challenge. Not for a moment.

But that could come later.

Taking a cleansing breath, Callie pushed herself upright, pleased to see that, somehow, she had managed to hold onto the bat. They had come full circle and were in a small park near Unicorn Field. It was chilly here under the canopy of these few trees. Or better said, it was getting late in October, and that meant it was damned cold. Her breath misted as she exhaled, and the sweat that dampened her baseball uniform made her shiver. With her free hand, she removed her baseball cap and mopped her forehead with her sleeved shoulder. Above, a cloud passed over the full moon.

"I don't think I can do this again," she said to Trace.

"Aye, it would be quite the effort. Though now that we've been through the lands of your realm, I suppose I could manage the path more efficiently."

In the dim light of Pattersonville's streetlamps, she saw his smile and felt better enough to laugh. "Leave it to you to find the bright side."

"Once you've returned from being turned to stone, you might find considerable upside exists everywhere you go. Besides, you're a fairy mage now. I trust you can do more than you think you can."

Her heart skipped a beat, and her hands gripped the bat. What he said was true.

She was a fairy mage.

Their magical race through Pattersonville proved that better than any classroom lesson ever could. And she had found a way to retrieve Trace from an eternity of despair once.

Maybe there was a way out of this, too.

This was no time to give up.

The hum of baseball magic calmed her heart.

With a deep breath, Callie scanned the area, remembering it fully. The smell. The slight hiss of breeze through the branches. The way Bradford connected to Bonaventure farther up the road—which was the corner they took when walking from Emily's place to the Thorns' place.

She froze, feeling a new truth. Yes.

The Thorns' place.

"Baseball magic," she said.

"Yes?" His reply said he knew there was more coming.

She hefted her bat. Its warm hum let her know she was on a good track. "If we can keep making baseball magic, I can keep casting the protection wards over the city."

Trace scoffed at that but didn't say what she knew he was thinking. That the baseball magic might be a little hard to come by right now.

She put her hand softly on Trace's shoulder. "Don't worry," she said. I've got an idea."

"Something we're badly in need of, I'd say." His ears twitched in anticipation.

"That way," she said, pointing at the corner. "I'll tell you about it while we go."

By the time Callie had finished her rounds and returned to Unicorn Field, the sun was coloring the horizon a gauzy shade of gold. Physically, she was as tired as she could remember being, but her mind was racing in cycles that were almost too much to deal with.

Gripping her bat let her know her protection spell, as expected, was waning. It might last the day. Or it might not. Hearing the impatient whines of the Hunt members echoing around the city let her know that the host had patience beyond their desire.

This really did have to work.

Even though her brain wanted to skid out into doomsday scenarios and other what-ifs, one of which included confronting the Leader again, she had to focus. Her fatigue made it harder. Each time she closed her eyes in exhaustion, she saw the smirking confidence that was in his gaze when she'd left him last night.

She and Trace arrived at the field before the others, which made sense.

She'd gone to Emily's first, expecting to have to argue her point-by-point to enlist her help. Instead, she'd found Emily in a strange mood of hard determination.

"Did Adrien send you?" Emily had asked.

"I haven't seen him yet. Are you...?"

"I'm okay. I know how to fix this."

"So do I," Callie had said, letting out a relieved laugh. "Come to Unicorn Field at dawn. Bring every Unicorn you can. We'll get this done."

Emily had given a sharp nod and closed the door with a snap.

Callie thought there was something more to Emily's demeanor. It tingled with a kind of baseball magic, different from what Callie had worked this evening. There would be enough time for her to figure that out later, though, and she had a list of things to do. She had left the DeWitt house as quickly as she could and made her last stop.

Now, Callie was glad she and Trace had that moment to enjoy the silence of Unicorn Field as dawn broke.

"Hey," Emily called from the far dugout as she, Jake, and Patsy came to join Callie and Trace at home plate. Jake and Patsy wore their Unicorn jerseys, but Emily wore her full Small Folk uniform.

"Hey," Callie replied. "Nice duds."

"You look like crap," Emily said. "Are you going to be able to pull this off?"

"I love you, too, Em."

"The rest are coming along," Patsy said. "Should be here any minute."

Callie peered through the morning gloom to see Patsy's eye was darkened even beyond the extra shadow and eyeliner she'd applied. "Are you okay?" she asked.

"It's nothing. Just had a little tussle with one of your fairy mates last night."

Callie couldn't help but hear the accusation in Patsy's reply. Not that she could blame her. Emily DeWitt wasn't the only person who could lay down a line of self-accusation. "Yeah. Sorry about that.

That's why we're here though, right? Try to stop this thing from happening."

Across the field and down the left field line, Lizzy Rodriguez and Jamal Douglass hopped the fence to join the rest.

"I don't see how we can stop this," Jake said. "Even if we get the whole team, we don't have enough players to make a right game of it. And without a full game, I thought baseball magic didn't happen."

"I told you I'd take care of that," Callie said.

"Like we want to play the Bulldogs again," Emily said as Pash Kulpari rolled up.

"It's not Marion."

Emily gave a brittle laugh. She was holding her mom's baseball in her glove, turning it over so nervously Callie thought she might rub the stitches off. Emily's gaze flitted to home plate, and Callie felt a cold breeze freeze her.

"I know that's what you said," Emily replied. "But who else do you have ties to that would answer your call to action while the Wild Hunt is roaming free?"

Callie and Trace shared a secret smile.

They'd had that same conversation a few hours ago at their second stop.

They needed baseball magic. The purer the better.

And when she thought back on her own life, she knew the one source that was better and purer than any other.

Callie put her fingers to her lips and blew a sharp whistle.

It was Adrien who emerged from the shadows first, his Unicorn warmup zipped up and his baseball glove shoved under one armpit, an equipment bag fully loaded with bats and balls slung over the opposite shoulder.

His eyes danced as other kids swarmed around him, voices trilling and yammering in ways that made Callie think about the Hunt.

The key word here, though, was *kids*.

"Sydney?" Emily said, eyeing the mass of kids who poured out of the wooded area behind center field and ran pell-mell over the outfield grass to come closer.

"Hi, Emily!" Sydney Thorn yelled with gusto as he led that race toward the infield. He wore his glove on one hand but waved the other wildly over his head. "Cousin Adrien said we were going to get to play on the big field!" He skipped so fast he nearly fell. He caught himself, though only putting the hand that wasn't wearing his baseball glove up to hold his cap kept it from flying off.

As the mass neared, Callie took them in, already feeling momentum build as she grasped the handle of her bat. Some of the kids, like Sydney, wore red and white uniforms that had been silkscreened with their sponsor's name, *Annie's Diner.* Their hats were red, trimmed in white. Others wore green shirts and caps with numbers on the front and the snazzy logo of Jackson's Sporting Goods stenciled across the front. But they all ran toward the field at breakneck speed, and they all arrived out of breath to gather into a single group at the pitcher's mound.

"Little Leaguers?" Jake said, finally recognizing that these kids Sydney had rounded up were all part of Pattersonville's Little League system. "We're going to play a bunch of Little Leaguers?"

"No," Callie said, her eyes glistening as she took in Emily, Adrien, and the rest of the Unicorns. "We're not going to *play* them. We're going to *coach* them."

TWENTY-ONE

Though still anxious that the gate to the fairy ring over Unicorn Field had been slammed shut, and worried about being trapped in the Fairy Realm, at least Benji didn't have long to spend in the dismal halls of Unseelie Castle. The queen, full of fury that flowed from her like raging tongues of flame, moved about her domain with undeniable power. "Come along," she said to Benji as she gave orders to shadows, commanded monstrous forms that lurked in corners, and bade piles of dusty bones to rise. "There's little time to waste."

All her servants were quick to obey.

Benji watched in horrified awe as the queen's army of servitude swarmed through the castle, packing enough trunks and preparing enough food to allow a whole baseball team to traverse the wilds of the Realm. Their fervor added to Benji's sense of inadequacy.

Benji, clutching the Web Gem close to their chest, followed the queen.

That they were in way over their head had never been more obvious.

Once having completed her directions, the Unseelie Queen took a seat on her throne, her spine stiff with anger at Emily, Callie, and her Designated Hitter. Benji, still clutching the Web Gem, sat beside her, distracted by the dark servants, but not so distracted to miss that her gaze kept darting to the Web Gem.

"What are we doing?" Benji said.

"Don't be foolish, Spider Child. We're going to look for the Octagon."

"Now?"

"Have you any other ideas?" the queen spat. Her eyes flashed as she glared at them. "The Octagon has the power to bring a whole community together to common purpose. Do you understand what that means?"

With the Web Gem glowering beside them, Benji put their mind to the queen's question. Her tone sounded as if she meant it to be rhetorical, but her following silence said she wanted her student to use their brain. If what the queen had already taught Benji was right, the Octagon was another of the great spiderkin artifacts, a cousin to the Web Gem that Benji's spiderkin relatives had assigned them stewardship over. A wave of understanding seemed to come from nowhere.

"It's a tool for gathering power," Benji said.

The queen nodded, and a flicker of satisfaction crossed her face. "And with the power of a whole community of sorcerers, much greater things can be accomplished than any one spellcaster could attempt on her own."

"Seems like a temptation for abuse, doesn't it?" Benji said unthinkingly.

The queen smirked. "Indeed. But in the hands of a proper wielder, namely, a descendant of the spiderkin that made it, such temptations need not worry your precious mortal morality. Of course, if we wish to utilize the power to the greatest extent, we need to place the artifact in such capable hands once we find it. Nothing less will allow the fairy ring to open again."

"I see," Benji said, feeling even more inadequate than ever. Benji could barely open a gate on their own. There was no chance their hands would be capable enough to do anything with an artifact like that. "But—"

"No buts," the queen admonished. "Perhaps you are prepared, and perhaps you are not. But the world does not wait for you to be ready. It is time to rise."

Embarrassed, Benji clamped their mouth shut.

Could they do this? Could Benji wield the Web Gem well enough to find the Octagon? They barely knew what it was. The idea of finding it and then using it to make any difference felt about as possible as calculating the 98th digit of pi. Benji kept replaying the queen's comment, *it's time to rise*, and kept feeling more morose with every replay. Benji had barely gotten to understand the first level of the Web Gem, better yet anything deeper.

Maybe they should give it to the queen.

She was the one who knew how to use it, after all. And she seemed to have been rehabilitated. The queen had had so many opportunities to wrest the Web Gem from Benji's untrained grasp, after all, and hadn't taken any of them.

A cold, creeping shadow crawled over the foot of the queen's throne. The awful hollow ringing of the fairy ring's closure pinged through Benji's veins. They felt lightheaded just sitting in the little chair beside the queen. Maybe, with this kind of emergency happening, it made sense to let her manage the Web Gem. Maybe that's what the Web Gem wanted. Maybe it would be better for everyone if Benji left the use of the Web Gem in her much more capable hands.

Questions floated through Benji's mind, but the black angles of the queen's face stifled any attempt to voice them. Instead, the two of them sat in stony silence, with only the furtive sounds of the terrible servants doing their work stirring the air.

Once the preparations were complete, Benji found themself climbing quite gratefully into the malodorous carriage that had brought them to the castle, and sitting on the bench opposite the Unseelie Queen. Even the momentary breath of fresh air after the dark stuffiness of Unseelie Castle calmed the spinning in their vision. The thought of moving even farther away from the place put a tiny spark of joy in their heart.

Yes, Benji still had a huge problem. But without the oppressive atmosphere clouding their thoughts, they could examine it so much more effectively.

With fresh resolve, Benji took in the Web Gem that sat beside them, then looked to where the Unseelie Queen was sitting back in the velvet upholstery of her seat, arms folded across her chest, her face tight with lingering irritation. It was time to delve more into the mystery of the Octagon.

Before Benji could form a question, though, the carriage door closed with the finality of a coffin lid, and the carriage lurched forward. Benji craned their neck to peer out the curtained windows.

"Where are the other carriages?" Benji asked, thinking of the piles and piles of trunks, the veritable feast tucked into a multitude of baskets.

"What other carriages?"

"For the ones coming with us."

The queen scoffed. "We travel alone, child. For a crisis such as this, I don't trust even a driver to keep his head— so to speak."

She gestured behind Benji's head, where the driver's seat would be on the opposite side of the carriage's wall.

Benji peered out the window but couldn't see if the seat was truly empty. "Then what was all that other packing for?"

"I am a queen," she said. "I never travel without the proper comforts."

"I see," Benji replied, removing their Unicorns cap, then replacing it.

"Believe me," the queen continued, "we will need such fortification on our quest. I told you before that time was of the essence, but your imbecile friends have just cut that in half at least."

The carriage gave a jolt as it crossed over an ill-kept stony bridge. Benji's head and shoulders bashed against the back of their seat.

Though the upholstery kept them from suffering injury, the bolt of pain that shot through them made Benji even more focused on their peril.

Benji rubbed the back of their head.

The pair rode in silence for some time, Benji's mind circling in never-ending cycles of self-doubt that grew more aggressive as each minute passed. Who were they fooling? There was no way that Benji Amberman, a just-graduated fresh-out senior from Pattersonville, could deal with the powers of ancient fairy lore.

Somewhere in their thoughts, Benji realized the carriage had stopped its rickety swaying.

The sounds of the Fairy Realm filtered into the carriage through chinks in the wood.

Crows croaked in the gnarled trees of the forest surrounding the Unseelie lands.

In the distance, a hag cackled, and stones clattered as some wayward creature's flight disturbed them.

The wind whistled through small gaps in the carriage's construction, smelling of mold and lichen, cold with the tingle of pure Fairy Realm magic, uncut by the faint touch of the mortal world.

"Why have we stopped?" Benji whispered. Suddenly afraid of even their own voice.

The queen gestured to where Benji's fingers had curled of their own volition around the Web Gem's base, clenching until the knuckles were white. Suddenly self-conscious, they let it go and felt an ancient power fade away.

They knew now why the carriage had stopped.

Why fear had risen inside that place within them.

The mortal realm could not exist without the Fairy Realm. And if that was true, the counter would also hold. No matter how aloof some fairies and their lords might seem, the fey folk needed congress with mortals in order to survive. And with the fairy ring closed, Benji themself, more mortal than spiderkin after all, might be the only scrap of sustenance within reach.

"It's yours," Benji said to the Unseelie Queen, grabbing the Web Gem and holding it forward to her. "I can't do this, but you can."

The queen reacted swiftly, shielding herself with a raised forearm.

"It's not going to be that easy, child," she said in answer to Benji's bewildered gaze. Her tone was clipped, and she didn't meet their eye as she declared this, glaring instead once again out the window. "I cannot lie to you, Benji Amberman of the spiderkin. I tried to scry for our quarry before we departed, but the Web Gem doesn't respond to me as it did before. True, I am not its rightful mistress this season."

"Why does that matter?"

A darkness came over the Unseelie Queen's face. Rather than answer, she lifted one hand idly, and between her crooked fingers a tiny thundercloud of inky magic coalesced, a casual display of her unquestioned power. Then, with a huff of disgust, she waved the magic away unused.

Benji bit back a bark of laughter. Why indulge in fearing creepy crawlies *outside* the carriage, when they willingly sat *inside* it with arguably the most dangerous fairy of all?

"You think I can do this?" Benji asked, baldly requesting the queen's pep talk. "You think I can wield the full power of the Web Gem because I'm spiderkin?"

The queen turned a surprisingly warm smile on them.

She looked tired, as if the anger that had fueled her since the closing of the Fairy Ring had abandoned her in one swoop.

"I think the Web Gem has awakened to the idea that finding its family is possible. Is it any wonder, then, that it would favor you?"

"I don't know," Benji replied.

She made a shooing motion as if to say *go on with you, scamp,* and Benji breathed an almost painful breath as they felt more deeply into the artifact cradled on their lap. An unnamed emotion settled in their throat, making it hard to swallow. But as they peered into the

Web Gem, that lump slowly loosened. A warm presence was waiting for them within.

Is she right? Benji asked the warmth. *Are you looking for your family like I am?*

The answer didn't come in the form of words, but instead in the form of a spreading out, a rippling of that warmth from the Web Gem, through Benji, and out, over the lands surrounding them. To Benji, that ripple was a cry of loneliness that pierced so sharply that tears burned in their eyes.

They were the same, Benji and the Web Gem. Both cut off from others of their kind. Benji had come here to the Realm seeking answers to their ties to the ancient spiderkin, but now found themself unable to return to the home they knew, to their friends, and to their mother and father back in Pattersonville.

The Web Gem had spent millennia separated from the rest of the artifacts the spiderkin made.

It was ready now to search them out.

Benji nodded then, feeling resigned and powerful.

"May we continue?" the queen asked.

Benji made their own shooing motion, then. A moment later, the carriage was rolling again.

***

THEY TRAVELED FOR A LONG TIME, following the tenuous signals the Web Gem gave to Benji.

Benji couldn't truly say how much time passed, but day and night flowed into one another in a meaningless shifting of light. They stopped as needed, both Benji and the Unseelie Queen emerging from the driverless carriage to find a lovely picnic laid out for them as if some shadowy servant had indeed preceded them to see to their needs. The queen laughed when Benji voiced their suspicions, but she did not truly answer the question.

Still, the food was delicious.

A kind of invigoration had taken hold of Benji as the search went on. Muscles that had throbbed earlier had recovered, and fatigue that had muddled the mind had dissipated. They never felt tired and, other than the picnics, required no rest to recuperate strength. Benji couldn't remember the last time they closed their eyes other than to delve deeper into the magic of the Web Gem and that inner place of connection within.

"Over those hills," they'd say with a gasp, emerging from the spiderkin magic with a burst that felt like breaking the surface of the ocean.

"Beyond that singing brook." "Under those hanging boughs." "Inside that tangled thicket!"

The pair of coal-black horses that pulled their carriage sans driver would snort, stamp, and then prance forward at their mistress's command.

They crisscrossed the Fairy Realm in this way, passing through lands controlled by other great houses. Everywhere they went, lesser fairies fled before the Unseelie Queen's driving force. Benji couldn't help feeling swept along with it all, the magic coursing through their veins like silvery threads of silk. They felt themself grinning as a pair of Seelie maidens abandoned the gold-sparked pool they'd been bathing in at the gloomy carriage's approach, sprinkling droplets of water like diamonds from their hair and their delicate butterfly wings in their flight.

The Web Gem gave an exuberant jolt as they crossed into the shadowed hollows and deep forests of the lands patrolled by the Wild Hunt.

Though Benji had been there only once before, the place felt strange with the absence of its caretakers. The standing stones around which the Hunt's ramshackle village center had been built echoed eerily like a ghost town, the wind whipping through passages and around the stones in blustering gusts that tugged at Benji's Unicorns cap as they stepped down from the carriage. The remains of cookfires long cold lent a faint scent of charcoal to the empty air. Piles of bones and animal skins lay scattered where they'd been left. Unlike the bones Benji had seen spring to life in the Unseelie Castle to answer their mistress's commands, these gave the place an apocalyptic atmosphere. The masters of the land that had made this place were gone as cleanly as if a plague had come through, or some marauding enemy had laid siege. Nobody lived here now.

From the thick forest growth, a bird let out a terse song of sharp and brittle tones, as if uncertain whether such liberties would be tolerated.

Beside Benji, the Unseelie Queen stood with her shoulders back and her head tipped to the sky. She drew a long, deep breath in through her nose and let out a slow sigh as if relishing the flavor of the air.

"Benji," she said, turning with a look of girlish delight on her face. It made a nice change from the strained expression she'd worn throughout this entire quest. Ever since the closing of the fairy ring, their mentor had carried a burden. "The Octagon. Can you taste it?"

Benji sniffed the air, too, cradling the Web Gem like a swaddled babe. Beneath the cold, empty scent of soot, and the only mildly unpleasant aroma of carcasses in the final stages of decomposition, a tingle came to their tongue.

"I think I can."

"Come here."

The Unseelie Queen stepped lightly over the grassy expanse that served as a plaza and came to stand before the largest of the standing stones. She lifted one pale hand to hold her palm a scant inch away from the rough-hewn surface. Her fingers trembled slightly, but only for a moment. With another breath, she mastered herself.

Benji came to stand beside her, watching in rapt attention as she slid her hand across the stone. Where her palm passed, the dark tendrils of her Unseelie magic left silvery etchings on the granite surface. They glowed like starlight. Benji felt them pulsing. Their power brushed against that same power inside the Web Gem.

There was a secret here. Something that had lain hidden for thousands of years. Perhaps for as long as the Web Gem had been alone in this world.

Eager, Benji moved to take up the threads of the spell alongside the Unseelie Queen.

She gave a nod of approval, but said nothing, keeping her attention on the task at hand.

Together, teacher and student unraveled strands of ancient magic. Benji felt that new place within them calling out, but they fought off the temptation to dive straight in. They were stronger now and knew the danger that waited if they gave in like that. Instead, they let the pool of power fill their spell the way the Unseelie Queen had taught them.

The Web Gem hummed in anticipation, gathering unspooled strings as fast as Benji passed them to it. Now it was Benji alone working, the Unseelie Queen stepping away as the magic turned more spiderish.

Caught up in the frenzy of unspinning, Benji didn't realize they'd finished until they reached for the next piece and found themself grasping at emptiness. They cleared their thoughts and returned to themself. The ground under their feet was hard, the wind curling around them cold.

The standing stone lay so utterly exposed before them that Benji couldn't avoid comparing it to the skinned carcasses of the creatures that had fallen prey to the Wild Hunt.

Symbols shone on every square inch of the stone, symbols that spelled out a tale Benji couldn't read, and yet as they looked upon them, their meaning became clear.

"There's a ley line here," Benji said.

The Unseelie Queen's excitement was palpable, and the girlish look was still on her face, her eyes shining bright as moonlight. She put a hand on Benji's shoulder.

"Oh, child," she breathed, then laughed, a light, airy sound. "You *have* done well. A ley line! That bright and shining river of power!"

Color came to her cheeks. "Such things used to span the length and breadth of the Realm openly eons ago, connecting baseball fields and the great houses one to the other. Did you know they flow through your world, too? Back in times when the worlds were more mingled than they are now— or were now, until your friends closed the fairy ring. The truth is, they aren't the first to make such a blunder. There used to be so many more such rings, and so many more baseball fields where games could be played, and power exchanged."

Benji stared at the standing stone. The queen's words brought a feeling of deep satisfaction that rose within them, a sense of accomplishment so much greater than acing a test or nailing a fantastic triple play that Benji nearly burst. Benji had found this line with their own hands and tracked the magic with their own birthright.

They followed the glowing symbols and traced the line of light until it disappeared into the dark depths of the forest, then saw it also stretched the direction they'd come from, back towards the rolling fields where tiny pixies danced by night and where the Wild Hunt practiced baseball by day. This place was just part of the ley line, merely a point along it where the Wild Hunt in ages past had tapped into the power that flowed beneath their lands.

Not a terminus.

Instinctively, Benji understood.

A nexus of two lines crossing would gather more power than flowed along a single line. And a terminus— a place where all that rushing magic gathered in the end— would be a place of such power as to hide a mystical artifact.

"If we go that way, we'll eventually find the Other Field, won't we?" Benji asked, pointing toward the fields.

"We would," the queen replied with a tone that confirmed their idea. The node there was dead now. There was no reason to go back.

The darkness of the forest, however, beckoned.

THE CARRIAGE WAS TOO bulky to pass through the dense trees, and only a mount trained to the ways of the Wild Hunt would dare traverse these woods.

Thus, Benji and the queen braved it on foot.

The foliage crunched under their feet, and branches thick with leaves and moss bent to clutch at their heads and shoulders. Benji ignored their shivery touch and pressed on, the Web Gem held tightly against their chest. They felt good now. Strong with the pull of spiderkin magic that they felt in places deeper than bone.

The Octagon, Benji thought. It had to be just ahead.

The queen, too, seemed unaffected by the dank surroundings. Her midnight black traveling dress sported streaks of mud and a smattering of twigs and leaves, but none of these discomforts dimmed the brightness that still lingered in her eyes whenever Benji cast a look back at her.

The ground they tramped over began to change. Stones tumbled up from the muck and moss, taking on the appearance of faces in deep repose. The residue of ancient magic caused the very air to grow darker than natural shadow. It was a comfortable darkness, though. Inviting like a pure midnight rather than oppressive. Nearby, the chattering of flowing water floated through the air, a sensation that was sweet and clean. The combination of sound and easy darkness made Benji's eyelids heavy.

The queen made a sound of warning, but Benji didn't need it to realize the water's song was treacherous. Dipping their consciousness into the sheltering facets of the Web Gem, they blocked the noise out as they scrambled over the sleeping stones.

Ahead lay a thicket, not unlike the myriad others the two of them had poked their noses into over the course of their quest. The brush was tangled with vines and thick with talon-like thorns. The trees around that thicket bent over it to form a vaulted ceiling to a chamber of solitude.

A deep thrumming came from within.

This is it, Benji thought.

With an exchange of glances, Benji and the Unseelie Queen pushed the brambles and thorns aside to enter the thicket.

A globe of woven branches hovered in the center of the grove. It spun slowly and in random patterns, rotating first on one axis, then shifting to another. As it turned, rays of light, gold and silver and green, spilled forth. Where the light touched, warmth built to an almost unbearable level until the light passed on and the cold forest air swept back in.

Benji stood in awe.

The Unseelie Queen stepped forward, her hand lifted as she had done with the standing stone. But a moment later, she shook her head and stepped back.

"This is not for me to untangle," she said.

Benji nodded, understanding. "It's spiderish," they said. "They've cloaked the power of the terminus in a web of forest stuff. That's how it's stayed untouched for so long. Anyone might stumble across it if they could brave the forest, but only the spiderkin can reach beyond the webbing to touch the treasure within."

"I believe you're right," the queen said, stepping aside.

Slowly, Benji approached to stand directly before the globe.

It felt warm. Welcoming.

The Web Gem pulsed in rhythm with the globe's rotation.

They watched it for a moment, then, heart racing, carefully set the Web Gem down at their feet and, touching the place within themself, cupped their hands together as if cupping a baseball. In the space where the ball would lie, they began to spin strands of silken power that coiled into thicker ropes, and then thicker still, until Benji held a baseball-sized ball of yarnlike power. This they looped through the facets of the Web Gem, then, like holding the reins on a team of feisty horses, Benji plunged both fists into a gap in the globe's tightly woven branches.

The heat inside was scorching. But the threads of power and Benji's spiderkin essence kept the pain at bay just enough to tolerate. Bearing down, Benji spun new threads through the interior of the globe, searching by feel, waiting for the vibrations to come back to them like a bat seeking a meal.

The Octagon, Benji said to themself. *Find the Octagon.*

It had to be there. Benji knew that now.

And it was.

There.

A presence called to the Web Gem and Benji alike, resonating along the threads of magic Benji spun faster and faster. A franticness came over Benji then. *The Octagon!* The magical artifact that would allow them to open the fairy ring once more, to go home, to reassure their friends that all was well between the worlds.

Fighting eagerness, Benji forced themself to move deliberately. They drew it in. Wrapped the threads of power around the artifact.

Steady.

Steady.

Bringing the essence carefully forward. Holding it firmly.

Once Benji felt everything was under control, they turned their attention to the woven globe itself.

There. A pull in that spot would undo the whole thing.

The woven branches came apart all at once and tumbled to the ground with a dull clattering sound. Benji, breathing hard with the effort, fought to keep from succumbing to a wave of lightheaded-ness. They had to see this through.

Gently, they set the thing they'd retrieved upon the soft moss and retracted their spidery ropes.

The Unseelie Queen gasped. Benji opened their eyes.

What lay before them was not the artifact they had expected, nor did it have eight sides.

It was a person, curled in on himself and blinking as if waking from a long dream. His black skin shone in the filtered light of the grove. His woolen baseball uniform was baggy but looked pristine. The cap on his head had a small bill of dark fabric.

He looked like a young man, perhaps a year or two younger than Benji. But to Benji he felt old. Not ancient, just old in the same way

Adrien Thorn was. A kid displaced from his own time rather than an unchanging being of immortality.

Benji and the kid stared at one another in bewildered confusion.

"Who... are you?" Benji asked.

The boy shook his head, never breaking eye contact. He looked frightened now.

"Dunno," he whispered. "Don't remember."

"The Octagon?" Benji tried.

The boy remained motionless.

The Unseelie Queen moved between them. Her eyes were wide, and she bit her lip as if it was the only way she could contain herself. She knelt beside the boy and placed one hand on his shoulder. Dark tendrils of magic writhed over him, and he flinched, trying to cower. The queen did not let him go.

"Hey," Benji said. They tried to step forward, to stop her. But their feet didn't want to move. Glancing down, they saw the fallen branches had woven around them, holding them in place as firmly as a spider's web.

Terror shot through Benji. Their heart pounded in their throat, and they tore at the tangling branches with their hands. But no matter how many they pulled away, more curled in to entangle them tighter.

"Help me," they cried, reaching a hand to the queen. "Help!"

"I understand now," she said as if she hadn't heard Benji. She grasped the boy by both shoulders, holding him in place as he tried to cower. "This boy is the key."

"No," he moaned, thrashing in her grip. "No!"

"Your Majesty!" Benji tried again. The branches squeezed them. Sharp points dug into their skin. The molten power of the ley line pulled incessantly at them like the strong current of a river rapid.

In a smooth motion, the Unseelie Queen stood.

The boy, now entirely wrapped in the dark tendrils of her magic, rose with her, floating a few inches above the mossy ground.

She smiled at Benji.

"You have come so far in your studies during our time together, Benji. I have no doubt you can handle extricating yourself from this web. But understand that I must see to the restoration of this poor wretch's memories. He can tell us what has become of the Octagon!"

"I can't get out," Benji gasped, reaching even more desperately for her. "Help me! It's pulling me down!"

But the Unseelie Queen was already leaving. Her cloud of black magic swirled up and around her, engulfing both herself and the struggling bundle behind her. A thunderclap sounded in the grove, and when the sound faded, the cloud was gone.

Benji was alone with the brambles and the roaring, sucking whirl of the power they'd unleashed.

And, as the silver-gold light of it closed over their head and the branches wove themselves into a new globe around them, they realized one other thing was gone.

The Web Gem.

CHAPTER

TWENTY-TWO

Megan couldn't tell how many days she and Essie had spent prowling around the Unseelie Court, poking their noses into every nook and cranny they found and digging into places where they certainly weren't supposed to be. Time was slippery in the Fairy Realm, and the dark and dreary weather of the Unseelie lands made it even more so. Every once in a while, a twinge of fear would run through Megan. How much time had she spent away from home? Would she return to find herself displaced from her own time, like Adrien had been? Could she return, even? She'd eaten a lot of fairy food by now, and she'd heard the warnings about that too many times to count. But hungry is hungry, and her way of thinking said it was better to be alive and trapped than it would be to die of starvation.

A few nights ago— if nights they were— even Essie had lain curled in a little ball, trying to stifle her wails as she, too, suffered from feelings of being *trapped, cut off,* and *bereft.* Megan, helpless to do otherwise, had been able only to hold the brownie against her chest as Essie sobbed variations of those words over and over. Meanwhile, her own loneliness and homesickness felt like a weight on her chest. It was hard to breathe sometimes. She missed her mom. She missed Adrien.

At least by the time the sky had lightened into what passed for morning Essie seemed to be over the worst of that one, whatever it had been. She'd remained drawn and pale all day, though, and nowhere near as bubbly as usual.

And Megan. Well, as Essie greeted the morning sun, Megan's inner terrier rose to the forefront. She hitched up her big girl pants and set her mind right again. She couldn't deny her own spirit. Fear, even as powerful a spell of it as that one, wouldn't last long for her. There were secrets still to discover here. She felt them in the cool mist of the morning fog, and this was who Megan Moore was. Indomitable. Relentless. A crack reporter on the chase.

Any fear she felt was doomed to be overridden by the thought of finding and making sense of the truth.

Essie's spirit, of course, as she settled, was just as indomitable. She could carry the Small Folk's entire cheering section by herself, after all. The brownie was also invaluable as a reporter's assistant. Her tiny size meant she could get into places Megan couldn't, but even that couldn't explain the downright uncanny ability she had for wriggling herself onto the other sides of locked doors.

"Has anyone ever told you you'd make an excellent investigative journalist, Ess?" Megan said with breathless excitement as she stepped through the latest such opening. "Or a hell of a thief?"

Essie gave her a smile that would have lit up a baseball field. "What, little old me? I'm just a humble brownie, doing the tiny jobs that smooth the way for the big folk to do their big things."

"Says the brownie that swiped the Web Gem to begin with," Megan said, waving away Essie's false humility with a laugh.

"I just picked it up from where it was sitting," Essie said, arms crossed and countenance suddenly stiff. "Nothing anyone wouldn't have done."

"I've heard that before," Megan said. "Next time, try it with a bit more of a raised eyebrow and a bigger wave of the arms as you're crossing them. It'll make you look a little more amused and a little less proud of yourself."

Essie's face clouded, but Megan snickered and used an index finger to "punch" the brownie's shoulder.

"Don't worry, little Ess. I'm on your side. I hope you know that by now. I think your special skills are pretty cool."

"Thanks," Essie said. "Sorry to be like that. I think I'm just missing baseball sooooooo much."

"Me, too," Megan said. "But I meant what I said. You'd make a brilliant investigative assistant. I bet you know some pretty big words, too. Newspapers like those."

By the time they got on their way, Essie was beaming once again, perched on Megan's shoulder and giving her directions for navigating in the dimness.

Days trawling about the gloomy surface world's landmarks had led them through gnarled woodlands and into corpse-riddled graveyards. They'd followed lead after lead, sorting through the branching paths of their discoveries to ensure they were piercing to the deepest, darkest secrets the Unseelie Court had to hide.

Now they descended into the tunnels that took them beneath the place where the queen of this domain resided and wrought her wicked spells.

The bowels of the castle in the heart of the Unseelie Court.

Darkness clung to the air, and a damp, mildewy taste coated Megan's tongue. She raised her phone before her like a torch, the flashlight app on. Its light cast a thin needle of illumination through the inky blackness, barely enough to show their full surroundings, which were as terrifying as they were tantalizing. Black stone walls with sharp, polished facets like obsidian. A floor of some porous stone that looked like it was made of thousands of compressed, tiny faces screaming in eternal agony. Around every bend, another door of thick, black wood, barred entrance.

But they hadn't bet on Essie the brownie coming knocking.

Each such door fanned the flames of discovery burning in

Megan's heart. These dark tunnels were the places of secrets. The terrier in her said they were in the right spot, and that everything she saw was important in some way. Even if they didn't apply to the specific story she was chasing now, each was a lead she could follow in the future.

Chamber after chamber, they progressed. Quick but thorough searches of each room were disappointing, though. After each she jotted quick notes in her phone's app, but they found nothing to do with the missing kids she was tracking. Then they moved on.

It occurred to her to wonder how her phone was still alive after however much time had passed since it had last seen the charger back home on her bedroom nightstand. The display said it was drained. No bars, either, but that was hardly surprising. Yet still the phone was operating.

Something to do with Fairy Realm magic, she assumed.

Do not question good fortune now, she thought as she lifted her phone light and crossed the threshold of the newly opened door.

Essie grabbed onto Megan's leg and clambered up to sit on her shoulder. Together, they looked upon their spoils.

Shelves, it seemed.

Shelves like a pantry in a ship's galley.

The room was deeper than it was wide. Cramped, with barely enough space for a bow-legged cook to squeeze down it by himself, let alone return with arms laden with ingredients. Megan's light did not penetrate to the far end, though, giving it the appearance of stretching off into forever. Which, she admitted, might be the case with a secret magic room deep underneath Unseelie Castle.

The aroma of ancient breath seemed suddenly stagnant here.

The sounds of their footsteps were oddly muted.

She swallowed a nervous giggle and examined the shelves nearest her.

They were built into the walls and made of a dark wood similar to the door. From floor to ceiling, Megan counted five shelves on each side. The eerie thing about them was how utterly empty they were.

"What do you think, Essie? Invisible treasure?"

Essie gave a sniff like a cat investigating a strange new piece of furniture, then grimaced. "I don't know. Smells weird here. Very stale. Worse than that graveyard somehow."

"Yeah," Megan muttered absently as she peered into the deeper darkness beyond her light. Then she tipped her head towards Essie. "Do you think we should turn back? Leave this one alone?"

Even as she said it, she knew the answer.

Essie's grip tightened on Megan's collar, and she snorted. "Should the Small Folk forfeit their next match?"

Megan grinned and stepped forward.

"Secrets," she said, feeling stronger again. "Here we come."

Methodically, she swiped her hand from side to side in the space of each empty shelf, making certain the shadowed cubbies truly were empty. All she felt was cold air, and sometimes a faint tingle, as if some magical trap might be thinking of springing on her. She snapped her hand back each time she felt that, then tentatively tried the space again to find it as dead as every other shelf.

As she walked on, the darkness of the back of the room stretched out even deeper with no sign that they were nearing an end. Soon, the front of the room matched it, cloaked in concealing darkness just as inky. It was a corridor, she realized. Not a room. Megan and Essie walked in a little hamster ball of light, feeling like they were being led forward, as if they were rolling down a piece of track made for a marble or a toy race car.

The shelves remained empty. After a while, Megan stopped checking them.

The feeling in the never-ending hall changed slowly and subtly.

A feeling of dread made Megan want to hunch her shoulders and hide. A sense of hopelessness told her to stop where she was, sit down, and never move again, because there was no point in moving on through this hallway and its road to infinity. It was draining work, too, this trek. Wearying to the point that even Essie's buoyancy was dragging.

Luckily, Megan had faced tedium before. Research was the cost of doing business, after all. And research could be nothing if not dry and boring. Doggedly, she kept on, and on, and on.

Eventually, the emotions the darkness pressed upon her shifted again.

Megan recognized this sensation, too.

It was like she'd passed through some kind of checkpoint, a gate that told whatever haunted this long path to stop its deterrence. She was coming to the end. Each step made her heart feel lighter. Even the beam of her flashlight seemed to brighten.

That didn't mean the place didn't still give her the absolute creeps.

When, at long last, the light touched what appeared to be the first sketched outlines of a back wall, she had a moment of trepidation.

Something lay there, waiting.

In the darkness ahead, it felt big and weighty with implication no matter its actual size.

There was a taste in her mouth that said she'd finally found what she was looking for.

The brownie was excited, too. Essie's short breaths puffed against her ear, and Megan knew Essie also sensed they were standing before something important in the Unseelie Court. Essie knew what she was doing. Friendly poking aside, the brownie *had* stolen the Web Gem from a place like this, and in doing so had set everything that had happened in Pattersonville and the Fairy Realm over the past two years into motion.

Megan wondered what events she was about to put into play now.

They pressed on. A few more steps and Megan found herself standing before the final shelf.

There, on the middle shelf, precisely in the center of its gleaming platform, lay an object.

At first, Megan thought it was a kind of small shield that knights once used in one-on-one combat, a buckler. But as she drew closer and pointed her light at it, she saw that wasn't it. The thing was more like a decorative plate, though all of a single pale pink color. She could make out no painted pattern or etched designs that would make it pretty. It had eight sides, was about half an inch thick, and was perfectly flat across its entire radius.

"It would make a nice trivet for serving a hot pot on, I guess," Megan said. She straightened, letting her spine crackle back into proper position after bending over at such an angle. A bolt of frustration shot through her. Roadblock. After miles of straight, unimpeded progress they'd hit a dead end.

She hated when that happened.

"What on earth does this thing have to do with my missing kids, though? Ess? Any thoughts?"

The brownie remained quiet. Silent, in fact.

But she was trembling, Megan realized. Now that Megan wasn't engrossed in examining her find, she noticed the faint vibration against her neck. Cold fear washed over her.

"Uh, Ess?"

"W-w-we're not alone!"

Megan spun around to find that, indeed, someone stood between them and the distant, shadow-barred exit.

The mistress of the castle had returned.

And there was someone else behind her, too, someone who was clearly not a willing guest, given the dark tendrils of magic that bound him.

The cold fear turned downright frigid. Megan couldn't feel her fingers as they clamped around her phone.

"Well, well, well," said the Unseelie Queen, smiling down at Megan and Essie so each one of her sharp teeth glimmered in the light of Megan's flash. "How *convenient*."

CHAPTER

TWENTY-THREE

As far as Emily was concerned, the morning's game was the perfect way to greet the last day she'd ever be able to play — and she wasn't even going to be on the field herself.

It started with Sydney's fastball, a pitch that came exactly as the sun crested the horizon. By then, Emily understood both baseball magic and the way of the fairy ring far too well to think the timing was anything but an omen.

Standing at the edge of the dugout, she gave her catcher the sign for another fastball by running her hand down the jersey of her Small Folk uniform. It made her think about Fennoc's fastidiousness in the dugout. That led her down the path of other remembrances, like the day Mellica and Jessebel had doted over her hair in between innings. The memory of Essie the brownie practically bursting out of Greeven the elf's pocket in raptures at the style made her giggle.

On the field, the singsong chatter of little voices was like warm darts to her heart.

Callie had been right. The baseball magic had welled up in that first pitch, and now the sight of every little body bent over in antici-pation of a ball batted their way, fists pounding into gloves, and faces scrunched up in concentration, carried the essence of the game to an even higher state. With every moment that passed, Emily became more certain her decision was a good one. She didn't need her baseball talent as much as she needed baseball magic.

Nestled in her back pocket, her mother's baseball exuded a wreath of comfort.

For an instant, it made Emily wonder.

"Come on! Let's have some fun out there!" she called out to her Annie's Diner Giants as she wrapped her hand around the dugout rail.

"Let's have fun" had been the crux of her pregame talk with the kids. She was the Giants' manager. Jake was out at the bullpen. Pash was sitting on the bench fretting over the batting order and thinking about advice he'd give to the kids as they went to the plate.

Adrien was managing the other team, the Jackson Sporting Good Hawks.

Callie, by the power of her increasingly interesting bat, was the umpire behind the plate. Trace, acting as the second umpire, roamed the back of the infield.

The batter swung. The ball bounced to third base where a kid named Helen Myrsovich scooped it up and fired to first base to get the out— the runner, dashing by, lost his helmet in the chase.

"Good arm!" Emily called, clapping her hands. "Great catch!"

On the field, Patsy was coaching first base for the Hawks. She picked up the first batter's helmet and handed it to the kid as he went back to the bench. "Keep it on your head next time," she admonished gently. "You don't want a bad throw to bop you on your noggin!"

The kid laughed and pushed it jovially back onto his head as he ran back.

Warmth suffused Emily as she watched the play. Perhaps giving up her baseball talent wouldn't sting so bad. If she could pass it on to one of these young sparks, it would feel more like a building of something than any paying of a price.

When the time was right, she'd make the transfer. Until then, she'd follow Callie's lead. Her old rival had something up her sleeve to deal with the rogue Wild Hunt, that much was obvious.

Sydney got the ball back and leaned in to get the next sign.

Fastball, Emily thought. *Don't change what ain't broke.*

BY THE TIME the game ended, the sky was a perfect blue and the sun slanted down from behind a single, billowing cloud so white its edges gleamed silver. The kids, tired but wound up from their incredible morning getting coached by the "big kids," still hung out in the dugouts and the infield. Baseball magic flowed off them in wisps Callie could see without any effort at all.

Her plan had been a success, at least the first part of it.

Time was running short, though.

Standing in the far reaches of center field, Callie gripped her bat. The baseball magic made it glow so brightly the sheen had to be visible to even the normal mortals. She held her breath as she tapped into it, almost afraid she'd drown in that power.

With a deliberate breath, she checked in on her spell. As she'd suspected, the fabric of last night's magic was frayed and fading. It would be only a short while before the Hunt Leader could break through.

"Are you all right?" Trace asked, concern on his face.

"Yes," Callie said, though she wasn't truly sure of that. "As all right as I have to be, anyway."

The baseball magic she held now was the purest form she'd ever felt. It pulsed through her body and throbbed at her temples, almost too beautiful to contain. She wondered if she could overdose on it. "Too much of a good thing is wonderful," she said to Trace as if trying to convince herself.

She knew what she needed to do, though, and that thought helped her cut through her euphoria and get down to earth.

"Are you ready?" she said to Trace.

"I am. I told Miss Em and the Designated Hitter to follow our trail, as you asked."

He braced himself, and Callie swung onto his powerful back.

Bat raised, she let her inner self rise to meet with the power of the baseball magic. Inside, she felt the heat of the Hunt she'd been so close to settling. Somewhere the essence of her Seelie heritage prickled her mind. With purpose, she let them mix together and felt the trail forming.

Prey, she felt. Lead me to my prey.

She gripped the bat harder and laid her head back to call a charge.

Magic swirled around her, and for a moment— though perhaps she was dreaming it— Callie heard Trace's voice once again calling her a fairy mage.

Then they were flying. Or more, they were hurtling through space, winding their way through the streets first, then rising over rooftops and the red and orange canopies of oak and elm and sycamore trees, following the sounds of hunters struggling against her bonds.

She knew where she would find them even before she arrived.

A large building of brick and glass.

A store.

The store.

McMasters Ball and Glove.

There was movement there, too. Crowds of people milled about as Callie and Trace raced forward. Trace's hooves clattered on the parking lot as he set them down, and the situation became clear. Mortal faces and fey maws turned to her, showing a mixture of fear, anger, and desperation.

People— citizens of the city— were pinned down in groups, quivering with fear as fairy creatures of the Hunt paced back and forth, corralling them into the shopping center's corners and the crannies made between parked cars. The double glass doors of the

Ball and Glove had been forced open, but Carol Dement, her father's office manager, stood at the entry, brandishing a large, wickedly hooked hockey stick and threatening a crooked-backed earth troll as it attempted to enter.

Behind the troll stood the target of Callie's mad dash.

"Stand your hunters down," Callie called to the Leader of the Hunt.

She slid off Trace's back, her baseball cleats clattering as she landed on asphalt. She clasped the bat in one hand and pounded it purposefully into the palm of her other as she made her way forward. Baseball magic flowed off it. She heard its whispers fully now. *Take what is yours, mistress. Take what is yours.*

She braced herself against the flow, holding onto the pure strength of human hearts that permeated the baseball magic itself, and realizing the bat's urging had come from someplace deeper and more primal.

She knew what she needed to do.

Ahead, the Leader growled.

He was fully a beast now. Locked into his animal form. His canine muscles bunched at his shoulders and over his strong chest, solid and hard-packed, formed of centuries in the wild forests of the Fairy Realm. He stood tall and strong, as if his presence alone would cause her to cower. His eyes narrowed, bloodshot now with the power of the chase bottled inside him, and his fangs gleamed white as he showed them in the late morning sun.

Callie stepped forward, bat held before her not in threat, but in supplication.

"Be stronger than this, Huntmaster. I know somewhere inside there, you're still the same Fairy Lord who played baseball to save this city. Call down your horde and let these people free. This is not who you are."

The Leader gave a sharp double yip. He tilted his head, and his jaw moved as if he meant to speak to her. But all that came out were more barks.

The answer burned Callie's heart. She had hoped it might not come to this. "Oh, Leader. You're that far gone, are you?" She shifted her grip to hold her bat like a two-handed sword, and felt the ancient power of the Hunt surging through the Leader's presence. "No, not that far gone, after all," she said. "Once I've taken care of this mess, I promise I'll find a way for you to set yourself right."

The Leader's fit of yipping and howling was the most derisive laughter Callie had ever heard. He still thought she couldn't take this from him. Even here in the mortal realm, he thought she couldn't match his power.

She swung the bat languidly and let the baseball magic calm her.

Time seemed to stop for an instant.

Then, from behind the Leader, the earth troll leapt forward, catching Callie off guard. "No mere mortal can lead us!" it roared.

Callie started to raise her bat but knew it would be too late. Not fair, her brain called. Not fair.

With a sharp, un-baseball-like crack, the wood shank of Carol Dement's hockey stick caught the lunging fairy in the side and sent it flying away to crash onto the parking lot with a yowl. She stepped back to protect the store, then, and Callie saw something deeper in her than she'd seen before. The building meant something to her beyond the job.

"Looks like mere mortals can do whatever we damn well please," she said, blowing a wisp of hair out of her face.

With a glance, Callie thanked Carol.

The Leader growled. His ears lay flat against his lupine skull, and his lips pulled so far back his black gums showed around his teeth.

Having regained her balance, Callie narrowed her gaze and waved the bat in the space between them. "You know I'm here to take your crown, don't you?"

The Leader bent into a tense spring, stepping slowly to the left, and encircling her. His eyes shone red with pure, unrefined Hunt magic.

Callie focused on his face more than his gaze, pivoting slowly to ensure she remained fully facing him as he circled like a shark. "I can lead better than you are now, Huntmaster. You've given in to pure instinct, and let that base instinct bring your host into a position where it cannot win. You know that. I know you do. Inside where that Leader who supported the mortals against the Seelies still resides, you know that the Fairy Lords will enact vengeance if you destroy this place."

Energy welled inside her. Fairy magic mixed with the power of pure baseball.

Beyond their little ring, the rest of the Hunt stood in vibrating anticipation, waiting to see the outcome of this confrontation. One of them had tried to come between the two already and faced the consequences.

The rest waited to see who they would follow into the future.

With an uncanny swiftness, the wolf who had led sprung forward, claws out, fangs bared, hot spittle flying as his dark form flew through the space between him and his challenger. The strength of the Hunt bore down upon Callie with a weight that came as if through the ages themselves, complete with the heated scent of forest foliage and fresh coppery blood.

Somewhere behind her, Trace called a warning.

But she didn't need it.

As the Leader leapt for her throat, Callie swung her bat, singing again, bringing forth the magic she'd begun to feel was as much a part of her as any single organ. She felt it all as it came together, and she felt it too, in the talismans of Emily DeWitt and Adrien Thorn— Miss Em's baseball and The Designated Hitter's glove— as her two friends finally made it on foot to the grounds of her father's old Ball and Glove.

Whumpf.

With their arrival, Callie's spell exploded in a massive surge that sent people and fairies sprawling so that only Callie, Emily, and Adrien remained upright.

The Huntmaster remained also.

Frozen.

Suspended in midair, jaws extended and fangs bared a slim inch from Callie's neck. His eyes now glistened with pure panic as he saw what was happening.

Callie didn't let his fear distract her. She kept humming, still weaving her spell, still adding the powers inside Adrien's glove and Emily's ball into the recipe as they made them available to her, making something stronger than fairy magic, stronger than human will, stronger even than baseball magic itself.

"Riders of the Wild Hunt, behold me! I am no *mere* anything!" Callie said through her exertion.

"I am mortal!" she cried as the spell work encased the Leader. With a twist of the bat, she sent him sprawling to crash hard against the wall of the Ball and Glove.

"I am Seelie!" she said as she stepped forward, panting, her bat smoking with the raw power it channeled.

"And I am the Hunt!" she said as she bent to rip a handful of dark fur from his pelt.

Holding the handful out, a few random hairs scattering in the wind, she turned to face her riders.

"I lead. What say you? Do you follow?"

There was a moment of stillness then in which the only sound was the feather whisper of an unseen bird of prey gliding over the sky.

Then came a Red Cap's yip.

Thacker, the Wild Hunt's catcher, sidled over to stand at her side.

A troll's groan rattled as Grangle heaved herself forward, too, stepping over her fallen brother with a pointed look.

The satyrs, led by Pyrgin, came forward as she scattered the fur of the past Leader into the wind.

As the strands floated away from the parking lot, the rest of the Hunt raised their voices into one howl of loyalty.

It was done.

Callie McMasters was the new Leader of the Wild Hunt.

But before she would lead a single chase, she crossed to where her predecessor lay panting on the asphalt. As his red eye rolled up to look at her, she knelt and placed a soft hand on his head.

A moment passed.

Then, with a gentle whine, the wolf who had led licked her hand.

Callie smiled.

"Calm, friends," she said to her still-howling host. "It is time we return to the field. We hunt."

CHAPTER

TWENTY-FOUR

Fred McMasters pressed himself into the farthest recess of a nook in the Victorian house at the corner of Calabash and Main Street, cattycorner to Mayor Culpepper's place. It was midmorning on this crisp autumn day. The Victorian's brick pressed into his back through his lined Ball and Glove jacket. He pulled the collar up closer around his neck.

Down Main Street, the storefronts, which had sported pumpkins and ghosts and witches' hats the night before, were all in disarray. The sounds of Hunt chaos still reverberated through the city, though, and the streets were empty despite the time of day.

He smirked.

Until now, holidays were always good for business.

The mayor's place was a two-story house, large, but not extravagant. About right for a public servant. He considered his play.

Natalie would be working, of course.

She was always working. Something that pissed McMasters off to no end. Wouldn't even take time off to do dinner with him, even though he told her he wanted to work on a new zoning agreement. Didn't she understand that he *was* business in Pattersonville? With

187

his wife run off, you'd think she'd have seen him for the catch he was. Being seen with Fred McMasters would pretty much guarantee her mayor for life.

Or at least he had *been* business in Pattersonville until this.

Damned kids.

Look what the hell they'd done.

Even Callie. His own daughter, who had gone bad despite all his best attentions.

Well. He could fix this part at least. That was his play.

He glanced up Main Street, comforted to see it was still empty. He wasn't afraid of the Hunt. Not too much, anyway. He carried the blood of Seelie royalty. They wouldn't harm royalty, would they? Of course, he'd watched the slavering horde of fur and scale-lined mouth breathers run freely over the streets last night and knew somewhere inside himself that he didn't want to be around when the Hunt got their blood fully up. Mistakes could be made, and even if a rabid dog gets put down, the innocent bystander it bites could wind up just as dead.

The street was empty, though.

No rabid member of the pack drifting along and looking for scraps.

With a confident breath, McMasters glanced into his reflection in the dark first-floor window beside him, used his fingertips to ensure his hair was properly coiffed, and stepped across the quiet street to Mayor Culpepper's place.

It took two knocks on the door before the curtains in the bay window moved.

The lock clicked back, and then the door— expansive and painted white— cracked open.

"Fred McMasters?"

"Good morning, Natalie. I didn't expect you'd be managing your own door."

The mayor, wearing a pair of creased black business slacks and a wide-collared plain white shirt with a button opened at the top, looked like she'd been up all night. Her blonde hair was down now, and frazzled ends seemed to dance with static in the cold, dry air. Normally Fred knew Natalie would keep him standing on the patio, but now she rushed him into the foyer, casting furtive glances up and down the street as she slammed the door shut behind him.

"We're a little busy right now, Fred. We've got a state of emergency to deal with."

"That's what I'm here to talk about. I think I can help you out."

"I. Um." The mayor hesitated.

"Come on, Natalie. You know I'm Seelie blood, right? It's all over the place. I mean, you can't pick up a local paper without another one of those hit pieces by the Moore girl slapping you in the face. She's got a lot of everything wrong, though, making it out like I'm some kind of an asshole when all I'm trying to do is make sure this city is safe to live in."

He paused and let his eyes grow soft.

"That's something we both care about, don't we, Natalie? Law and order? We both know that if we keep the people safe, everything works out. But let the freaks run wild, and... whatever." He gave a gentle gesture out the window. "But it's true I'm a Seelie, Natalie. As much as the girl reporter gets wrong, she's got that part as right as a rainout. And that means that if we can work things out right between us, I can use my bloodright to set this right."

In the muted distance, another round of wild howling crackled over Pattersonville.

"What do you say, Nat? Wanna work together?"

Natalie Culpepper's colorless lips pressed into a thin line. She really could use a touch of makeup, McMasters thought. Presentation is everything. After this was all settled and things were back to normal, he would help her with that, too.

"All right," she said with a weary sigh. "Come on in. Can I get you some coffee?"

"A cuppa Joe would be great," McMasters said, shedding his jacket and making himself comfortable. "Just black."

. . .

ALONE IN HER KITCHEN, Natalie Culpepper hated herself as she poured freshly brewed coffee into a cup for Fred McMasters. Even the smell of the rich liquid, made from freshly ground Colombian beans— one of the only indulgences she allowed herself anymore— wasn't enough to calm her nerves. The sound of it flowing around into the cup made her stomach burn.

The man was a drop-dead boor.

She couldn't trust him as far as she could throw him. Or, to be fair, she could trust him completely to always be out for whatever was good for himself. That was the constant with Fred McMasters. His Ball and Glove, for example, had extended itself too far in this whole fairy ring fiasco, and that had been the real start of all her problems because it turned out that his business, as one of the largest employers in town, had gone and built out past where their zoning license had allowed them to.

Which made him subject to extra taxes and additional penalties.

Which he couldn't pay.

When called on it, McMasters had just waved a hand and made a suggestion that if everyone just looked the other way a bit longer, he'd have the votes to make it all fine and good— meaning, she supposed, that he thought he could use some kind of Seelie magic to get his way, and that any penalty he had to pay would be bad enough for the city that he should just be allowed to get away with it, anyway.

Asshole. No wonder his wife and then his daughter both ran off.

That he wasn't totally wrong about his status made it that much worse.

When the feces had hit the rotating device last spring, she thought the Ball and Glove's demise was going to kneecap the entire city. Only the fanatical following of the amazing Unicorns as they chased and eventually won the State Champion had kept enough people coming into the city to keep it afloat.

Now her city was cowering as the Wild Hunt ran free in the street, and McMasters and his greasy grin was here to squeeze as much as he could from her. All she could say for sure was that whatever happened, this wouldn't be the last she heard from him. Fred McMasters was the bleeding ulcer that kept giving. The communicable disease that spreads forever.

Unfortunately, though, nothing she was doing was helping. It was to the point where her only option left was to grab that Louisville Slugger she kept in the corner behind her desk and go out to defend the streets herself.

From her office, the staticky call of the police radio announced another run.

That she had to listen to McMasters was infuriating.

She poured herself a topper, too. At least her tenth cup since late last night, but who was counting? Then she picked up the two cups and went back to her office.

"All right, Fred. What can you tell me?" she said as she stepped into the room where she'd been working all night. He was, of course, lounged back and sprawled on the leather couch she had placed across the far wall.

She proffered the cup and watched as he took a big swig. "Mmm. Good Joe."

"Yes," she said, barely letting the corner of her lip twist into a wry grimace as she thought about the source of the beans that had gone into the coffee. "I'm sure it is good Joe."

"Here's the thing, Nat," McMasters said, putting the cup on the clean coffee table set before the couch.

He'd taken a glance at the documentation on her desk when he stepped in and saw her computer screen had a display of Pattersonville's map, complete with multiple sites tagged red for attacks, orange for disturbances, and yellow for locations where distress calls had been received from, but not yet addressed. A police radio sat on a stand beside the desk, spouting blasts of static between short reports from the few officers who were out patrolling the streets.

"Just cut to the chase, all right, Fred?" the mayor said as she sat back behind her desk. Her gaze scanned the screen, looking for changes. "I don't have time for the soft sell."

"All right, then." He grinned, the whites of his capped teeth blazing. "Wham bam, thank ya, ma'am. I can dig it." He rubbed his hands together, then motioned to the computer screen. "You got a real problem on your hands. But if you think the city can forgive my debts, reinstall my business license, and tweak that little zoning line we discussed last summer, I think I can bring my royals here and take care of the Hunt."

"I don't believe you. Besides, last I looked, you've also been found guilty of wanton endangerment in the use of an automobile. The fact is, now that you're here, I should call someone and have you locked up."

"Natalie!" McMasters shook his head. She was going to play it feisty, of course. "You know I love it when we play hardball."

The mayor sipped her coffee. "When are you planning to cut to the chase?"

"That is the chase, Mayor. Wipe my slate clean and get your city back. Otherwise, just deal with it." McMasters grabbed his cup and took a healthy sip, wiping his lip on his sleeve as he watched the game play out on her face. "The question is how much are you willing to sacrifice to save your people? Because that's what matters, right? At the end of the day, all these arbitrary rules are great and all that, but all that really matters is what's best for everyone in the long run, right? Who wins, and who loses?"

A red blob appeared on the Mayor's screen then.

The report of fairy creatures raiding a garage or warehouse down by the river came across the radio. Then another. A disturbance at the Ball and Glove had apparently resolved some time before, but the mass of the Hunt had left and was racing through the streets again, heading down Main Street and toward her office.

McMasters saw the situation harden on the mayor's face.

She was going to cave.

Of course, she was.

He was right, after all. This was how the game worked. You followed rules until the rules didn't help you get where you wanted to be. Then you made new rules. Or didn't. It wouldn't matter, because, in the end, people with power were all the same. Malleable.

No matter how high and mighty Natalie Culpepper talked about morals, she was no different from anyone else.

He smiled, feeling triumph rise inside him.

He couldn't help one more comment. His coup de grâce. His pièce de résistance.

"Then, of course, when we've got this all worked out, we can talk about the future over dinner, can't we?"

The comment snapped her head around.

"You know we'd make a great power couple," he crooned. "And I could get used to this Joe."

She stood up then, staring at him. "I think we're done here." She turned to grab hold of the baseball bat she kept in the corner, then stepped around her desk.

McMasters' heart jumped to his throat. "What are you doing?" he said, raising his hands in self-defense.

She scoffed at him. Unattractive, to say the least.

"Oh, grow up, Fred. I'm not going to bean you with a baseball bat simply because you're a crappy human being." She shouldered on a jacket.

"Then... what...?"

"I'm going out to defend my city. There's no way I'm letting you, your Seelies, or even the Wild Hunt control Pattersonville."

McMasters stood up. "You're going to get yourself killed."

A third voice broke the tension snapping between them.

"Not if I get a say in it."

Both McMasters and Mayor Culpepper turned to the open entrance to the office.

"Callie?" McMasters said.

His wayward daughter stepped fully into the office. She had a feral look about her— more than the usual, that was. And yet, for all that, her casual body language said she felt completely in control of the moment. Her baseball uniform billowed about her frame as if caught in a breeze Fred McMasters couldn't feel.

A clicking of nails on the hardwood floor drew his attention to the creature that accompanied her. A faithful hound, it seemed, standing easily at heel beside her. It growled as it stared at McMasters, its blood-red eyes trained on him, and its ears pinned back.

"I'd be careful if I were you, Father," Callie said. "I don't think he likes you, and I'm not sure I can control him that well quite yet."

———

CALLIE WATCHED her father process the moment.

"What is this? Aren't you a bit old for jokes?" he said. He was stalling for time, though, she knew. His expression was beginning to show the feral fear of someone who knows he's lost and lost big.

Across from him, Mayor Culpepper pressed her thumb and fore-finger to the bridge of her nose. "Do I want to know how you got into my house uninvited?"

Callie tossed a smile her way. "You haven't got a thing to worry about, Madame Mayor. Everything with the Hunt is under control. Your city is safe. For now, anyway."

For a moment, she let herself enjoy the way the release of tension smoothed Mayor Culpepper's face and loosened the hunch of her shoulders. Then Callie focused on her true quarry.

"The time has come for you to answer for your follies, Dad."

He scoffed, looked from her to the beast who was once the leader, then outside the window, to where the rest of her Hunt waited with varying levels of impatience, pacing, groaning, and calling with jaws clacking.

His eyes widened. His breath came faster.

He knew the truth, even if he wouldn't admit it out loud.

"Come on, Callie girl. You're not seriously thinking of putting your own father to the chase?" he said, laughing. The sound grated out of his throat, forced against the friction of unease.

Callie's laugh came light and easy.

"Don't worry. *My* Hunt doesn't work like that."

Then it was her father's turn to chortle. It was cute the way he thought she couldn't read his relief in his weakening posture or smell it in his sweaty stench. "That's what I thought."

"You think I'm weak?" she said. She let one hand drift down to stroke the wolf's head, enjoying the bristly roughness of his fur. Her companion leaned against her thigh. His flank heaved with his breaths, rapid with anticipation. "I'm pretty sure you raised me to be otherwise."

"What are you going to do? Make me sit in timeout for a week?"

"Something like that. At first, anyway."

"What the hell does that mean?"

Quick as lightning, Callie pulled out a baseball. Her bat was in her hands, too, pulsing with magic, both Hunt and baseball. The baseball hovered before her, waiting.

Her father stared, wide-eyed, slack-jawed, still unable to admit to his fear of her.

Gently, she batted it to him.

He flinched, which made him fumble it, and it fell to the couch, where he picked it up.

She chuckled. Outside, her Hunt horde built up a yapping cacophony.

"I wonder," she said, hooking her magic bat across both shoulders and letting her wrists dangle from it. "You've sold baseball gloves, batting helmets, and even jock straps for decades. Exactly how long has it been since you played a real game of baseball, Dad?"

Her father's eyes narrowed. "What do you mean?"

"You know what I mean. I think it's time we see what Dear Old Dad can do on the field."

Callie's father spluttered, apparently unable to call upon his cherished Seelie blood to lend himself poise in this moment.

Culpepper let out a bark of laughter. "Oh, hell. I am not missing this. After last night, I need a stiff shot of fun."

Callie felt her lips spread in a grin that was downright wolfish.

Mayor Culpepper was absolutely right.

This was going to be fun.

CHAPTER

TWENTY-FIVE

Standing in the parking lot outside Unicorn Field, Emily waved goodbye to Sydney and Helen as the two left to walk back home.

She hadn't been expecting to see them here when she returned from the Ball and Glove. It was a good hour since the game had come to its end. She expected she'd be alone in the boneyards of a silent Unicorn Field. But it was clear now that none of the kids had wanted to go home. So, even though Emily and Adrien had raced off to go help Callie corral the Wild Hunt, the Little Leaguers had stayed behind, swapping stories and telling jokes for a long time, some asking the remaining Unicorns for extra hints and others practicing swings and defensive stances. Slowly they had dissipated, though, leaving when their parents showed up in cars to drive them away, or — the ones who lived nearby the schoolyard— walking, baseball gloves tucked under their arms or still on their hands, clinging to the game day baseball magic for just a little longer.

Despite the sense of resolve that had fallen over her, joy filled Emily as she watched Sydney and Helen walking away, jabbering as they went.

They were neighbors, Helen's family living just down the street from the Thorns. They went to school together, too. It was clear that Sydney liked the girl, and that the girl liked Sydney, but then Emily knew Sydney well enough to know that all it took for the kid to like someone was that they could talk a good game of baseball. It didn't take long to see that Helen was the same way. Only the luck of the preseason Little League draft process had kept them on separate teams.

As the two rounded the corner and disappeared from Emily's line of sight, she drew a breath. Then she turned to the field she finally had all to herself.

Except apparently, she didn't.

Adrien stepped up beside her, shouldering the once-again bulging equipment bag.

"Can you believe Callie McMasters is the Leader of the Hunt?" he said.

Emily fought to hide her surprise at his presence. She'd thought he'd headed home after the craziness at the Ball and Glove. "To be honest?" she said. "Yeah. She's always had an edgy side, right?"

"I suppose she has."

"The real question is what comes next."

"Right. I worry she's bitten off more than she can chew."

Emily privately agreed. But a wave of loyalty made her shake her head. "She's got a sense of purpose driving her now. She took off to Hunt her dad, right? Which I totally think is a good first step."

The memory of Fred McMasters trying to trick her into signing a contract that would have made him her agent brought her a shudder as hard as the idea of Benji and Megan in trouble. At least Callie was doing something to right a few wrongs. Emily, standing in the middle of the nearly empty Unicorn Field, felt her own inaction building up uncomfortably. Her baseball talent felt like it was burning a metaphorical hole in her metaphorical pocket.

They stood together there for an awkward moment.

Emily expected Adrien to peel off and go home at any moment

now that he'd collected his baseball equipment. But, instead, he just stood there with her. His closeness made her anxious. Did he know what she was planning?

Hiding her nervousness again, she reached her mom's baseball from the back pocket of her Small Folk uniform and turned it over and over in her fingers. The same sense of joy she'd felt earlier watching Sydney and Helen pulsed through it, and instantly she felt better. *I know, Mom. It's time.* Emily glanced back to the pitcher's mound. Its pull was strong. It was time for her to go there, alone, and enact the baseball magic that would open the fairy ring again. Time to sacrifice her baseball talent.

"Are you okay?" Adrien said. "You look a little down."

"I'm great," Emily replied. She pressed her cap down further on her head. "I feel great."

"That's good, because I can't imagine spending a couple hours watching those kids play baseball and not feeling pretty good about life. Besides, the Hunt is under control again. Even if we can't fix the fairy ring right away, that's one huge weight off our chests."

"Yeah," Emily said.

Adrien frowned at her. "There it is again."

"What?"

"I don't know. You look... not sad, really. But something."

She sighed.

"Melancholy!" Adrien blurted. "You're looking melancholy." He took a dramatic pose. "'It is a melancholy of mine own,' or, I guess, your own."

Emily nodded and smiled as warmly as she could. It did make her happy to hear him quoting Shakespeare and indulging his newfound enjoyment of theater. Adrien deserved better from her. He deserved to know. But if she told him what she was going to do, Adrien would do something to "save" her, and the last thing she needed was for him to get tangled up even further with the Fairy Realm. After a century of indentured servitude, he deserved a full life.

Besides, after coaching the kids of the Annie's Diner Giants all morning long, Emily was certain she was doing the right thing.

"I'm fine, Adrien. Really. I am. Just thinking back to when I was their age and how great the game was for me."

"Yeah. It would be nice to be able to just play again."

He shifted the bag.

"You'd best get back to your Aunt and Uncle's place," she said casually, definitely not as if she were giving him a hint. "I'm about ready to turn in, myself. I can watch kids play baseball all day, but Callie fair wore me out."

Adrien chuckled. "Callie can be a bit of a Fairy Realm tornado sometimes, can't she?"

"Says the Unseelie Queen's Designated Hitter."

Adrien feigned a wince. "Well played, Emily DeWitt."

"Besides, you need to check on Sydney and Helen. They might get so caught up arguing about whether Nolan Arenado is a better third baseman than Brooks Robinson was and forget to go home."

"Brooksie all the way," Adrien said. "Arenado is great, but I'm taking it on faith that Robinson had the blood of immortals running through his veins. Did you see that play in the World Series? I could watch that video forever."

Emily nodded sagely. "I see where Sydney gets it."

"All right," Adrien said, finally capitulating. "I can tell you want to be alone, so I'll get out of your way. See you tomorrow."

Emily smiled in a way that she knew still looked melancholy. "Yeah, see you tomorrow," she said, knowing she might be lying. Magic in the Fairy Realm was more than unpredictable. She wasn't sure if the baseball magic would force her through the portal or not when she did her thing.

It was time to find out, though.

Ready for whatever was to come, Emily breathed in the fresh October air.

As Adrien stepped away, a commotion came from up the street. Growling. Yowling.

Emily turned, biting back frustration and worry in equal measures.

A parade of padded and cloven feet charged in unison toward Unicorn Field. At their head was Callie McMasters, riding on Trace's back like a queen leading her army into battle. One hand brandished her bat like it was a pennant. The other held a lead line. A hunched and harried figure stumbled along on foot beside her, struggling to keep up with the pace of the horde as he was pulled along.

"Callie," Emily said under her breath. "And her Hunt. What are they doing here?"

Adrien stopped. "Is that... Mr. McMasters?"

A sense of panic rose in Emily. She was so close. Reluctantly, she shoved her mom's baseball back into her back pocket, feeling a sudden pang of anger and desperation mixing at the sight of her friend parading forward.

"Emily!" Callie called in glee as the Hunt raced forward. "And Adrien, too! Perfect!"

As the Hunt arrived, McMasters was out of breath and red-faced. His hair flew in wild wisps that even the copious product he always used couldn't keep in place.

The large, dark-furred wolf stayed beside Mr. McMasters, keeping him in line.

"The Huntmaster," Adrien said under his breath as he returned to Emily's side. "She managed to tame him after all." His gaze grew a new admiration for Callie McMasters.

Callie dismounted from Trace. "Just the two I need," she said, leaning on her bat, now.

"What do you mean, just the two you need?" Adrien said.

Callie pulled her father's leash and he nearly stumbled headfirst into the asphalt. "I say my dad needs to serve a penalty for what he's done to both Pattersonville and the Fairy Realm. Mayor Culpepper and I had a good long chat about it, and we agreed that the Real World's system is lacking."

"Now it's my turn to ask what you mean," Emily said.

But Adrien laughed, catching on immediately. "A challenge. How sweet."

"I still don't get it," Emily replied.

"Law enforcement is different in the Fairy Realm, Emily," Adrien said. "The rule of the fittest works for the big stuff, but when two parties disagree over more trivial matters, the arguments are often resolved in ways that are, maybe, a little more arbitrary."

"In other words," Callie said. "The ball doesn't lie."

"A challenge," Emily deadpanned, slowly beginning to catch on. "You mean, like, if your dad wins a game he gets off free but if he loses he's got to pay up?"

The sadistic satisfaction in Callie's smile was all Emily needed to see.

It hit her all at once, like a bat upside the head. Her friend— the rival of her entire childhood— was a *Fairy Lord*. Her whole air was more mystical now, complete with her subtly billowing baseball uniform and her downright wolfish grin.

Emily swallowed. "Well, you *are* the Hunt Leader now, aren't you?"

"I am," Callie said, confidence dripping. "And that means I can set the rules. So, everyone listen up." She tugged at the leash again, and when her dad glared up at her through a flopping lock of greasy hair, she smirked. "I say if Dear Old Dad can strike out a Unicorn, he's off free. Otherwise, he gets a hundred years in servitude to the Small Folk, say working as Essie's subordinate mending gloves and tending to the team's practice field. You know, work he's suited to, what with all his experience running the premier sporting goods store in town."

McMasters' glare turned sour, showing how he took that insult. But he was apparently capable of learning, at least when it came to saving his own skin. Not a single word of complaint passed his lips.

Emily chuckled. "Are you sure you want to do that to Essie?"

Callie's grin widened. "She can handle it."

"Maybe."

Mr. McMasters scowled at the conversation, but he was still breathing too hard to make a comment.

"What happens if that doesn't cure him?" Emily said.

Adrien replied. "The usual thing, I assume. If he still hasn't changed, he'll be set free in the wilds of the Fairy Realm to fend for himself."

"That's harsh, isn't it?"

"Fairy Realm justice has its essence. At least he won't be able to hurt anyone."

Callie broke in, staring at Emily. "All I need are a couple of Unicorns, and I can't think of anyone better than the two of you."

"That sounds great, but I'm Small Folk now." Emily lifted the chest of her brown Small Folk jersey, emblazoned with the number eleven.

"Good try," Callie said. "But I've heard someone say that once a Unicorn, always a Unicorn, so I think it will be all right." She gave Emily the unicorn salute.

"I think she has you there," Adrien said to Emily. He, too, had his finger raised from the bill of his cap. A smile tilted across his face.

Emily grumbled. She couldn't see a way out of this. But then, the idea had merit, too. She could kill two birds with one baseball: help Callie dispense well-deserved justice on her slime of a father and pay the toll to open the fairy ring at the same time. If nothing else, doing what Callie wanted might get them out of here quicker.

"All right," she said, raising her hands in surrender.

Callie smiled.

Emily pointed to the equipment bag over Adrien's shoulder. "You think you've got a bat in there I can use?"

He unsheathed a bat. "I believe I do," he said, proffering it handle first over one arm. "Milady?" he said with a courtly bow.

Emily took it, and the warmth of baseball magic tingled in her palm.

"Hunt!" Callie called. "To the field!"

The calls came thick, then. Callie pulled on her father's leash and the man followed her. The sky suddenly darkened with clouds, and a distant thunder rumbled.

The game was afoot.

Baseball magic began to flow.

TWENTY-SIX

Floating in midair, with her toes dangling a few inches above the polished marble floor of the Unseelie Queen's inner sanctum, Megan wriggled once more against her bonds, but the black tendrils of magic that held her refused to budge. She'd lost feeling in her extremities. Her breath came short and rapid. The stink of fresh sweat laced the air under her nose.

Beside her, hovering at the height of Megan's shoulders, Essie gnashed her blunt teeth at the tendrils that held her own tiny body, to no avail.

Struggling only served to make them spin sluggishly one way, then the other, like sitting on the world's most evil computer chair.

The boy the queen had brought with her when she found Megan and Essie poking around in her basement storage closet was bound, too, and also floated alongside them, but he didn't struggle. Instead, he wore the blank expression of someone who'd already experienced a lifetime of horrors and knew it was simply best to disassociate this time around.

"Pssst," Megan hissed at him again, already knowing she wasn't going to get anywhere, but needing to do something other than spin lazily and twiddle her numbed fingers. "Kid! Who are you? I'm Megan Moore, reporter at Pattersonville West High School, and this is Essie," she added with as much of a gesture as she could manage with her chin. "I see you're wearing your baseball uniform. Do you play for one of the teams in the area? Are you one of the ones who disappeared through the fairy ring under Unicorn Field? Do you have a statement you want to make about your experiences in the Fairy Realm?"

She might as well have been babbling gibberish for all the reaction she got.

Maybe there'd been a glimmer of something when she mentioned Pattersonville, but she could have been imagining it.

Desperate minds conjured all sorts of useless details.

On the far side of the room, the Unseelie Queen stood at a long table that was draped with a silken cloth. Light from the fey fire torches that lined the walls rippled off the cloth like moonlight off the surface of a smooth lake. On top of the cloth, the queen had placed three items: a bowl harshly carved from some kind of wood, a long, narrow candle not yet lit, and the strange eight-sided pink plate Megan and Essie had found in the dark basement chamber. Megan still had no idea what the thing was or what it did, but the queen was smiling down upon it as fondly as a mother would look at her child.

It wasn't a good sign.

Unable to stop herself, she wriggled again.

A moment later, she faced the left-hand wall rather than the queen and her toys.

A light titter of laughter slithered across the room, and the tendrils of magic that bound her spasmed. Megan gasped as a sharp pressure forced air from her lungs. Luckily, once she was facing the queen again, the tendrils loosened enough for her to breathe. Unluckily, she'd been dragged much closer to the table, as had Essie and the mystery boy.

"Let's not tarry any longer," said the queen. "I've been patient for a hundred years already. I don't fancy continuing to do so."

Megan couldn't help but ask questions. "What are you planning? What do you know about the kids who've been pulled through the fairy ring over the past hundred years? Did you kidnap them? And what is that weird plate thing?"

The queen smiled like a snake and stroked one long, pale finger along the edge of the pink plate. "This, sweet scribbler, is the Octagon. Merely the first of the spiderkin artifacts to fall directly into my hands, although in truth there is nothing *mere* about it. It's going to help me take over the realms."

Megan scoffed. "Yeah, right. Everyone knew you were up to something when you didn't field a team for the Fall Season. And even though Benji thought they were being sneaky enough about it to keep it from the rest of us, I know they've been keeping an eye on you. It's only a matter of time before you're stopped again."

She narrowed her gaze. *And only a matter of time before I'm getting the story of every one of your too-many-to-count, unsurprising crimes out into the public consciousness,* she added mentally.

The queen appeared unmoved. "At the moment, my dearest Benji is a bit preoccupied with more magic than even a descendant of the spiderkin can withstand. I don't think they're coming to your rescue anytime soon. But don't worry. I intend to broadcast my own story far and wide very soon. And you, my sweet little reporter, are most definitely going to be of great service."

Megan forced herself not to recoil, wondering if the queen had heard her thoughts or if her reputation was simply strong enough that the queen had just gotten lucky. "I won't be your mouthpiece."

"Oh, no," said the queen. "That's not what I meant at all. I meant that you're going to serve as my mortal sacrifice when I perform the ritual to awaken the power of the Octagon to my command. You and the Small Folk thief there. The combination of mortal and fey sacrifice will make a perfect lever. And when we are finished, I *will* control the realms."

She flicked a finger at Essie, who growled around her mouthful of black magic.

The queen picked up the bowl, swirled her hand above it, and continued her monologue. "The boy, of course, is mine. He's the first one I took, even before Adrien Thorn. He slipped away from me, though, soon after I pulled him from your world. But I never *lost* him. I knew he'd fallen into a nexus of ley lines. I simply didn't know which one or how to retrieve him. I made a start at narrowing it down while the Web Gem was in my possession, and Adrien, of course, once I had him, did such a good job of keeping it in my hands that I had time. And while I searched, I was hardly idle. I did pull more mortal players across. Do you want to know where they are, scribbler?"

The queen cast Megan a glimmering smirk.

Megan struggled to keep panic at bay. She'd been in tight spots before. That's what happened to reporters— to good ones, anyway. The ones willing to go the distance for the story. But she was beginning to suspect that there was perhaps a very small chance that this time, she had gone a step too far.

She'd come too far to *not* get answers, though.

Almost unwillingly, she responded to the queen through gritted teeth. "Of course, I want to know."

The queen set her bowl down softly and tapped the Octagon. Her nail's impact gave forth an almost metallic peal.

"Where else? I've got them all safe and sound right here. Seven souls snugly packed up, simply waiting for the missing eighth to join them and awaken the power of the Octagon. For a little while, I considered trying to use Adrien as that eighth, despite his usefulness as my Designated Hitter. But I knew better." The queen let her languid glance fall over the boy. "I knew who the eighth had to be. When Adrien truly did escape me, I thought that was a setback at first, but I know better now."

Megan wracked her brain trying to come up with some kind of

plan for her, Essie, and the boy's escape, but all she managed to accomplish was a splitting headache to go with her numb hands.

The queen picked up the candle and stepped around the table to place one hand against the floating boy's cheek.

"Luckily, I still had you, didn't I, Tommy Mathison? Tucked safely away in the eddies of the ley lines. It was only a matter of time, and only a matter of finding a spiderkin descendant willing— or desperate— enough to do the work I couldn't before I had you back in my collection."

The boy, Tommy, shuddered passively.

The queen smiled another dark smile and took one step back. She snapped her fingers above the candle's wick, and a flame sprang to life with a soft *whoosh*.

A familiar scent filled the air. At first, Megan couldn't place it. Then: popcorn. Ballpark popcorn. It was so unfitting a smell for this dark chamber of evil that she almost laughed. But what was happening to Tommy then killed the sound in her throat.

He began to fade, his body going translucent as the queen waved the flame beneath his nose like a smelling salt. Every inhalation was like loading a weapon. Every exhale sent more of his essence floating into the flame. Already, the fire was burning brighter.

"Stop it!" Megan shouted.

The queen ignored her.

Three breaths later, Tommy fully disappeared.

Tears burned in Megan's eyes, some spilling over to splash onto the tendrils wrapped around her chest.

The candle flame, now flush with Tommy's essence, burned as brightly as a captured star. The queen carried the candle back to the table with one hand cupped protectively around it. Then, lifting the bowl, she tipped the candle so the wax dribbled into it.

Once the bowl was full to the brim, the candle flame went out.

The wax now carried a glow.

The queen swirled one hand above the bowl just as she had done prior to lighting the candle. Then she poured the contents over the flat surface of the Octagon.

Megan held her breath.

There was a horrific slurping sound as the wax sank into the pink surface. Light flashed along the eight sides like a movie house marquee.

The queen let out a genuine cackle of triumph and picked up her prize.

"At last, at last!" Her cheeks flushed with deep satisfaction. "All it needs now is the finishing touch. The final polish. How fortunate that Samhain is upon us. Come, my sweets," she said, beckoning to Megan and Essie as if they would follow her of their own accord. The tendrils, obediently, floated the captives forward. "It is time to return to your precious mortal world."

"You won't get away with this," Megan said, hating the cliché as it nevertheless left her mouth. But it was all she had, and even that was diminishing as she watched the Unseelie Queen bend below her table and reemerge bearing what else but the Web Gem.

Never in her life had Megan felt as hopeless as she did then.

If the queen had the Web Gem, then Benji was truly in trouble. By now Megan knew better than to hope the queen couldn't use the artifact or to assume she even needed it to accomplish her sinister intent.

For the first time in her life, Megan truly felt the fear that came from thinking she might be killed.

She could do it, Megan knew. The queen could kill them all.

She hoped Adrien would forgive her. She slid her gaze over to Essie, floating beside her. "I'm so sorry," she whispered. "I got you all mixed up in this."

Essie returned her tearful look. "I'm sorry, too. I hope my poor Greeven won't be too heartbroken."

Then the Web Gem flared, and everything went white.

TWENTY-SEVEN

Standing with Unicorn Field dirt under her cleats and Pattersonville's swirling autumn chill in her nose, Emily DeWitt knew for sure that this was her last baseball game. Her last time batting. Her last time experiencing the intimacy of a field as only a player can.

Thanks to Callie's ingenuity and sheer willpower, the crisis of the Wild Hunt running free in her home had been averted. But Halloween was only a half hour away now, and the power of Samhain moaned in the night air.

It was Emily's turn to do her part.

Time to open the fairy ring and rescue their friends trapped on the other side.

Coaching the Little League kids had been great. Encouraging, even, given what she meant to give up tonight. But coaching and playing were two different things. It felt good to be in a uniform. Felt good to be on the field. After weeks spent watching from the stands, it felt right to be here with her friends.

She focused on her warmups, playing pepper with Adrien and Callie. Up in the stands, people were huddling under blankets against the late-night cold as they watched the strange proceedings. This wasn't going to be a game so much as a trial, but the people of Pattersonville had answered when Mayor Culpepper had sent out the call for spectators. The town needed to see that Things Were Under Control here, she'd said. She'd even volunteered to serve as umpire for this little shindig.

From the size of the gathered crowd, Emily could tell her fellow townsfolk were as bloodthirsty as any fairy when it came to seeking justice.

On the field, Mr. McMasters finished his warmups. He looked awkward toeing the pitching rubber in the glare of the field lights. His work slacks were wrinkled, and his silky jacket seemed to bind him up as he pressed the ball into his glove. The Samhain wind swirled leaves around Unicorn Field and blew his thinning hair into strange little spikes. The windup for his first warmup pitch had been all herky and even more jerky. The ball spun off his fingertips in a big looping path that bounced before it got to home plate.

The people in the stands laughed. Pyrgin and his satyrs yipped as Thacker flung his squat little Red Cap body after the errant ball.

But after his first few comical warmups, it looked like Callie's father could actually pitch.

In retrospect, that made sense. Callie's athleticism had to come from somewhere, and Emily knew Fred McMasters had played as a boy. The Seelie blood he carried meant he would have been smooth and athletic at some point, even if those years were quite a distance in the past.

As Emily recalled, he had been good enough to arouse scouting interest.

Regardless, McMasters had taken off his Ball and Glove jacket now, and he'd loosened his collar even further. His baseball cleats looked goofy under the dress slacks, but he'd figured out the right spots for his feet to land as he pitched. His curve had a solid break. His fastball was as good or better than the average high school pitcher. She and Adrien would have to be careful. It was possible they could strike out. If that happened, McMasters would go home free.

On the sideline beside the home team dugout, Emily felt the stares from the Unicorn fans. They seemed tentative toward her, uncertain of how to feel about their star player wearing her Small Folk uniform with its stitched #11 on it.

It was okay. She understood. It didn't settle fully though until she saw Dad and Elaine arrive. There was something sad in the way he watched her warmups, sitting there in the bleachers with his White Sox cap perched up high on his forehead. It was as if he, of all the people at the ballpark that night, understood exactly what she was doing. Elaine pressed close beside him as if body heat would make things better.

Emily curled a half smile and nodded as her mom's baseball sent a comforting wave through her.

"Let's do this," she said, feeling suddenly spritely as she tossed her mom's baseball to Adrien, who used his magic glove to scoop it to Callie, who, whispering to her bat the whole time, popped a gentle liner back to Emily.

The glow of it was like a hug inside Emily's mind.

Her feeling was right. It *was* time.

Gripping a bat from Adrien's equipment bag focused her thoughts. She swung it twice, letting its heft and momentum loosen the last of her tension.

As McMasters finished his last warmup, Callie raced up and down the sidelines in full Leader of the Hunt bluster, waving her bat full of fairy magic like it was a scepter and exhorting her Hunt host to play their best. "No lollygagging out there, my team! I want a fair challenge. No mercy to my father for what he's done! And the rest of the Fairy Realm gets no appeal if he goes free! Have fun, my legions! Play your best!"

The team on the field clamored and howled even harder.

In center field, the pacing lupine figure of the ex-leader roamed, ready to run. At third base, Trace took his stance. Thacker squatted behind home plate, his gloveless hands raised in readiness.

On the mound, McMaster set his jaw and dialed in his gaze.

"Play ball!" Mayor Culpepper called, pressing her Unicorn cap further onto her head.

Emily watched as Adrien stepped to the plate, "leading off."

The deal was simple. McMasters would pitch to Adrien first, then Emily. If either struck out, McMasters was free. Emily knew from personal experience how hard it would be to strike the Unseelie Queen's Designated Hitter out. And, indeed, after two pitches wide of the plate, when Fred McMasters tried to get a fastball past Adrien, the booming crack of his bat against the ball shattered the air, and the ball rose high into the sky out to direct center field. The park didn't hold it, and Adrien rounded the bases for his ceremonial celebration.

Baseball magic crackled over the field. Emily tasted ozone.

"Your turn, Em," he said as he crossed the plate. "Send it out of here." He gave her a high-five as he walked to the dugout to watch.

The intensity of the moment came over her. She gripped her bat, letting her fingers tighten over the handle and then grow loose.

The magic was drifting towards her now, attracted to the price she was offering up.

"I let him hit it because I wanted to face you," McMasters taunted her from the mound.

"Good luck with that," Emily called back.

If Fred McMasters thought he could intimidate her, he had another thing coming.

She stepped to the plate, feeling more centered than she'd ever felt before. *Bring it on, asshole,* her thoughts came. *You're going down.* The bat felt perfect in her grip. She held the label up and saw it had the Jackson's Sporting Goods logo burnt into it. *Pattersonville's Finest Bats* arcing in the space below it.

Seeing the city's name gave her even more energy, and when she looked at her father in the stands, everything came together.

She thought suddenly of Benji, and their constant refrain on how this town deserved to know about its connection to the magic of the Fairy Realm. For the first time, she truly felt that sentiment within herself. This was what she was giving herself up for, not just saving her friends. And it was worth it.

She dug into the batter's box, feeling the grit of the dirt as if it was part of her body.

She dried a hand off on her thigh, then extended the bat barrel to tap the far corner of home plate. A lazy practice swing later, she looked up.

"Bring it on," she said to McMasters.

Callie's father went into his windup, and Emily prepared. It would be a curve. She knew it would be. McMasters knew she was a dead fastball hitter. He wouldn't bring heat until later in the count. But there would be no later. She was sure of that. She was going to hit this pitch out of the park, and when she did, the rift would come. The ring would open, and both she and McMasters would be transported.

McMasters reared back.

The ball whipped out of his hand.

By the spin, Emily knew she was right. Curveball. Big and fat. Hanging there.

She went into her swing, feeling the bat arcing so beautifully she could hear the tone of her mother's voice from back when Emily was a little girl, explaining the poetry of the game. No one loved baseball like Emily's mother had. Now she felt that joy filling her.

Her baseball talent welled up. The feel of a swinging bat gave her the deepest solace she'd ever felt. The baseball magic rushed towards her faster than the pitch, coming to claim its prize and do her bidding in return.

Suddenly, with a pull that felt like her heart being ripped out, the baseball magic wrenched away from her, leaving her gasping for breath, and her talent untouched. From the deepest part of left field, a bolt of fiery lightning split the air, and the crashing of thunder came so loud it might break eardrums.

Players, McMasters included, ducked and stumbled as they crashed to the ground.

Fans screamed and covered their ears.

Emily's connection to the ball shattered. Her swing crumbled, and the ball sailed past, but both Thacker and the mayor behind the plate had fallen over backward due to the shock wave. Her unbroken momentum tumbled her to the ground and into a cloud of dust that swirled with little wind devils before fading into the ozone-thick air.

What? she thought, her mind going numb with despair.

This was her time. Her moment. What had gone wrong?

But she knew the truth even before she managed to lift herself from the ground. It was in the magic that coiled over the field now. Oppressive and bitter. She'd felt it before.

The Unseelie Queen.

She and a baseball team's worth of her court members rode as a grand procession, in from the outfield. Their massive mounts snorted and frothed as they trampled Adrien's fine groundskeeping. The beasts were Hellhounds, Emily saw. Terrifying black dogs built from the darkest of all magics. The beast the queen sat astride was the largest of them all, its eyes burning with a malicious green fire and poisonous strings of saliva dripping from its exposed fangs.

The queen cast her authoritative regard over the field, the Hunt, and then the spectators. Her black-painted lips curled up in a wicked smile.

Emily's heart froze when she noticed the limp form draped over the nightmare dog's neck before the queen.

The reporter was magically bound before the Unseelie Queen's saddle, trussed with shifting black tendrils. She wasn't alone, either. A tiny lump wriggled within another bundle of the queen's binding tendrils, and Emily recognized the muffled shrieking as belonging to Essie.

"Megan!" Adrien screamed, racing from the dugout.

Swallowing against anger, Emily grabbed for Adrien, holding him back from doing anything stupid.

"How did she make it through the ring?" she asked.

Adrien's angry gaze snapped to her, then he shook his head. "She didn't. At least not on her own. But it's midnight, Emily. Halloween. Samhain. The veil between the worlds is thinnest right now for those powerful enough to tear a way through. And she had a boost." Adrien pointed with his gloved hand.

Emily looked, and to her dismay saw the telltale crystal glint of the Web Gem tucked against the queen's saddle with a loop of belt.

But it wasn't the only tool the queen had on display. As Emily watched, the queen raised one hand to display a radiating, eight-sided artifact over her head. Emily had held part of the Web Gem for long enough that she didn't need a road map to tell that whatever this new thing was, it held power beyond her ability to imagine.

Blue and red threads of electricity crackled over its pale pink surface.

"Come forward, my Unseelie court!" the queen called, her tone haughty and disturbing as she met Emily's stare with a cruel twist of her lips. "It is time for this world to see what true power looks like!"

Power flared from the thing she held, and the ground surged under Emily's feet. Silvery light erupted from cracks in the dirt to reach like beacons up to the black night sky. Emily raised her arm to shield her eyes from the blinding brightness.

Then the light seemed to coalesce into a single point right under the pitcher's mound.

Fred McMasters stumbled off it in a hurry.

The queen turned the eight-sided thing, and the light flared again. A beam of silver shot up from the pitcher's mound, and a roar like a raging river filled the air as the beam grew into a torrent of glowing power running underground.

A newly revealed river of magic flowed from Unicorn Field down Main Street.

Adrien let out a gasp of wonder and terror. He was gripping

Emily tightly, and she suddenly realized that he had been doing so ever since the first eruption. "A ley line," he said. "Running right under Unicorn Field this whole time!"

Emily didn't know as much about the Fairy Realm as Adrien did, but she had heard of the lines of power that were said to crisscross the Realm. The idea that the Unseelie Queen had an artifact that gave her control of one right here in Pattersonville, *right under Unicorn Field*, made Emily want to scream.

The queen, as if reading their thoughts, smirked and turned her procession to cross the field and parade alongside the silvery flow, Hellhounds leaping and racing with great strides.

"Stop her!" Adrien called.

But Callie the Huntmistress was already on the task. She stood forward, bat glowing with Fairy Realm magic, baseball uniform billowing wildly about her as she worked her spell. A bolt of pure baseball magic sizzled across the distance between Callie and the queen, aimed directly between the queen's shoulder blades.

The queen, without even glancing over her shoulder, casually snapped her fingers, and the bolt fizzled out, melting into the silvery flow of the ley line. Callie's bat burned with too much power, and the bat flung itself from its mistress's grip, leaving Callie crying out in dismay.

"Ha!" the queen called to her cohort. "Look how far the lowly Hunt has fallen! You see now how easy this will be."

The queen gathered herself and turned back toward the fence running down the foul line. "To the terminus, my pets! And the power that awaits our ritual there!"

Her Hellhound mount reached the edge of Unicorn Field and, upon stepping onto Main Street, the Samhain procession was underway in earnest. Emily could guarantee Pattersonville had never had a Halloween parade so horrific in its entire history.

Adrien dashed forward, pulling his magic glove from where it hung on his belt loop. "Come on! We have to stop her."

Callie let out a growl that rivaled her predecessor. She clutched at her hands where her bat had rubbed them raw. "My father is getting away."

Emily glanced back at the pitcher's mound.

Sure enough, McMasters was gone.

She picked out his shadowy form scurrying away beyond the dugouts.

Adrien whirled on Callie. "There's no time for him now! Whatever the queen is trying to do, she's going to sacrifice Megan and that little brownie in order to do it!"

Emily tore her gaze away from McMasters' fleeing figure. She realized her mom's ball was already in her hand, her fingers already perfectly placed to pitch a fastball. Baseball magic swelled around it, mingling with the baseball talent that, despite her efforts to sacrifice, she still yet possessed.

She met Adrien's eye and nodded. "We'll stop her, Adrien. No matter what it takes."

Callie came to join them. Her bat was once again in her hand, resting against her shoulder. Her Wild Hunt thronged behind her in building anticipation of a chase.

But for half a moment, Callie did not give the order to run. She stood with her eyes closed, swaying slightly. Her nostrils flared in hungry anticipation.

When she opened her eyes again, they glowed gold like a wolf's.

"I know where the ley line goes," she said, determination deepening her voice. Then she laughed.

"You do?" Emily said.

"Of course I do," Callie said. She laughed again in a tone that was almost a bark. Her lips drew back to reveal teeth that flashed white in the Samhain moon. "Where else but the good old Ball and Glove? Come, my friends. Let us run the chase. I know a shortcut."

CHAPTER

TWENTY-EIGHT

Benji fought to hold their breath as the molten flow of the ley line surged with silver flares. The strange globe of twigs and branches had completely rewoven itself about their body. They were caught, mired in a whirling eddy of raw magic, just as that young baseball player had been until Benji had stupidly, stupidly done what the Unseelie Queen had asked and opened the trap.

Now the queen had walked away with the prize, and Benji had taken that player's place.

A part of Benji wondered who the boy had been, and why the queen had so obviously wanted him.

But Benji burned with the magic in the trap, and they didn't have the energy to waste trying to puzzle that one out. Instead, they were too busy panicking as the roaring river of magic battered them against the sides of their cage and as the fire threatened to char their skin, flesh, and bones to ash.

Their lungs screamed for air that did not exist.

In another moment, they would have to take a breath. Then everything would be over.

Regrets? Plenty. But everything was too late.

Unable to hold off any longer, they opened their mouth and gasped as flames consumed them.

Miraculously, horribly, that was not the end.

Benji continued to exist as a writhing lump of agony and shame. But now the ley line was inside, sending silver-hot feelers coursing through Benji's body, scouring them. Burning them. Searching for the pool of inner power it sensed within them.

Benji jerked reflexively against that probing. They tried to curl up around themself, to protect that innermost essence of their being from being washed away in the raging flow. Compared to such surging power, Benji was insignificant. A mere drop or two of water in a frothing white rapids. The attempt at survival was purely instinctual. Benji wished it would stop, though. Wished they could give up instead, hating themself enough that they ought to be seeking the oblivion of burning up and washing away.

How full of themself they'd been.

How arrogant, to assume they could read the Unseelie Queen's impeccable acting as true recalcitrance. But perfect stagecraft or not, she was still the Unseelie Queen, and only an utter idiot would ever believe a word she said. Only a cocksure ass would apprentice themself to her.

A part of Benji's instinctual drive nudged them to reach out for the Web Gem.

They'd gotten so used to having it at hand they almost tried it. But the Web Gem was far away now, back with the Unseelie Queen to whom Benji had practically handed it on a silver platter.

She'd turned it down so many times. Clever. She must have been biting down on her laughter so hard this whole time. It was a wonder her lips weren't a ragged, tattered mess.

Did the Octagon even exist? Or was it a figment of her imagination, a pretty lure to draw a faltering spiderkin descendant to her side?

Benji didn't know.

They were alone in a burning river of magic, and probably, given the way they'd found that boy here, would remain here, so alone, until the Unseelie Queen could dupe another sucker into pulling Benji out. Whenever that would be.

Benji wished they'd said goodbye to their parents.

They would worry. They would wonder. And it seemed they were doomed now to never know what had become of their child. Benji would be another statistic. Gone from the face of the mortal realm, never to be recovered.

Another stinging silver needle of the ley line tried to squirm its way inside Benji. They thrust it away with a harsh twist of ashen hands.

"Why do you not let it weave your silk into its flow?" a small voice said.

Benji started.

A spider dangled steadily in the twined globe with Benji, riding the silver flame-waves with her eight legs splayed over the surface to keep herself in place, her multifaceted eyes flashing prismatic sheens. The spider was not large or monstrous like the creature that had served as the Seelie King's umpire in the fateful game last spring. She was simply a spider of proper size and proportion, with a soft gray coloring. Little tufts of white at her feet gave her a bit of a balle-rina's presence.

She'd been there for some time, Benji realized. Or maybe she'd also only just arrived, appearing out of thin air— very thin here in the depths of the coursing magic— a split second before she'd spoken. Or maybe it was a split second after.

Still startled, Benji lost their concentration and let the buffeting river bash them against the woven cage.

Anger bubbled again once they'd righted themself.

"Help me!" Benji shouted. "I'm trying not to get washed away!"

They pushed another probing bit of silver out of their space. How much longer could they keep this up? What state would the Unseelie Queen find them in whenever she decided they would be useful to her again?

The spider, unhelpfully, tipped her body to first one side and then the other and blinked all eight of her eyes at them. She watched Benji tumble about inside the cage for a while.

Then, she said, "I simply don't understand. Is it that you *don't* wish to know all the worlds?"

She sounded prim, like the matronly lady who worked at the Pattersonville library and who thought every child should have a natural interest in reading about actuarial tables.

Benji paused in their latest attempt to keep the ley line out. They looked at the spider.

"What?"

"Because, as every spider should know," she said, her voice turned lecturing, "one cannot utilize the web of ley lines without providing one's own bit of silk. It's a joint effort, you know."

Benji let themself lay pressed against the cage where the flow held them pinned. Their chest heaved despite the fact there was no air to breathe. They met the spider's eyes and shook their head to clear it.

"I'm not trying to utilize it. I'm— I'm trapped here. I need to get out. Can you help me?"

"Oh, dear," tutted the spider. "I'm dreadfully sorry to hear that. I'm not sure how such a thing could have happened."

She looked at Benji like she was trying to decide how a child had gotten the square peg stuck in the round hole after all. *This shouldn't even be possible*, her many-eyed body tilt said. *How embarrassing, though I can't decide if it's for you or for me.*

An answering swell of humiliation rose in Benji at that perusal. If they could, they would have shuffled their feet and looked at the ground to avoid it.

"The Unseelie Queen tricked me," they admitted. Bitterness flooded their mouth, just as silvery magic tried to flood their essence.

The spider waved her front two legs. "Oh, *her*. Well, she does get the best of many. Bound to happen with one who's always spinning her next scheme. There's no shame in it." *I would never fall for such a trick, though*, said the quiver of the spider's pedipalps. She made a sound like she was clearing her throat. "But, just so I know what her latest trick is, do tell me what it was?"

Gossip-monger, Benji thought.

But they had no reason not to tell the whole of it at this point.

"She told me she was searching for the lost spiderkin artifacts, and that she needed my help. She said she wanted to return them to their rightful owners as a way to atone for her past transgressions."

The spider let out such an unladylike laugh that Benji gaped. She stifled the sound with a soft murmuring a moment later but swiped one front leg at her eyes as if wiping away a tear of mirth. "I do apologize, but, oh, dear, how *funny!* The spiderkin artifacts aren't lost. They can't be. I mean, does a spider not always have access to her own silk?"

Benji, feeling rather fed up with her know-it-all tone, pushed another rush of silver away. "I suppose so, but what with the clamor over who gets the Web Gem, it seemed like a reasonable thing when she told me her plan. But now I see it was all a string of lies. There is no such thing as the Octagon, is there?"

"Oh, there is. She's had the care of part of it for far longer than anyone has had any of our toys. And..." The spider went still, and her eyes took on the far-off look of someone lost in thought. "Yes, she still has it."

Benji frowned.

Of course, the Unseelie Queen had had the thing they were searching for in her possession the entire time. Of course, she did.

But, "How can you know that? That she has it right now?"

The spider peered closely at Benji, and when she next spoke, her tone was the slow, deliberate cadence of someone trying to drill a very simple concept into an imbecile's head.

"Because my silk is in the ley lines, and I always have access to my silk. Really, it would behoove you to pay better attention."

Benji nearly scoffed at the further riddling.

Then understanding burst over them like a wave of cool water in the midst of the river of silver fire.

"This power inside me is my spider silk?"

The spider's silence felt like a confirmation.

"The Unseelie Queen told me I would lose myself if I used it directly. Another lie."

"No, that was probably not so much a lie as a mistake. The Unseelie Queen is not above overestimating her own intelligence. I think that bit of misinformation was probably a genuine lack of knowledge on her part. Unseelie magic is so different from the elegant work we do. So transactional." The spider waved a front leg in a *how gauche* gesture. "How could she possibly understand how the warp and weft of spider magic never ceases?"

"So, you're saying if I let this torrent in, my essence won't wash away? I'll just... be tied into the flow?"

"That's simplifying things a great deal, but yes. Oh, but, if you weren't interested in knowing all the worlds and only wished to leave this little trap, you needn't do it, not if you didn't want." Again, her tone implied that Benji would be a fool indeed to pass up such an opportunity.

"I don't? Then how do I get out otherwise?"

"You *are* the mortal world cousin who was granted stewardship of the Web Gem, aren't you?"

Benji wasn't sure how to feel about the question. "Oh! Well, yes, I am. But the queen took the Web Gem when she trapped me in here, and—"

The spider made an exasperated sound, and all four of her front legs rose such that she almost lost her balance amid the flow. She recovered gracefully enough, though, even as she rolled her eyes and twisted her body as if shaking her head.

"I simply must track Grissa down and give her a piece of my mind. She made such a muck of the whole thing if she didn't even take the time to explain the fundamentals to you when she bestowed the stewardship. Too caught up in enjoying her baseball, most likely. Listen, child."

Benji's head was whirling already, hearing this tiny creature speak about the monstrous spider lady who had umpired the spring game like she was a toddler to be disciplined. But they forced themself to set that aside and pay attention.

A true teacher was finally giving them a lesson.

By the time it was over, Benji had a new understanding, not simply of themself, but of the universe. More significantly, they knew their place in it. A sublime awe filled them.

Determination burned as hot as the fury of the ley line.

Benji had been using the Web Gem all wrong all along. Everyone had, in truth. But only Benji had the capability to do it properly, to tap into the spider magic of the artifact, except they hadn't known.

But now they did know.

The Web Gem didn't open portals; it *was* a portal.

And the Octagon... Benji knew its truth now, too.

The spider sat back, satisfaction rolling off her. "Will you add your silk to the ley line and see the worlds?"

"Later, for sure," Benji said, dipping into their spooled silk. "But I have something to take care of first."

Then Benji reached for the Web Gem as easily as if it were right beside them. Easy, because their silk was in it, and had been since the moment the umpire lady had given the artifact into their keeping.

And they always had access to their silk.

Benji felt self-confidence grow within them, sharp as a fresh blade forged in the fires of their new determination.

Now, the Unseelie Queen was going to get what was coming to her.

TWENTY-NINE

Victory still tasted so sweet, even after a century of relishing its flavor.

The Unseelie Queen let her laughter flow as she promenaded down Pattersonville's Main Street, the ley line she had leashed to her command rushing along beside her. With its power splashing everywhere, the mortal world air did not smell so stale as it had during her previous visit. She breathed deeply, letting the spice of magic fill her lungs. Then she laughed again for the sheer joy of it.

She stroked her Hellhound mount, telling him what a bad boy he was and how proud she was of the work he was doing. He shivered at her praise and marched onward.

She flung bolts of pure dark magic into the screaming Samhain night, striking her enemies or not. She didn't care much what happened to them now.

Nothing they could do could stop her.

The Octagon was nearly complete. The eight mortal souls she'd spent the past hundred years pulling from the baseball fields in this world were now finally contained within the plate, and all that remained was the proper sacrifice.

As if sensing her thoughts, the bundle that lay slung over the saddle before her twitched.

Megan Moore— implacable human reporter— had tenacity, the Unseelie Queen had to give her that.

"What's your endgame, here?" the girl said, just as sharp as if she were conducting an interview rather than being held prisoner in readiness to have her blood spilled in an ancient ritual.

The Unseelie Queen frowned and squeezed her hand into a fist. The black tendrils slithered around her captive and covered the girl's mouth once more. Annoying, that she kept finding ways to wriggle out of that gag and pepper the queen with her incessant questions.

Out of an abundance of caution, the queen turned her attention to the much smaller bundle. This one had already proven herself irritatingly resourceful in thwarting her Unseelie Court's work, and it was better to ensure the little brownie was well in hand than to discover the inconvenient way that her second prisoner had escaped.

But the brownie was safely contained, scowling out from between the tendrils like a fierce little shrew, and the queen threw her head back and laughed up at the Samhain moon.

The Wild Hunt had done a lovely job of priming this place for her. The fool mortals screamed their heads off as she and her procession approached, and many ran off into the night as if that would save them from her cruel touch. Imbeciles. Poor little idiots. They had no idea how far she would be able to reach once the Octagon was fully awakened. They'd all fall under her command, no matter how far they ran.

And it wouldn't be long now. The terminus of the ley line was close. She could feel it throbbing through the ground, the trees, the unwieldy buildings these mortals made, and the very air itself. She felt it quivering in her own deep-flowing blood.

There. Right at the crossroads.

On the corner past the metal poles with the heavy, yellow-encased tri-color lights dangling from them.

The rush of the ley line's power expanded and swirled into a maelstrom that whipped and tossed magical mist before sinking down, down, down into the earth. Beyond that spinning whirlpool stood another of the ugly little mortal buildings, made of its sturdy brick and its delightfully fragile glass, helpfully labeled with a gaudy sign.

The Ball and Glove.

But the Unseelie Queen was not the first to arrive.

"Adrien!" the reporter shouted.

The queen flicked a furious glance at the once-again loosened tendrils of the reporter's gag and squeezed her fist once more. Her way to the stone steps that led up into the shop and that would serve as her sacrificial altar was blocked. Her own Designated Hitter was indeed standing there, feet apart and magic glove on his hand, and he wasn't alone.

"It will go better for you if you return to your Unseelie Court on your own, won't it?" said the constant irritant known as Miss Em, her tone even more insulting than the fact that she dared to speak so while wearing the uniform of the insignificant Small Folk. Miss Em tossed her charmed pure white baseball to herself with a steady focus. "Before we make you, that is."

"My Red Caps would love a chance to shred you to tiny pieces," said the Mistress of the Hunt from her place astride her glowering Centaur mount. Her enchanted bat glowed green and purple in her hand. "They've never tasted royal flesh before."

Baseball magic crackled around all three, discernible even over the roaring of the ley line.

"How quaint," said the queen with a sneer as she saw the truth of Callie's position. "A mortal who thinks they can take the seat of a Fairy Lord. And so clever of you to get here before me. But it will do you no good."

She lifted the Octagon so that its radiant sides cast their red and blue light over the terminus. Though it was not yet fully awakened, the artifact could already do some delightful tricks.

The reporter tried to shout a muffled warning, but the tendrils held this time.

Still, when the Octagon threw out a bolt of blue lightning to crack upon the stone steps, her Designated Hitter managed to leap forward, glove outstretched, to catch it. He tumbled and rolled with his stretch before bouncing up to stand upright again, holding the glove out as if to show his prize to a nonexistent umpire. He struggled against the power for a moment, though, obviously trying to rework the magic into something he could use.

"Tsk tsk," the queen said, shaking her head and feeling the joy of haughty sadness. "You never could learn to leave things well enough alone, could you? You should have stuck to what you were good for."

With a turn of the Octagon, the Unseelie Queen made the magic grow hotter and hotter again until the threads that held the glove together grew scorched and the leather cracked. With a shout, the Designated Hitter dropped the magic and shook his now gloveless hand. A look of rage covered his face.

"Oh, hell no," said the Huntmistress. Undirected, her Centaur lackey gathered himself and leapt over the whirlpool in a graceful arc full of fierceness. When he landed, sparks flew from his hooves, and the Huntmistress swung her bat straight for the Unseelie Queen's head. Magic flared along its length.

But another turn of the Octagon held the queen's attackers in place, utterly frozen.

Only their eyes moved, wide and white as they filled with growing fear.

Slowly, crystals of ice formed and spread over them, turning them into lovely, glassy sculptures. As the ice reached the bat, the magic in it flickered and died along with the wood.

The Unseelie Queen cackled as her spell work subsided.

The artistry in the sculpture was perfect. A captured Fairy Lord and her trusty steed. Perhaps she would have it moved into her throne room, once all this was over.

A pale white blur shot across the whirlpool, then, and the sharp crack of ice shattering rang out as her spell fell apart, leaving the Huntmistress and her mount to crumple to the ground, shivering but annoyingly alive.

The Unseelie Queen swung to look at the steps.

Miss Em stood there, her ball back in her hands and a look of smug satisfaction on her ugly little face as the Huntmistress and her little pet crawled away, dragging the deadened length of wood with them.

"Still got my skills," Miss Em said, raising a know-it-all eyebrow. Then she shifted her stance and placed her fingers against the stitching for a fastball. "I told you to leave before we made you."

The queen smirked.

This moment, this rematch between herself and the upstart Miss Em, had been a long time coming.

"Go on, then," she said. "Make me leave."

Miss Em narrowed her eyes, and with a whiplike movement, she pitched.

At the same time, the queen lifted the Octagon higher. Another bolt of lightning, red this time, shot towards Miss Em.

Miss Em dodged. As she twisted away from the sizzling beam, she performed magic with her fingers and wrist.

Screwball, the Unseelie Queen thought, surprised.

None of her reports said Miss Em threw such a pitch, but the disgusting little ball spun backwards, arcing for the Unseelie Queen's nose. Baseball magic spun in sparks off the pitch, and Miss Em wore a look of confidence as her missile approached.

The Unseelie Queen turned the Octagon a third time, though, and the ball halted in midair. It spun there for a moment, its momentum winding down. No ice crawled along its surface, nor did any flames erupt from within its compact sphere. It just sat there, slowly coming to rest.

With a quirk of her lips, the queen made it explode.

Fragments of fluff, shreds of red thread, and charred bits of leather floated down into the swirling flow of the ley line and disappeared.

Miss Em's choking sounds of dismay tasted almost as sweet as victory itself.

Her sacrifice thrashed against her bonds then, but the queen ignored her futile attempts in favor of savoring the way her enemies fell to their common weakness: friendship and caring. Instead of regrouping or pressing the attack, her former Designated Hitter and the Huntmistress ran instead to Miss Em's side.

Then again, attacking her without the aid of their talismans would be akin to suicide.

"Your toys are nothing to the power of a spiderkin artifact," the queen said. She watched as her three enemies huddled together. Then she shook herself out of her moment of gloating. She had work to do.

Her Hellhound started forward again. Its hard claws gave eerie clatters on the flagstone pathway. With a few steps, she arrived.

The queen savored the power of the ley line maelstrom as it swelled from, to, and around this place. As she drew near, the wild aroma of raw existence grew sharp and bold. The Ball and Glove was a massive terminus, she realized. A gathering point for many ley lines, a return that collected up and recycled all magics, including the baseball magic. No wonder even someone as inept as the Seelie King had once been able to hide the Web Gem here.

Her heart pounded in joy as the maelstrom unleashed pure magic to tumble like a crystalline waterfall down the stone steps.

It was all hers.

All she had to do was spill a little blood, and nobody would be able to challenge her again. Everyone would march in lockstep, an entire community brought together to enact her purposes.

With a wave of her hand, the Unseelie Queen's magic tendrils lifted Megan Moore and the knot that was the brownie from her Hellhound and placed them on the steps alongside the rushing streams of ley line magic. She, too, dismounted, letting her midnight-colored skirts swirl about her in a moment of dramatic display. Then she placed the Octagon at the very bottom step, where blood and power could run down over it.

The reporter had finally stopped wriggling, too frozen with fear to do more than stare wildly through the tendrils. The queen loved that moment dearly, the exact instant when her victims understood just how much power the queen held over them. The reporter had just witnessed her only hope of rescue falling one by one to the might of Unseelie power and the Octagon. Her fear was ripe and juicy.

The Unseelie Queen brought out her silver knife.

"This is a momentous occasion," she said as she knelt beside her sacrifice. "You should be honored to play such an integral role. Know that this sacrifice I make costs me dear. Your skills could be turned to wonderful, wicked purpose under my command. But instead, I give you up."

She raised the knife.

Above her head, the edge of the blade caught the entwined lights of the ley line and Samhain moon.

Her fist tightened around the knife's handle.

Megan Moore let out a whimper.

The shining blade arced downwards.

But a sharp pain blossomed in the queen's ankle, then. She flinched and cried out, drawing a breath deep with anguish.

The knife clattered against the bare stone.

"What?" she growled, twisting to touch the place that throbbed.

The brownie stood there, wiping blood from her tiny chin and glaring in defiance up at the Unseelie Queen.

"Tell your Red Caps that royal flesh tastes terrible," she said to Callie in a voice far louder than her diminutive size should support. She turned her head and spit something red and lumpy onto the steps.

"How dare you," the queen said. Fury burned through her. Her flesh, her own perfect body, desecrated by such *vermin*. And at this pivotal moment.

With lightning speed, she caught the brownie up in her hands and squeezed and squeezed. She would make this interloper wish that all her queen had done was sacrifice her upon this altar. When the ritual was finished and the power of the Octagon was completely under her command, the Unseelie Queen would—

"Blood has been spilled, and baseball magic has joined with the terminus. As the representative of the masters of the ley lines, I accept this sacrifice."

Confusion and an unknown terror fell over the Unseelie Queen. She released the brownie, who skittered toward Megan. The voice had come from where her Hellhound stood at the ready. Now, the beast was twitching nervously as something emerged from its side, where the Web Gem hung safely in its belt loop.

Legs. Huge and long, gray and spindly, incorporeally ghostly. They waved as they sprouted from the crystal of the Web Gem, growing longer and longer, feeling their way up and out into the mortal world. But they carried not a bulbous arachnid body at their connection point, but a thin human shape instead.

Benji Amberman, descendant of the spiderkin.

Their baseball uniform shimmered with gossamer silk in the moonlight, but instead of a ballcap, a diadem of six enormous sapphires encircled their head, each gem twinkling like another eye.

Their ghostly spider legs, angled like wings from a pixie's back, worked together as Benji stepped delicately to the pavement of the crossroads, their body held aloft to look down upon the Unseelie Queen. All of their eyes, both the human ones and the six spider gems lining their temples, shone with disappointment.

From the opposite side of the whirlpool, the queen's enemies shouted in horrible jubilation.

"Benji! Benji, oh my god, look at you!"

"You're all right!"

"Get her, Benji!"

Desperation welled in her. The flow of ley line magic gave a crackle of panicked futility. In response, she made herself as hard as possible. She was the Unseelie Queen. She was on the cusp of ultimate victory. She need not cower before anyone, no matter how much their friends cheered for their untimely arrival.

"Benji, my most excellent student. You managed to extricate yourself from the ley line. I told you you would."

But Benji shook their head and held one hand out, palm up in expectation. "The Octagon, if you would."

The Unseelie Queen laughed. "Now, my child? Be patient a moment, and I will finish the ritual. Then we may see what gloriously horrific wonders we can work together."

For some moments, Benji did not react beyond the quirk of one eyebrow. Then they took one giant step with their impossibly long spider legs and scooped up the Octagon.

The queen made a noise of outrage, but Benji ignored it. "The ritual is already complete, Your Majesty. I accepted the sacrifice of blood and baseball magic, and in doing so I have awakened the Octagon— the true Octagon— in the name of those who made the sacrifice. Emily, Adrien, Callie. And most importantly, Essie. I invite you all to come take what's yours."

Then, holding the plate of the Octagon out over the whirlpool of magic, Benji tapped one finger right in the center.

A flare of light blinded the queen. When she blinked her vision clear, she gasped.

"No. No, you fool! You'll ruin everything!"

But it was too late. All her hard work had been undone in an instant.

The souls— all eight of the players she'd gathered from this plane of existence and painstakingly fed into the Octagon— had emerged. Like specters they stood upon the curb of the sidewalk, their various baseball uniforms flowing in an unfelt breeze. Ethereal lights as bright as candle flames bobbed from within each one, right where their hearts would be. Their hatred of her and their anger borne of their long imprisonment rippled outward in a tangible wave that left the queen feeling like she'd been kicked in the chest.

Behind her, a breathless voice spoke rapidly. "That's them! The eight missing kids!" Megan Moore— implacable reporter— was free of her bindings and, instead of running away like a smart little girl, she pulled out her ridiculous pocket rectangle and began dictating. "*The incredible sight of their long-awaited emergence carried an unforgettable sense of absolute triumph.*"

Benji gave a beatific smile. "Everyone, I present to you the Wills-o'-the-Wisps, the eighth and final team of the Fairy League Fall Season. Now, at last, the season can come to its final series."

The entire gathering, including the host of the Hunt, gasped.

"Oh," Benji said, turning to look upon the queen again.

She couldn't help recoiling.

"The Unseelie Court will be fielding a team, of course, Your Majesty."

"Absolutely not. I refuse to be part of this sham, this utter usurpation, this—"

"I'm afraid you haven't got any choice, though. Not even the Unseelie Queen is free from the power of the true Octagon, and the Web Gem, in the hands of a spiderkin descendant. I'm bringing my community together to common purpose: defeating you. Hence, Your Majesty, you will field a team."

And, as Benji pointed one spindly spider leg at her, the Unseelie Queen fell into a dead faint. Better that than to feel the moment the power bound her to a mere child's will.

CHAPTER

THIRTY

Behind the plate, Nash, the Small Folk's gnome catcher, flashed two fingers, then patted his thigh.

Curveball. Inside.

Emily fought to keep from outwardly smiling. Perfect. Start Jamal off with the bender. Take advantage of his adrenaline. Her one-time Unicorns teammate had turned into a good hitter. She would have to be careful if she wanted to keep him off the basepaths.

The grit of the mound felt firm under her cleats. The wind had fallen to a gentle breeze that swelled with anticipation.

The fairy ring below Unicorn Field was fully open. She could feel the raw ebb and flow of magic between the realms like a calming sigh. She felt, too, the round surface of her mother's baseball in her back pocket, though now it was nothing special, except in what it meant to her. All its practical magic had been washed away in the ley line by the time Benji plucked it back out for her, whole and pristine.

There was new blood coming into the Realm, and into Pattersonville.

She'd felt it in Callie's ascension to the Hunt, and in Adrien's new comfort in the modern world of the mortal realm.

She felt it, too, in the closeness of her Small Folk teammates as they chattered behind her in preparation for the first pitch of the game, Greeven at third base, Shady Marie at short, Delananey at second, and Maddoc at first. It was a good infield. Sure-handed and dependable. Their voices were the perfect baseball choir, and the pixies working the outfield added a beautiful descant that made the air of the mortal world shimmer.

But mostly she felt it in the way the Unseelie Queen had been so truly fearful as Benji had laid down the rules of this challenge.

Four games on four fields to manifest the full powers of the Octagon and finally bring stability to the realms through properly shared bounty. No more would the power balance bounce from one court to another with each passing baseball season, leaving the lesser houses to scrounge what recourse they could from tiny scraps of baseball magic. No more, either, would the Fairy Realm and Pattersonville be two separate places, forever locked away from one another unless the proper sacrifices were made. They would be a community, mortals and Small Folk and Seelies and River Kin and all the rest, sharing and being shared with. The perfect fall ritual, to be celebrated with a final festival thereafter.

If the series was successful, anyway.

If not, the queen would have her way.

This had to work, though. This ritual that Benji had commanded.

The four games needed to create immense waves of the baseball magic to engage the Octagon. Otherwise, the spell would fail and the artifact would fall into her hands for who knew how many more centuries.

Emily wasn't worried about *this* game, at least. In truth, of everyone working the spell tonight, she had the easiest role to play. Baseball magic wasn't about winning, after all—though winning made a difference by enhancing the purity of the play that the Web Gem, and therefore the Octagon, demanded to fuel their machinations. The joy inherent in the quest for the perfect bunt or the well-timed jump to steal second base was enough to prime the pumps.

Baseball magic was much more about the players, the moments, and the games themselves than it was about deciding the actual victors. But winning could add that special spice.

Tonight, Emily DeWitt was playing for a team she loved, against, and in full camaraderie with, another team she loved, on the field she loved more than any other.

Unicorn Field was vibrating around her. The stadium lights cast silvery cones through an inky darkness. The string of lights that Adrien had built into the baseline fences danced with the power of the fairy ring that encircled the field. Candles inside the Halloween jack-o'-lanterns that lined the wooden fence rails flickered with waxy aroma. Crispness in the air carried the full flavor of autumn. And, while her Small Folk teammates scattered their magic about the field, her Unicorns classmates filled the air with the warmth of their enthusiasm.

Patsy Pell with her makeup dark and her baseball uniform dramatic. Jake Nesbitt with his lucky Taylor Swift T-shirt peeking out from under his jersey. Pash Kulpari and Lizzy Rodriguez laughing together on the dugout bench. And Jamal Douglass facing Emily down from his place in the batter's box, waiting with keen anticipation for whatever pitch she gave him, his wide grin saying he would hit it out of the park anyway.

She'd just see about that one.

All these people she'd spent an entire four years of high school playing baseball with and growing up with. All of them on the cusp of moving into the next phase of life. And behind her, the family she'd found with the Small Folk stood, blossoming with the baseball magic they'd helped her rediscover after years of grief. Fennoc tapped a pen against his clipboard as he twirled a long blade of grass between his lips. Little Essie cheered so loud she put the entire Unicorns support block to shame.

Together, the moment caught in her heart.

Unicorns vs. the Small Folk at Unicorn Field. It should be a great game.

The only ones missing were Benji and Adrien. But they were busy with their own game, joining the Wills-o'-the-Wisps as they faced off against the Unseelie Queen and her team on Dark Field out on the scraggly outskirts of town. They had a hard night ahead of them, make no mistake.

The dark queen would be doing everything in her immense powers to sabotage this process. If she succeeded, there would be no baseball magic grown from that game. But if the rest of the games could be perfect, the night might be won yet. It depended on Callie and her Hunt finding the joy as they faced off against the Seelie Court, and on Lady Marne and her River Kin working tightly with the Hags of the Wood to pull off something truly spectacular.

It was a lot to think about. Especially with Jamal "Jammy" Douglass staring her down, bat waggling with determination.

Focus, Emily said to herself as she drew a sharp breath and straightened her shoulders.

She gripped the baseball inside her glove. The rough thread of the seams felt glorious against her fingertips. She rocked back, then, and as the powers around her rose into a hushed silence, she threw her love of pure baseball into the first pitch of the game.

———

"DAMN IT!" Callie threw her baseball mitt to the ground and, by the fading fairy light that covered the practice field, she threw herself onto the tree stump that was part of the dugout. Her hand scraped hard against the rough edge of the barky seat, and the meat of her palm welled with a thin layer of crimson.

She'd made a throw so errant that even Trace stretching at first base wasn't long enough to corral it. It had cost the team a run, and now the Seelie Court's lead was four runs to two. Maybe it wouldn't have been so bad if the Seelie King hadn't smirked all the way to home plate as Trace had chased the ball down.

Only two innings remained.

The soily scent of the field stagnating around her made Callie that much more desperate. The baseball magic lacing the air was too thin for this late in the game. If things didn't pick up, she— and her royal Seelie cousin, for all he cared— would fail at their part in this overarching ritual.

She sucked on the hand, and the taste of her own blood made her that much angrier.

Around her, the Hunt yapped and yipped, preparing for their turn at the bat.

"I'm sorry, everyone. That was my bad," she growled, angry at herself.

"It's all right, Hunt Leader," Pyrgin said as he gave a practice swing. "For is it not so that errors are part of the game?"

"Of course they are," she snapped back, feeling rebuked. Some Leader of the Hunt she was turning out to be. She couldn't get her head enough in the game to make the amount of baseball magic they needed for this ritual, and now her own players were spouting her words back at her.

That *errors are part of the game* line was what she'd given the team back when she was first practicing them up, and it seemed to have stuck. The whole Wild Hunt baseball squad had gone through a phase of making error upon error in those early days. Thacker, as the team's catcher, had made such a string of errant tosses as he tried to throw out base stealers that Callie had wondered if he could ever learn. *"It's all right,"* she'd told him back then. *"The Hunt is relentless. The prey might elude us one night or the next, but we win out in the end because we never quit. Do it again. You'll get it. Don't be afraid to make a mistake."*

Now the errors were fewer, and that admonition was probably the leading cause.

If next season was good to go, Callie was convinced that her horde would be the best defensive team in the Fairy League.

She was still prickly, though. Pyrgin's use of her own words against her now felt... She ground her teeth together.

Annoying.

Playing for playing's sake didn't mean she didn't want to win. But enjoying the game for the spectacle that it was took the pressure off any particular moment— pressure she'd never truly known she'd taken on as her father exhorted her to win at any cost.

You're a McMasters! her father said again and again like it was an invocation. *And that means you're a winner! No matter what, a McMasters wins!* Then he would turn to her with his steely gaze and in a low, cold tone, add, *Always.*

That was wrong. She knew that now. Sure, if you were good, you won. If you were really good, you won a lot. But a *winner* was the person who did their best regardless. A *winner* was the one who could focus through it all, and who played hard. A *winner* was proud of that no matter what the ultimate outcome on game day might be.

Win or lose in any one game, a *winner* was someone at peace with themselves.

She stared out at the practice field and breathed in its essence. The sky above was a dome of darkness that was just beginning to grow light at the distant horizon. She felt the baseball magic that flowed in the field's simple existence, and suddenly, she knew another truth.

The practice field was her favorite baseball field of all time. She liked it for its ragged nature. When she was younger, her father would take her around to all the fanciest baseball stadiums in the Real World, making a point to call out all of their latest big screen displays, towering sound systems, and spotless concrete and brick hallways that were lined with concessions where you could pay five times the price for the same hot dog that you could get from the vendor outside.

Being in those parks made it harder to see the true magic of baseball.

Not impossible. But harder.

The practice field was the opposite of that in every way.

Its infield was hard-scrabbled and covered in wild grasses that grew in wavy greens and yellows, the baselines were marked with nearly haphazard rows of early-breaking winter wildflowers. The outfield fence was grown of brambles and thicket that she swore would move on whim.

And the fairy lights.

The fairy lights glowed with the baseball magic all night, too, flashing warm and excited colors when the best plays were made. Growing cold when a player lollygagged around the bases. The spectators—whether, elves, sylphs, gnomes, or pixies, cloven-hooved and horned, winged or lithe—lined up around the playing field without benefit of stadium seating, calling out their cheers three and four deep, bringing their own refreshment and snack foods and staking their claims to their watching spaces in ways that reminded Callie of how her mother had been when they would go to picnic in the park outside the Ball and Glove.

That was before she ran off, of course. Mom, she began to remember, had always been more Hunt-like when compared to her dad's Seelie smarm.

Callie wondered what her mom would think of her now.

A familiar sensation rose along her back. The sense of the Hunt filled her mind. For the first time in a long time, Callie wondered if it might be possible to find her mother.

The sound of the umpire calling the game to start again broke her from her thoughts, though. She focused her mind.

Benji had made a perfect call on assigning her this field tonight, and another perfect call pitting her Wild Hunt family against her Seelie Court relatives. Competition drove her like nothing else. The only thing that would make beating the Seelie King any more satisfying would have been if he had somehow convinced Dear Old Dad to sit on their bench beside him. Alas, her father was long gone—another problem for another day, if he was worth a thought at all anymore.

Either way, Callie was beyond his touch forever.

She picked herself off the bench and pumped her fist.

"Pyrgin's right," she called. "Let's go out there and get some runs!"

The pack's hunt call rose in that wave of excitement that came with every fresh burst of adrenaline.

Newly determined, Callie grabbed her bat. While no longer charged with Fairy Realm magic as it had been, it was still hers. And it had still been made for her from the Fairy Realm's wood.

If she got her chance, she would use it well.

In the batter's box, the previous hunt leader, who was now answering to the name Antor, led off the inning in his human form by lacing a single into right field. The clean hit kicked up a shower of baseball magic that rippled outward as it landed. More baseball magic welled as Antor reached first before the Seelie elves could coordinate their throws.

Trace was going to the plate with a runner on. Callie would follow.

On the field, Antor danced off first base as if he was going to break for second, distracting the Seelie King as he pitched. Trace took advantage of a thick fastball, drilling it hard back up the middle and forcing the King to duck lest he lose his head.

Callie thought Antor would push on for third, and she prepared to call him to heel. But, instead, he wisely put on the brakes and stayed put at second as Trace galloped safely to first base.

She grinned then. She gave her bat a practice swing, enjoying the clean burn of using her muscles. Then she strode to the plate.

She was going to hit with two runners on, while the Hunt had a two-run deficit.

This was the moment. The prey was afoot. The moment was at hand. With everything on the line, there was nothing left but to make things happen.

It was, she realized, exactly what she lived for.

She looked at the Dullahan umpire, standing with head in hand.

"Isn't this an amazing game?" she said.

"It is at that, Huntress," the umpire said, smiling surprisingly pleasantly from the crook of her own elbow. "It is at that."

Callie felt the baseball magic then, coursing over the field in ways she was sure had happened before but was equally sure she'd never truly felt. Its power was intense. Its beauty sublime. For an instant, she thought she might actually cry.

She swallowed hard and whipped her bat back and forth.

"Come, come, Ms. Rival, it's time to see what you're made of," the Seelie King goaded her from his place on the pitcher's mound by using her original Fairy Realm name. He rubbed baseball magic into the ball's seams as he paced.

"That's Huntmistress to you," Callie replied sharply, digging into the batter's box. "And I think it's time to see what *you're* made of."

She was a winner either way, but she was a member of the Hunt now. And a member of the Hunt is relentless.

A member of the Hunt never quits.

A moment later, the Seelie King delivered a fastball right down the middle.

Callie McMasters tracked it in. Watched the seams spin in the early morning gloaming.

Timed it as best as she could.

When she swung, it was like magic.

THERE WAS something special about Benji, Tommy "Center Field" Mathison thought.

And about the white boy, too. Adrien Thorn.

Benji Amberman was Jewish, unapologetically neither a man nor a woman, and full-forcedly both mortal human and the terrifying kind of spider fey that ought to give Tommy nightmares for years. And Adrien Thorn was... not like anyone Tommy had ever met before. White, yes. And a boy only a little older than Tommy by eyesight. But Adrien carried himself like a man grown, something that made sense once Adrien explained that he, too, had been captured by the queen and forced to be her Designated Hitter. That shared aspect of their life made Tommy feel strange, too. He'd never had something in common with a white boy before. Until now Tommy had never played baseball with anyone who wasn't black like him.

But Amberman and Thorn stepped onto this new, strange team of vagabond players like they'd never considered anything different.

Time was weird.

A century away played with Tommy's mind.

Just being on this field on the outskirts of Pattersonville was balm enough for his soul, though, even though that, too, was weird.

So much of the grounds were different now. Overgrown in ways that his Daddy would never have let happen and ringed with the rows of sleek and shiny automobiles that sat parked in the huge flat-lands of a strange, cracked parking lot and shined their bright head-lights on the field to let them play in the nighttime.

Imagine that.

Baseball at night.

Tommy wondered what his Daddy would think of it all.

Daddy had worked hard in the old textile factory outside of town — a place that Tommy had learned eventually became home to a shop called the McMasters' Ball and Glove, but back then was about the only place in town where a black man could get a fair wage. But working in the factory wasn't what Daddy had wanted out of life, and instead, he spent all his spare time tending the park that those in town derided as Dark Field, but that Daddy always called the Oscar Charleston Ballpark, after his favorite player, who he'd met once on a train while he was coming across the country to find work.

"You gonna be a center fielder like Oscar," Daddy would say as he laid fertilizer down on the outfield. "I know that's true."

Tommy thought of Daddy as he threw a warmup toss to Jughead Brown in left field, who had a similar story as Tommy. They all did. Captured by the Unseelie Queen from across time and space and thrown into the horrible artifact she called the Octagon. Johnny Two

Bones was their catcher. Jazmine Freeman played shortstop as slick as any person ever did. Bossy Bill Foster was on the hill now, warming up himself. They called to each other, teammates building camaraderie as if they weren't each from different years and ages. As he listened, the smell of cold grass grew suddenly rich and bold against the harsh scent of dead leaves.

Tommy felt it then. The powers welling up around him that he recognized from his time in the Fairy Realm, but bolder now. Stronger.

There was anger here.

Fear.

The need to scream out with the urgent desire for vengeance.

His Daddy hadn't put any of *that* into this field, but it was there all the same, and Tommy couldn't say he didn't have his own share in it.

At first, none of the eight players who had been released from their Fairy Realm prisons wanted anything to do with playing baseball, but then Benji Amberman explained things, and to a person, the entire team set their sights on putting things right.

Together, with Benji and Adrien, they were the Wills-o'-the-Wisps.

And tonight they were going to make their voices heard, though to be true, Tommy wasn't certain if any of them could play ball anymore. No one had done so for those missing years, and weird timing or not, a sliver of fear stuck in Tommy's craw. Benji had been so adamant that the queen had to be stopped, and that it was this "baseball magic" they would create that would do it. It was up to the Wills-o'-the-Wisps, as well as the other magical teams playing their games tonight, to make that magic happen.

"The queen isn't going to make things any easier, though," Benji had explained. "She's going to do whatever it takes to break us down. Trust me on that. So, we just need to go out there and play that much harder."

Now Benji was at third base, chattering with the rest, and Adrien

Thorn was hitting infield practice and encouraging the team, and Tommy, Jughead, and "Little Sam" Samantha Pierce were throwing long toss in the outfield.

It was chilly to the bone that night, Tommy thought as he stretched to get his blood warmed.

Unnaturally so.

The sky was the gauzy kind of dark-on-dark that comes from clouds that arrive on conjured winds, swirling with eldritch tendrils thick with rain and arriving fast to blot the stars and the moon. The smell of pre-thunderstorm ravagement came with each leaf-rattling gust. Fairy light flickered in hazy dark blots. The taste of electricity came thick against the back of tongues, and the cold of the wind cut deep into exposed skin.

It was shit weather for baseball, but at least it wasn't raining yet, and the game needed to be played.

He gave another warmup toss to Jughead and let his gaze go to the clotted dark clouds over the park. He shivered as he waited for the ball to return.

This was the work of the Unseelie Queen. He had known that, even without Benji's warnings, from the minute the clouds and the queen arrived at the same time. *You cannot defeat me,* the brewing storm said, looming overhead like a cudgel waiting to fall. This base-ball field had always been a refuge when he needed a way to get over the slights of the world, but now the intensity of unnatural magic crackling across the sky made it feel like the park itself was against him.

When he caught Jughead's return throw, he felt better though.

Focusing on the ball helped calm his mind.

He turned his torso to stretch, and windmilled his arm, letting his long fingers wrap over the seams in that familiar way. He gripped the ball and smelled something that seemed fresh and warm. Grass. Summer heat. *The baseball magic.* That's what Benji had called it.

He whipped a long toss back to Jughead and felt even better as he watched his throw arc gracefully into the nighttime sky.

Crickets gave harsh chirps from woods outside the field, and the breeze picked up to rattle with dry leaves and clacking bramble thicket.

On the opponent's bench, the Unseelie Queen sat cloaked in shadows as her team worked on their preparations, swinging bats and throwing spells of magic around in ways that Tommy was sure were meant to be both disruptive and intimidating. His eyes locked on hers then, and as her fingers twined magic his way, her velvet-smooth voice rang in his head.

"Perhaps we can come to an arrangement, Tommy Center Field?"

"What's that?" he said aloud in a combination of surprise and fear.

He didn't like fairy magic one bit. It gave him the hives.

"There is power here, young mortal," the queen said. *"You feel it, don't you? In your bones now, right? Power that is yours for the taking."*

Tommy's heart stopped.

It was true. That was what he'd been feeling ever since he'd arrived. That energy. The thrumming that was so obvious, yet too low to hear. It came to him in ghosts of people who had lined up to cheer on the games when he was a boy. The memories of young mothers mopping their brows as they unpacked picnic baskets and shook fingers at their rambunctious kids, who tumbled and ran and tried to make it out to the field despite the rules to stay aside. Young men and women throwing balls across the yard. The time-hollowed cracks of bats.

The ghosts were as real as the people in his life had been, Tommy realized.

They were all dead by now. But people had played here even though no one much paid attention back in the day, and even though no one much remembered that now. As Tommy stood still, the ghosts seeped through time. Pulling at him. Reminding him that they had once lived as he, too, had once lived.

He glanced down at himself, and he didn't flinch when he saw the little candle flame of his soul bobbing within his chest. He was just as much a ghost as them, though his time spent trapped in the flow of magic had rendered him different from these more earthly spirits.

There *was* power here.

And that power *could be* his.

The Unseelie Queen's presence grew inside him. The force of fairy magic burst in a spiced scent that hissed with gold and purple sparks.

"All you need to do is miss a ball here or there, Tommy Center Field. No one would notice. No one would even see. They can't hold your lack of practice against you now, can they? Take an extra strike at the bat? Make a bad throw? Do that, and I assure you all the power you need to take back this place."

Tommy gritted his teeth as he tracked Jughead's toss back to him, the ball white in the bright light of automobile headlights, sailing through dark skies.

"You want this place, right? This field? It's yours by rights, Tommy Center Field. Your Daddy made it what it was, and look at it now, all gone to rot? It's yours by blood."

What she said was true. This park should be his. He tasted that ownership like it was part of him.

And he could have it, too.

The ball fell toward him, arcing sharply, falling in a line straight for his head.

"Join me, Tommy Center Field. Join me and take it all back."

Yes, he thought.

Yes.

But another thought slipped into his mind then. A sound, really. A tone. Then a movement, and a thing so sweet Tommy's heart nearly burst.

It was his Daddy's voice, singing as he lined the field before a big weekend's brace of games. The way Daddy would straighten up after the work and look down the line to make sure it was straight and true. Then the sound of satisfaction that rode the little "Just so," that came as he welcomed the first players to the field. It was his when he worked on it; it was theirs when they played.

Barely in time, Tommy blinked back into the moment, took a sharp breath that cleared his mind, and plucked the ball out of the dark air.

He glared at the Unseelie Queen.

"Not falling for that one, no ma'am," Tommy muttered resolutely to himself, though a deep expression of anger creased the Unseelie Queen's eyes and confirmed that she could hear him.

He turned his back to her, then, and threw another perfect strike to Jughead.

"Just so," Tommy intoned with new strength in him. "Just so."

———

UNDERSTANDING the full import of the moment, Megan Moore, intrepid reporter, sat wedged into a nook in the same ancient oak tree she'd used to watch the Seelies play the Unicorns back before Benji had taken stewardship of the Web Gem. Against the chill of the night, she pecked out more words of the story she hoped the world would live through long enough to be able to read.

Megan had first considered attending the River Kin's game as they faced the Hag Sisters of the Wood. She enjoyed watching Lady Marne and admired the lovely iridescent colors the River Kin wore, and she knew what was going down over on that side of the veil was history-making on its own. But that idea passed quickly. No way was she going to miss the story of the newly formed Wills-o'-the-Wisps, led by the long-lost Tommy Mathison, taking on the Unseelie Court on the old field outside Pattersonville.

So far, the game had been appropriately nail-biting.

It was the top of the ninth inning, and on the field below, the Unseelie Queen slithered to the mound already wearing a triumphant smirk. The dark drape of her baseball dress whipped in the suddenly strong winds of her growing magical storms.

On the grassy patch of ground assigned as the Wills-o'-the-Wisps' dugout along the first base line, the team of humans and strange spirits that included Benji, Adrien, and the eight kidnapped players from the Octagon stood huddled together, also deeply aware of the problem they faced.

The game had been hard-fought, but the Unseelies, fueled by the queen's incessant stream of confounding magics, were ahead by a run.

Three outs and it was over.

Of course, it wasn't so much about who won this game. The important thing was the baseball magic. But the more victorious the Unseelie Queen felt, the more capable she was of quashing what delicate strands of baseball magic the Wills-o'-the-Wisps managed to conjure.

Benji Amberman could compel her to play via the power of the Web Gem, but by Fairy Realm rules, they couldn't stop her from using her innate power.

With every twist of her spell work, the night grew colder and damper.

With the rain threatening to blow harder, and with the baseball magic the team had been building pressed back farther than ever, that one run might as well be a hundred.

It wasn't all doom and gloom yet, though. News from the other three fields had been coming in through links to the Web Gem and the Octagon— which Benji had given to Megan for safekeeping during the game. Reports of great swells of baseball magic flowing from Unicorn Field made Megan optimistic. After first sensing only worrying dribbles early on, tales of a final firework burst of baseball magic from the practice field made her practically giddy. Maybe, Megan thought with more desperation than she thought she could ever feel, if the Wills-o'-the-Wisps could just hold their own, the other games could create enough baseball magic alone to engage the artifacts fully.

But the queen was as resourceful as she was vengeful, and she managed to not only staunch each new flow but to use the cracks that fresh waves of the baseball magic created as ways to add to the strength of her magics.

Still, it shouldn't be possible. The queen should be tiring by now. She should be running dry. But each play that started in a rush of new baseball magic ended in a cloud of consuming darkness, and the Unseelie Queen hadn't even broken a sweat.

Now the wind smelled of ancient blood and the sky cracked with her Fairy Lord magics.

The queen's work was almost done, and Megan was nearly overcome with anxiety.

One more inning. Three more outs.

Darkness swirls over Dark Field, she typed into her phone. Then she backspaced. *...over Oscar Charleston Ballpark*, she wrote this time. *The end is drawing near.*

The queen finished her warmup throws with a corkscrewing pitch that Megan knew no mortal could hit.

The gleam in her gaze was sharp and hungry.

Cold tree bark bit into Megan's back as Tommy Mathison, gripping his bat, stepped to the plate.

Before stepping into the box, the young man surveyed the land around him.

Despite the howl of the wind, Megan heard him address the queen.

"You were right about this field, Queen. By blood, this ballpark is mine."

With that, Tommy ran his hand across the buckle of his uniform belt and cut into fresh blood. All eyes turned to him as he dribbled crimson drops onto the handle, smearing the blood as he took his grip and readied himself for the pitch.

"Your blood is meaningless here, spirit," the queen scoffed.

At her words, the crimson turned to greenish silver, matching the ghostly candle flame that flickered in Tommy's chest. Wisps of steam rose from the cut on his hand as if his blood was evaporating.

Tommy barely glanced at it. Instead, he gripped his bat harder.

The queen wound up quickly, then unleashed a wild, looping pitch that dipped and rose and twisted and turned so fast that it seemed nearly invisible.

Tommy swung.

The crack of the bat on the ball raised a rush of the baseball magic so large it sent gusts of wind that smelled of oiled leather and fresh-cut grass to crash against the foul stench of the Unseelie Queen's magic.

Tommy raced to first base and turned toward second.

The dark elf in right field retrieved the ball and sent it rocketing to the infield, but Tommy's speed was too much and his hustle was sublime. By the time the ball arrived at second, Tommy was already standing on the base, chest pumping with great gulps from his sprint.

He glared at the queen, then. It was the ninth inning. If he scored, the game was tied.

"You're going to lose, queen," he called out loud.

"Anyone can get lucky, little bloodletter," the queen cackled. "Be careful your tongue lest I pick you off the base."

Tommy took his lead off second as she bent to pitch to Little Sam Pierce, the one-time star of a tee-ball team from twenty years ago, who held her bat out in preparation of sacrificing herself to get Tommy to third.

It was a play they had discussed in the space between innings. "If I get on," Tommy had told her, "Here's what I want you to do…"

The queen held the ball behind her back, waiting to pitch, twirling the ball between her fingers in a mesmerizing pattern. Megan felt the attention of the whole stadium drawn to the motion. Adrien was on deck, and even he was fixated on the queen's fingers as they twirled and twirled. The reek of Unseelie magic rose again, blocking the baseball magic that had been there moments before.

Megan wrinkled her nose, and the twitchy motion snapped her out of her mesmerization.

"Watch out!" she called.

At second base, Tommy had taken his lead, but his eyes were glazed with the effect of the queen's spell. Megan's shout came just as the queen whirled to throw to second base, and he dived back in — just barely safe.

"Hah," the queen snapped, glaring at Megan, then pointing at Tommy. "Lucky twice, deadly thrice."

"Go on," Tommy called. He let a drop of his still-glimmering blood fall to the soil. A thin, smoky trail of spirit vapor curled up from his hand. "Like knows like."

This time, as the gaze passed between the queen and Tommy Mathison, there was no wave of baseball magic, just as there was no swirl of Fairy Lord influence.

The queen's eyes narrowed in suspicion, and her fingers twitched around the ball she held.

"Pitch your pitch," Tommy called to her as he twisted his back foot into the dirt in preparation to run to third if the time came.

The queen did pitch then, throwing a ball down the middle without a bit of confounding magic to let Little Sammy Pierce do her sacrifice.

But Little Sam pulled back her sacrificial bat to instead take a full cut swing, and as lumber hit baseball, a crack resonated over the field. The ball rose into a sky that was now growing lighter at the eastern horizon. Tommy waited at the base for a moment in case he needed to tag up, but the ball bounced well past the elven outfielder, and both Tommy and Samantha ran, Tommy scoring and Little Sam making it all the way to third base before the ball had been retrieved.

"Not fair!" the queen called, stomping around the mound with the ball in her hand and glowering at the little runner at third. "You were supposed to bunt!"

"We can think for ourselves, Your Majesty. Think about that next time you kidnap one of us," Little Sam said.

Dirt devils rose around Samantha Pierce's feet then, and the greenish candle flame inside her flared with defiance. Megan felt the tides turning. So, it was apparent, did the rest of the players, both Wisps and Unseelies. The Wisps held themselves straighter, the light of vengeance brightening in their eyes. The Unseelie minions shuffled nervously, claws and fangs and leathery wings clacking and flapping in growing uncertainty. They'd been winning, and now they weren't.

"The score is only tied," the queen snapped as she went back to the mound.

Adrien Thorn stood at the plate.

The queen's smile was suddenly wicked. "The irony is so lovely, isn't it, dear Designated Hitter?" she said. "Or should I say dear *Adrien Thorn?*"

She said his name in a heavy tone that implied the press of magic. But to Megan, the air felt empty.

Adrien's reply was a simple practice swing that swirled with eddies of the baseball magic.

The Unseelie Queen's face twisted in angry confusion. Her use of his true name hadn't garnered even a reaction. And now, instead of kneeling to obey her command, he was making more magic with each casual swing of his bat.

Megan wanted to cry out for him. Wanted to cheer him on. The trill of a whippoorwill came from somewhere in the woods. The morning horizon glowed orange from beyond the oppression of Unseelie magic.

The queen pursed her lips, then twirled and pitched a twisty pitch to Adrien.

His gaze tracked the ball.

His bat struck it hard and square, drilling a liner that fell into center field. When the dust had cleared, Little Sammy Pierce had pranced home and Adrien stood safely at first base.

They were winning!

Megan was so excited she nearly fell out of the tree. Her heart pounded, and for the first time in her life not a single headline was running through her head.

They were winning!

When Benji followed with a double, and No Shoes O'Neill squibbed a dribbler down the first base line good for an infield hit, the lead was three. A moment later, Jughead celebrated the rising of the sun by crushing a massive home run into the deepest part of the woods.

It was undeniable now.

All around them, the baseball magic was embracing the baseball field, chasing away every remnant of the Unseelie Queen's work.

The queen let out a screech of fury that rent the air. "This isn't possible! I have stores of dark magic at my command, *why isn't it answering me?*"

Pacing back and forth around the pitching mound, she threw her glove down into the dirt and tore at her hair with both hands. Her face was no longer pale and beautiful, but twisted and horrific, her eyes wide and wild with uncontrollable rage.

As if in answer, the Octagon and the Web Gem pulsed where they lay beside Megan.

Benji, casual and graceful, stepped away from the dugout and reached with a translucent spider leg to touch the two artifacts. Light blazed forth, and an instant later, the woods surrounding Oscar Charleston Ballpark were filled with merfolk, kelpies, selkies, and a coven of witches young and beautiful and old and gnarled with knowledge.

They were players from the other games, Megan realized, flowing in now to watch the ending of this one.

Lady Marne stood at the first baseline, tossing a baseball to herself and smiling with sharklike satisfaction. "You know, Unseelie Pitch isn't nearly so horrific a place to play when the Unseelies aren't there," she said.

The coven mother standing beside her swirled her black baseball robes and tipped the brim of her pointed baseball hat back. "We had a lovely game there, and all that Unseelie magic hoarded below the field responded so wonderfully to our transformation incantation.

It's all baseball magic now, my pet," she said, nodding meaningfully to the Unseelie Queen.

"*What,*" spat the queen. Her fingers crooked into talons, and she plunged them into the space before her as if reaching for something Megan couldn't see. When she closed her fist and pulled it back, a fountain of baseball magic spewed forth from her clenched fingers.

"*No!*"

"Yes."

Megan said the word under her breath, just as Lady Marne said it, and as Adrien Thorn said it, and Tommy Mathison said it. The woods were growing more crowded now, as the Web Gem flared and flared, bringing Unicorns and Small Folk, Wild Hunt and Seelies to join the spectators of this final game, all of them saying "yes" in their own voices and with their own inflections.

Emily DeWitt said it as she came to stand in the Wisps' dugout. Callie McMasters said it as she slid down from Trace's back and slung her bat over her shoulder. And Benji Amberman said it, walking towards the queen on their gossamer spider legs, the Web Gem held before them.

"Yes, Your Majesty," Benji intoned from behind home plate. "It is so."

The queen scowled, her face angled up at Benji, her teeth bared as if she would tear them to pieces at the smallest chance. "How dare you touch what's mine. I'll kill you all for this. Enough of this frivolous baseball game. I'll make you all grovel before me in the end, I'll—"

"Perhaps that is so," Benji replied calmly. They lifted the Web Gem, and a twinkle of morning sunlight glinted from its commanding facets. "But for now, you'll pitch."

Jazmine Freeman drew a four-pitch walk.

Bossy Bill blasted a double to left.

Little Sam drove a single between the shortstop's legs.

Then Emily DeWitt, batting for the first time, popped a triple over the center fielder's head.

Callie McMasters slid a slick double just along the third base foul line.

Maddoc took a turn next, then one of Lady Marne's selkies. A trio of witches scored a trio of runs, and the Seelie King smirked as he ran the bases. Trace galloped to third before sending a spray of dirt up into the Unseelie baseman's gargoyle face, and then Essie screamed in delight as Greeven laced a triple that sparkled with such intense fairy light that for a moment the entire sky lit up in golden flares.

Adrien Thorn smashed a home run. He did it again the next time he came up in the batting line, and again the next.

It wasn't ever going to end. Megan knew it now. Everyone knew it now, even the queen.

The Unseelies had nothing left. The queen was in her own prison of sorts, facing a never-ending parade of hitters wrapped in blankets of the baseball magic that made them invincible.

This game was over.

The Wills-o'-the-Wisps were going to keep hitting and hitting.

"I give!" the queen finally cried, falling pitifully to her knees on the mound, her hands covering her head. "I give!"

Benji came to the roots of the tree to reclaim both the Web Gem and the Octagon.

"So be it declared," they said.

The sun rose high over the woods then, bold and golden in the morning sky.

It was over.

The queen was defeated.

And the Octagon flared to life.

EPILOGUE

Emily sat on the top stair of her front porch. She'd changed into jeans and a Chicago Cubs sweatshirt but hadn't felt right swapping out the Small Folk cap that she wore pushed up over her forehead.

It had been unnaturally warm for the first of November, so the door was open to the fresh air. Inside, the sounds of Dad and Elaine rattling around the kitchen and working on his latest batch of victory lasagna brought Emily a sense of comfort. He was going to be all right. Whether Elaine was for him or not, in the end, Dad was going to be good. They would both miss Mom forever, but knowing he was going to make it through made Emily relax in a way she hadn't known she needed to.

The abrupt sound of rustling leaves beside her made her tense up all over again, though, and she gave a hushed gasp.

She turned defensively to find Fennoc a few arm lengths away.

She let out a relieved breath and smiled at him.

He wore his uniform, still spotless, of course. His tawny fur was freshly curried, and his eyes danced with the jubilation that came with winning. The reed that dangled from the corner of his lips was long and loopy, vivid green in the late sunlight. "I'm sorry to disturb you, Miss Em," the faun said. "I can leave if you'd rather."

"No, that's all right," she replied, scooting over to give Fennoc space to sit, and patting the porch with her bare hand. "I think I'd like the company."

Emily'd come out here so she could be alone rather than lonely like she sometimes felt when she was stuck in her room. She liked the feeling of the open sky and the red and magenta colors the setting sun painted on the wisps of clouds that had formed over the horizon. They made her feel bigger, somehow. But Fennoc's appearance made everything that much better. She enjoyed watching Fennoc, with his slightly bowlegged gait, amble over and take his seat. The faun's body heat so near was a warm glow.

She was going to be all right, too, she thought.

She still had her baseball talent, so she could play if she wanted to. But she wasn't sure if she did or not. She pictured her mom's baseball, upstairs now, on the bookshelf next to her ereader and her trophies.

Fennoc reached the reed from his lips and held it out to droop over the front yard's still-green grass. "The world's a big place, iddn it?" he said.

Emily gave a chuff in agreement. "Especially now that our two worlds are mingling."

"Makes ya think that maybe even baseball magic can't hold it all together."

"Things seem good now," Emily said.

"Aye, they are, lass. Aye, they are."

Sitting quietly with her manager, Emily reviewed the whirlwind of activity that had happened just today. Every piece was momentous in its own way but also seemed natural and perfect as if it had been meant to be.

Benji had declared the Unseelie Queen's reign over, invoking spiderkin spellbinding to keep her in the sights of the Octagon's eight eyes at all times. They'd capped it off by declaring any further follies on her part would result in her banishment for a thousand years.

Callie, too, had so confidently renewed her claim as the new leader of the Wild Hunt, announcing her intention to make the Fairy Realm her home, as well as her plans to run hunts through Pattersonville at pivotal times throughout the year.

Emily was proud of her. She saw the truth about her one-time rival. Callie McMasters was a young woman of power. She was a leader. The Hunt had always been her home. Emily was happy Callie had Trace by her side, too.

"I'll keep an eye out for your dad," Emily had told her earlier as Callie prepared to return to the Fairy Realm.

"I don't think he's going to be a problem anymore," Callie said.

"I'll look out for him anyway," Emily replied.

Callie hugged her then, and as her arms folded Emily to her, Callie whispered, "I know you can take care of yourself, sister. But if you need me, I'll be there."

Sitting on the porch, Emily's throat clotted a little at the memory.

Callie McMasters was as loyal as she was fierce. Her word would be her bond. And, in that moment with her hug wrapped so tightly around Emily's shoulder, the Huntmistress—her old rival for best-damned baseball player in the city—had called her sister.

It was a lot to take in.

"I'd say Miss Reporter is going to be busy with her storytelling for a while now," Fennoc said, knowingly or not continuing Emily's litany of events. Megan had practically salivated over the celebratory post-game feast, not because of the magical food the Seelie King and Lady Marne had conjured in together, but because of all the juicy interviews she could conduct.

She chuckled. "Megan will find a way to get it all down, though."

"I'd say she and the queen's Designated Hitter seem to have made a good team of it."

"Yeah. They're good together."

"I'm glad to see you're happy for them, Miss Em. I thought for a while that it would be you and young Mr. Thorn that would make the pairing."

"Adrien's my friend," Emily said simply. "I'm happy they are together."

Fennoc slid the loopy grass reed back into the corner of his mouth, but just sat back to give Emily space to think.

Adrien needed Megan now, and Megan needed Adrien. She would help him sort out his history, and he would help ground her in what was important. Already Emily saw their first collaboration happening even if they didn't see it themselves: Developing Oscar Charleston Ballpark back to its full splendor.

The Wills-o'-the Wisps were finished now. Having played their part in defeating their captor, the Fairy League's eighth team had already disbanded. They'd spent too long immersed in the raw magic of the sleeping Octagon— and, in Tommy's case, the ley line— to return to their human lives the way Adrien had. The team members instead became less a gathering of vengeful spirits and more a new collection of ethereal fey beings, like true will-o'-the-wisps or some of the lantern sprites that made homes in the Halloween and Samhain jack-o'-lanterns that still lined the street along Emily's house.

They were free, though. Free for the first time since their kidnapping.

Maybe someday they would come back to play baseball together, but that sometime was not now.

Adrien, having already won his freedom from the queen, was stepping away from the team, too. And stepping away from playing baseball, although not the game itself. He was going back to his life in the mortal world—which, for him, would always mean designing baseball fields.

Arriving for that epic final inning, Emily had seen how Adrien had bonded with Tommy "Center Field" Mathison. If ever there were two people cut from the same cloth, they were Adrien and

Tommy as they talked about the field. But while Adrien couldn't bring himself to live in the Fairy Realm, Tommy's existence as an ephemeral wisp meant he couldn't be comfortable in the mortal world.

"I'll make it right on my side," Tommy said to Adrien after the Unseelie Queen had been dispatched. He'd stared lovingly out at the ballpark that his Daddy had made so beautiful back in his time. Then he had peered at Adrien with so much hope and desire that Emily thought her heart might burst. "Could you...?"

"Yeah," Adrien replied to the question Tommy couldn't quite finish. "We'll work on Oscar Charleston Park together, okay?"

Tommy's smile lit the place up brighter than the string of automobiles ever could, and Emily thought the grass in the outfield turned a deeper shade of green.

"But I'm thinking it needs a pavilion or something, right? A place kids can play around in while the games are going on? I can see it now, can't you? Seesaws and swings and calliopes?"

"Sure. That sounds good," Tommy said.

"And that'll need a name of its own, I think."

"A name?"

"Yeah," Adrien said. "Things are always more powerful when they've got a name."

The two of them paused, then, Tommy's brow furling.

"What was your Daddy's name?" Adrien said softly.

"Harold," Tommy said.

"Harold Mathison Playground," Adrien replied. "I like that."

Emily saw it all playing out now. Adrien and Tommy would work their magics together, Tommy sprucing up the practice field in the Fairy Realm, and Adrien making Oscar Charleston Park a place to play baseball that would rival Unicorn Field. And Megan, with her spindly fingers casting her stories like magic spells of their own, would help. Attention was the fuel that drove change, Emily saw now. And if there was something Megan Moore's terrier nature excelled at, it was drawing attention.

Funding, Emily thought, would never be a problem for any project Adrien Thorn put his mind to.

And that would go beyond baseball fields. Megan was probably always going to be a reporter of some kind, but Adrien was harder to pin down. Architect? Thespian? Sportsman? The future was wide open for Adrien Thorn, and along with Megan, he was better for it.

"And what about you, little one?" Fennoc said, turning his gaze to Emily. "What does the future hold for my favorite Miss Em?"

Emly shrugged. "I don't know."

"Sure ya do."

Emily started to argue, but the knowing expression on the faun's features and the deep compassion that filled his gaze made her stop. She wrapped her arms around her knees and pulled them to her chest, taking a deep breath of the evening air, then letting it out. Fennoc was right. She knew what her path was. Or at least what the next step in that path would be.

"I hear you were really good," she said, deflecting for a moment.

"I admit I was a very good player of baseball," Fennoc replied.

"Why did you do it, then?" she said.

The corners of his eyes crinkled in a smile that almost made it to his lips. "You mean, why did I give up my baseball talent?"

"Yeah. You're still a strong fairy. You could have played for a long time."

"You already know the answer. I gave it up for the same reason you were going to."

"To save your friends."

"Well that, and the other thing, too." Fennoc chewed his reed. "You do know what I mean, right?"

Emily thought about her mother then. Remembered the stories about her playing baseball and enjoying every minute of it. She thought about her fairy friends on the Small Folk team. Shayla and Twy, and Mellica, who had done up her hair for the festival with so much excitement. Izusa and Jessebel who danced with such glee. She saw Maddoc, Fennoc's gruff brother as he blushed at every appearance from Lady Marne, and Shady Marie and Delananey. And, of course, Greeven and little Essie. She felt a swell of closeness to Adrien, then. And Callie. They were all great baseball players. Amazing in their own ways. But they were more than baseball players, and while the baseball magic played a large part in all their lives, there was more for them than being just one thing.

Even Megan, who would probably always follow stories, was made of more than a single thought. Who knew what lead she would be following next?

Emily was no different.

And Emily knew now that she had to leave Pattersonville. Had to leave both the Unicorns and her Small Folk teammates to pursue her college dreams.

"Why is it so hard?" she said.

Fennoc put his hand on Emily's knee. "Butterflies have to claw out of their cocoons, Miss Em. That's just how it is."

"You're saying my baseball talent is my cocoon?"

"Maybe." An errant hair from the manager's brow twitched. "Or maybe not. You've still got your talents, anyway. You can play baseball even as you're taking to your study books and finding out just who you really are. Maybe you will be a baseball player after all? Or a counter of something that needs counting? Who knows what the future could bring? This time last year, no one would have seen the Fairy Realm and the Real World coming together, now would they have?"

"No," Emily said.

"Maybe someday you'll even decide you should be a manager, maybe?"

Emily smiled and put her hand on the shoulder of the faun's Small Folk uniform.

"Thank you," Emily replied.

"Dinner's on!" Dad's voice called from inside, followed by a peal of laughter from Elaine.

"Coming!" Emily called back, then turned to Fennoc. "You up for a little victory lasagna?"

The faun stood, then brushed the creases out of his uniform. "No, Miss Em, I think I'll pass on the 'victory lasagna.' Wonderful though I'm sure it would be."

"All right, then."

Emily stood up, feeling her muscles stiffen from the cooling air. "I hope to see you again sometime soon," she said to her manager.

"Me, too," Fennoc said, tipping his cap. "Until then, though, I hope you have fair winds always blowing out to left."

"Except when I'm pitching, right?"

"Indeed, Miss Em. Except when you're pitching."

Fennoc left then.

Emily stood on the path leading to her porch that led to the front door that led to her house. This was her home. Pattersonville. The people in it and the places she'd been.

It would always be her home, no matter what.

And now it was in good hands, both mortal and fey.

"I said dinner's on," Dad said from just inside the screen door.

"Yeah," Emily said. "I heard you."

It was, she decided later, the best dish of victory lasagna she'd ever had.

ABOUT BRIGID COLLINS

Brigid Collins is a fantasy and science fiction writer living in Nevada.

Her fantasy series *The Songbird River Chronicles* and *Winter's Consort*, her fun middle grade hijinks series *The Sugimori Sisters*, and her dark fairy tale novella *Thorn and Thimble* are available wherever books are sold. Her short stories have appeared in Fiction River, Feyland Tales, and Mercedes Lackey's Valdemar anthologies.

Sign up for her newsletter at www.brigidcollinsbooks.com/newsletter-sign-up/ and get a free copy of *Strength & Chaos, Mischief & Poise: Four Cat Tales*, exclusively available to her subscribers!

Website: https://brigidcollinsbooks.com

Also by Brigid Collins

<u>Novels</u>

Songbird River Chronicles (4 books)

Winter's Consort (4 books)

Home Run Enchanted (with Ron Collins)

<u>Novella</u>

Thorn and Thimble

<u>Collections</u>

The Sugimori Sisters series (3 volumes)

Three Tales of Faeries

Three Tales of Powers

Three Tales of Monsters

Strength & Chaos, Mischief & Poise

ABOUT RON COLLINS

Ron Collins is a best-selling Science Fiction and Dark Fantasy author who writes across the spectrum of speculative fiction. You can find his work at all major online retailers.

His short fiction has received a Writers of the Future prize and a CompuServe HOMer Award. His short story "The White Game" was nominated for the Short Mystery Fiction Society's 2016 Derringer Award.

He holds a degree in Mechanical Engineering, and has worked to develop avionics systems, electronics, and information technology before chucking it all to write full-time.

Website: https://www.typosphere.com

Get Free Books!
Ron's Reader List: Newsletter: http://typosphere.com/newsletter

ALSO BY RON COLLINS

<u>Novels</u>

Stealing the Sun (9 books)

Saga of the God-Touched Mage (8 books)

The PEBA Diaries (2 books)

The Knight Deception

Wakers

Home Run Enchanted (with Brigid Collins)

<u>Collections</u>

Tomorrow in All the Worlds

Picasso's Cat & Other Stories

Five Magics

Collins Creek (3 volumes)

<u>Nonfiction</u>

On Writing (And Reading!) Short

On Creating (And Celebrating!) Characters

<u>Poetry</u>

Five Seven Five

Acknowledgments

The authors would like to thank Sharon Bass, who is a beta reader extraordinaire, and Lisa Collins, wife, mom, and most excellent last reader.

Insert standard disclaimers: All errors are our fault.

All right, who are we kidding. If there's anything wrong in this book, you can pretty much take it to the bank that it's Ron's fault. [grin!]

Thanks also to the Kickstarter people who backed *Home Run Enchanted*, and *Curveball Cursed*, the first two books in this series. Without you, book 3 may not have happened! Final thanks goes, of course, to these wonderful people who helped bring *this* volume, *Outfield Magicked*, to life on Kickstarter:

Amanda Balter - Carl Spitzer - Cortney Babcock - David H. Hendrickson - Dean Wesley Smith - Elizabeth W. - Erin R - Gary Olsen - Greg Levick - Hannah Garrison - Janine - Jessica Ness - Jonas Jackson - Jonathan Kurts - Joseph Procopio - K. "Cy" Stauffer - Katherine Malloy - Laura Ware - ledzeplisa - Lisa Silverthorne - maileguy - Marlene Renteria - Mary Jo Rabe - Michael A. Burstein - Michael Lucas - Phoenix - Rajasekaran Senthil Kumaran - Richard Novak - Rowan Stone - Starcy - Stephen Kellat - Zach Lee

www.ingramcontent.com/pod-product-compliance
Lightning Source LLC
Chambersburg PA
CBHW031806200726

48289CB00014B/510